Silver Moon

HAVE A C...
OF 75 GREAT NOVELS
OF
EROTIC DOMINATION

If you like one you will probably like the rest

A NEW TITLE EVERY MONTH

Silver Moon Readers Service
109 A Roundhay Road
Leeds
LS8 5AJ
United Kingdom

http://www.electronicbookshops.com

If you like one of our books you will probably like them all!

Write for our free 20 page booklet of extracts from early books
- surely the most erotic feebie yet - and, if you wish to be on
our confidential mailing list, from forthcoming monthly titles
as they are published:-

Silver Moon Reader Services

109A Roundhay Road

Leeds

LS8 5AJ

United Kingdom

http://www.electronicbookshops.com

or leave details on our 24hr UK answerphone
08700 10 90 60
International acces code then +44 08700 10 90 60

New authors welcome
Please send submissions to
Silver Moon Books Ltd.
PO Box 5663
Nottingham
NG3 6PJ
or
editor@electronicbookshops.com

Slave to her Desires
by
Samantha Austen

Chapter 1

Toni Galt stared down disconsolately on the garden below. It was a dreary day, the raindrops chasing one another down the glass as the old sash window rattled with the force of the wind. She glanced up at the dull, leaden skies, searching in vain for a glimmer of sunlight, but there was none.

She sighed and rose from the wooden seat that ran round the bay window. There would be no chance of a walk outside today, she decided. She looked about her, taking in the austere white walls of her room and the old, plain wooden furnishings. At that moment, life seemed to stretch out before her like an endless procession of rainy days and sleepless nights.

She walked across to the full-length mirror that stood by the door to her room, pausing in front of it to take in her reflection.

What she saw was a lovely, shapely girl, five foot three inches tall, with long, flowing brown locks. She had a classically beautiful face with high cheekbones and a perfectly sculpted nose, her pretty lips soft and kissable. She gazed into the deep green depths of her eyes, eyes that would have stopped any man short across a room with a hundred other girls in it.

She looked down at her body. She was wrapped in a towel, having stepped from the bath about ten minutes earlier. Glancing about her, as if feeling guilty to be naked even in her own room, she checked that she was alone. Then, dropping the towel to the floor, she examined herself critically.

Toni was a true beauty. Her breasts were firm, with large brown nipples that pointed outwards and upwards. Her waist was slim, her belly flat. Her mound of Venus was covered in a pelt of dark, short hair that drew the eyes down to the thick lips of her sex. Below were a pair of slender legs, shapely ankles and small, pretty feet.

She wondered what a man would make of her body, and

an odd shiver of excitement ran through her as she imagined being seen as she was. She reached up and cupped her breast, stroking the nipple and sighing as she felt the strange sensation of pleasure that always accompanied such a caress. Then she moved her left hand down and ran it between her legs, and a shiver ran through her as she touched herself so intimately.

Toni looked into her own eyes, and saw that her face had gone red. Instinctively her hands left her skin and she snatched up the towel, hugging it to her body. She had been experiencing these odd feelings for some weeks now, and found it hard to understand the responses she had been receiving from her young body. Sensations she had never imagined coursed through her whenever she caressed herself. She wanted desperately to understand what was happening to her body, but there was nobody to confide in. She knew she daren't ask her aunt or uncle about them. Somehow the feelings seemed to make her feel guilty, though she didn't know why. All she knew was that there was something happening to her, and she wanted to share it with her contemporaries.

Toni sighed for a second time. There was no doubt that at nineteen, she was as lovely as any model on the catwalk. Under any other circumstances she should have been out partying every night, surrounded by young men. As it was, her life was drab and boring, with no sign of any relief ahead.

Toni had lived with her Uncle Carl and Aunt Gwendolyn ever since the car crash in which her parents had both died. At the time she had been at boarding school, and the tragedy had not greatly affected her life. Her parents had lived abroad and she had seen little of them anyway. At the end of the term, however, her aunt and uncle had arrived at the school and announced that she was leaving to live with them in their house in the country.

Toni had been sad to leave her friends, but had had no choice, since her parents had named her aunt and uncle as her guardians until she was twenty-one, and her inheritance had

6

been put into trust until then. She had been even less happy when she had seen the grim, grey edifice of the house in which her guardians lived. Set a long way from any town, the building was old and draughty, with few concessions to the comforts of the modern age.

Since then Toni's life had been a miserable one. Her aunt and uncle, themselves childless and clearly unhappy with the unexpected duty their relatives had placed on them, gave her no more than the necessities required to exist. Her clothes were bought for her from jumble sales. She was allowed no money of her own and, since her relatives never went out, was forced to spend her days and nights in her room, or wandering about the gardens.

Down the corridor she heard a door slam, the signal that her aunt and uncle had retired to their respective bedrooms for their regular afternoon nap. She knew now that she had the rest of the house to herself for at least the next two hours. The cook and maid would not be back until the evening and Simmonds, the butler, always went into the village during the afternoon, ostensibly to visit his mother, though Toni knew that he was far more likely to be found in the bar of the Red Lion.

She began to get dressed. Her underwear was drab and functional and the dress she put on was shapeless, buttoned to the neck and making no concession to her figure. Going to the mirror, she reached behind herself and bunched the waistband at her back, pulling it tight and allowing the cheap cotton material to hug her figure. The transformation was instant, the outline of her body suddenly quite clear. She wondered what it must be like to have clothes that fitted her properly. One day she would know, she promised herself. She slipped on a pair of flat shoes, then opened the door and headed downstairs.

This was her favourite time of the day. Time when she could relax with a good book or, on a better day, stroll about the garden without fear of interruption. She let herself into the living room and slumped into an armchair, glad of her solitude.

But today she didn't seem to be able to relax. Try as she might to absorb herself in the novel she was reading, she couldn't. Her concentration was gone, and her eyes wandered down the page, reading the words but failing to take in their meaning. Eventually she threw down her book in frustration and rose to her feet.

The rain was still falling hard, so she wandered out into the corridor and began prowling about the house, feeling more than ever like a caged animal.

As she passed the top of the stairs leading down to the kitchen she paused. Unusually the door stood open. Toni had never been into the kitchen. It was a place her aunt never went, and her uncle only to berate the servants for some misdemeanour or other. Now the place would be deserted, and she felt a sudden desire to see what was down there. She glanced about her. Nobody would know if she went down now, and at least it was a kind of way of passing the time. Walking on tiptoe, she made her way down the stairs.

The kitchen was large and old-fashioned, just like the rest of the house. Toni moved around, fingering the implements and running her hand over the hard, smooth surface of the heavy old kitchen table. A narrow passage ran from the back of the kitchen, its walls lined with wooden panelling, and she wandered down it. On one side was a laundry room, with a linen cupboard opposite. At the end was a door marked 'Private', which she guessed was the entrance to the butler's accommodation. She turned back, then stopped. There, on the floor by the wall, was a piece of paper. Curious, she stooped to pick it up, but when she tried to lift it, it slipped from her fingers as if it was stuck to the carpet. She examined it more closely, and was surprised to discover that half of it was apparently jammed under the wall. She pulled gently at it and it slid out.

Toni examined the sheet, and at once her eyebrows rose.

It was a page from a magazine, a photograph of a girl. She was standing with her back to the camera, gazing back at it. But what captivated Toni was not the girl's face, but her body. She was completely naked.

Toni ran her eyes up and down the girl's form. She had a plump, pert behind and a slim waist. Her body was twisted, so that her right breast was visible, the nipple erect. Charlie could scarcely believe the audacity of the girl in allowing herself to be photographed in such a state, and found herself staring in total fascination at the image. There was something strangely exciting about the sight of the brazen girl, happily displaying her body to the cameraman. Something that kindled an odd feeling in Toni's belly.

She began to wonder where the picture had come from. It seemed so out of place in this house. Then there was the mystery of the way she had found it, apparently forced under a crack at the foot of the wall. Overcome by curiosity, Toni crouched down again and, placing the picture flat on the floor, attempted to push it back under. She couldn't.

She began to examine the wall and, in particular, the panel above which she had found the picture. She ran her fingers down the edge. There was a slight, almost imperceptible crack between it and the adjoining panel. It was the same on the other side. She pressed the panel, and it rattled slightly. All at once she realised that it must be a door. She moved her fingers up and down, tracing the smallest of cracks that surrounded it. She tried pushing, then pulling, but it stayed firmly closed. Yet someone had opened it recently. How else could the paper have become stuck where it was? She began to look about for some other means of opening it.

It took her about ten minutes to find the secret. One of the coathooks on the wall felt slightly loose, and, after pushing, pulling and twisting, she heard a click and the panel moved slightly.

Her heart thumping, Toni pressed the wood, and it swung silently open. Beyond was darkness. She stepped inside and

9

fumbled up and down the wall. Then she found a switch and snapped it on. At once the room was flooded with light.

Toni looked about her in astonishment. The room was like none she had ever seen before. It had no decoration as such, the floor being bare stone and the walls plain brickwork. It was lit by a series of spotlights, each casting a harsh glare so that there were virtually no shadows or dark corners.

But it was the furnishings that were really unusual. Bizarre almost. One wall was hung with a variety of silver chains, attached to a series of pulleys and wheels. On the loose end of each chain were what looked like shackles and manacles, as well as other leather devices that meant nothing to the innocent young Toni. Stranger still, in between each set of chains was a mirror that ran from ceiling to floor.

She turned to the wall opposite. This bore plain wooden racks containing all kinds of extraordinary devices. There were whips, canes, tawses and handcuffs, as well as a series of smaller chains and clamps the purpose of which she could only guess at. Once again mirrors were placed at intervals, reflecting the chains on the wall opposite. In the centre of the room was a wooden frame and a long, low bench bearing yet more chains.

Toni was flabbergasted. The place was more like a mediaeval dungeon than a room in her aunt's and uncle's house. She wondered that they had ever allowed it to stay like this. It seemed so out of character. Then it occurred to her that maybe they didn't even know it was there. After all, the room was carefully concealed. She herself would never have found it if not for the piece of paper. Perhaps her relatives had no idea that the secret room existed.

Remembering the piece of paper brought her up short. In order for it to have got where it was, somebody must have dropped it whilst exiting the room. But who? Once again she realised that her aunt and uncle were the least likely candidates to have had a photograph of a naked girl. Someone else must have been in here, and recently too. After all, the picture could not have lain on the floor for long without somebody seeing it.

All at once she felt anxious. What if someone should come along and find her here? Despite the fact that she had every right to be in the house, there was something about this particular room that was different. Something that made her afraid to be discovered here. It was as if she was trespassing. Better close the door, she decided.

She checked that it had a conventional handle on her side, then clicked the door closed. It was only then that she noticed the rack of books and magazines. They were on the wall to the left of the door, so that she hadn't seen them on entering. There were dozens of them, all with glossy covers depicting young ladies in various states of undress. The titles were unfamiliar to her. She had never seen such magazines in any newsagent's. She pulled one from the rack and began to leaf through it.

At once her jaw dropped in astonishment. It was full of colour photos of women, all of them totally naked. This time there were no backs turned. They stood, facing the camera, their legs wide, staring out at her. Toni flicked through the pages, studying each photo, wondering at the brazen way the women allowed breasts, backside and sex to be photographed so intimately.

She replaced the magazine and picked up another. Once again, the photos were all of girls in lewd poses, displaying themselves. Two others she tried were the same.

She moved further down the rack and picked out another, allowing it to fall open in her hands. Then she gave a gasp, almost dropping the publication in her shock at what she saw.

The picture depicted a beautiful young girl kneeling nude on the floor. Before her stood a naked man. To Toni's astonishment, he had his erect penis pressed into the girl's mouth. Toni couldn't believe what she was seeing. She stared at the man's image. She had never seen a man without clothes before, and the sight was somehow fascinating to her. She ex-

11

amined the thick shaft of his penis and the puckered sac of his balls at the base. Then her eyes went back to the girl. Amazingly, she appeared to be enjoying what she was doing, her eyes closed in rapture as she fellated him. Toni wondered what it could possibly feel like to have such intimate contact with a man, and was surprised to discover how much it excited her.

She flipped over the page, and was presented with the sight of the girl on all fours, her legs spread wide so that her open sex was clearly displayed. The man knelt behind her, holding his penis in his hand , his eyes fixed on the girl. Toni turned over again, her hands trembling, only to be confronted with a picture of the man burying his penis in the girl's vagina whilst she gazed back at him, her face a picture of desire. Almost unconsciously, Toni dropped her right hand to her crotch, running her fingers between her legs, pressing the material of her dress against the gusset of her panties as she studied the picture.

Toni put the magazine down on the bench and continued to turn the pages, whilst still rubbing herself. The couple in the magazine went through a series of positions, the camera catching each clearly so that no part of their coupling was hidden from view. For Toni it was both shocking and astounding that anyone could allow themselves to be photographed whilst performing such an intimate act. At the same time, though, she felt an intense excitement welling up inside her as she studied the images, and there was a warmth in her crotch such as she had never before experienced.

She turned the final page and let out a gasp of surprise. The girl was lying on her back, her face turned up toward the man. His cock was ejecting a spurt of semen, which was directed into her open mouth. There was a white blob of it already on her tongue, and more trickled down her chin, yet the expression on her face was almost eager as she accepted her partner's sperm.

All at once Toni had to touch herself. She didn't understand why, but she knew her love bud was hard as a nut, and the sensation of her fingers against her clothes was no longer enough. She looked across at the door, checking once more that it was securely shut. Then she slowly began to lift her skirt, tucking it up about her waist, raising the hem until her panties were completely exposed. Her hand shaking, she took hold of the waistband and pulled them down her thighs, halfway to her knees.

She felt for her sex, amazed at how wet it had suddenly become. She rubbed her finger over her clitoris and gave a groan as a spasm of pleasure shook her lovely young body. She gazed down at the photo of the girl, her bare breasts thrust up at the camera as she raised her face to her partner's orgasm, and all of a sudden a new urgency overtook her. She pressed a finger into her vagina, feeling the muscles inside contract about it as she slid it deep within her. Then she began working it back and forth whilst her thumb continued to caress her love bud.

Toni glanced across the room, and caught her reflection in the mirror. For a moment she almost stopped. Could that really be her, standing there with her dress tucked up about her waist, her knickers pulled down, her legs spread as she thrust her fingers into her vagina? It seemed incredible to her, yet the sight served only to spur her on, her breathing coming in short gasps as she masturbated herself.

She came suddenly, without warning, a groan escaping her lips as the most exquisite pleasure she had ever known coursed through her. She had to bite her tongue to prevent herself crying aloud, her fingers working back and forth, each movement bringing a new spasm deep inside her. The orgasm was shattering, like nothing she had ever imagined, and she went on caressing herself until she could take no more, then slumped forward across the bench, her chest heaving.

It was fully five minutes before she felt able to raise herself. Once again she stared at her reflection, still not quite able to believe what had just happened. Then she reached

13

down and slowly pulled up her panties before allowing her dress to drop back down.

She pulled a handkerchief from her pocket and wiped her hand, suddenly guilty at her extraordinary behaviour. She had to get out of this strange room and back to the normality of the house. Hurriedly she closed the magazine and flung it back into the rack. Then she made for the door.

She placed her ear flat against it, afraid that someone might have heard the noises she had been making, but all was silent. She opened it a crack and peered out. The kitchen was still empty. She slipped out and closed the door behind her. Then, her heart still thumping, her face red with guilt, she hurried back to the stairs and up to the main house.

Meanwhile, in the secret room, the light continued to burn.

Chapter 2

That night Toni could scarcely sleep at all. She lay in her bed, tossing and turning, trying to come to terms with what had happened to her in that strange room. The images in the book ran through her brain time and again. The man with his stiff penis that spurted such copious amounts of semen. The girl, wanton and shameless, giving herself totally to him, careless of the fact that her breasts and sex were bare, and that her image was being captured by a camera. Then Toni saw herself, standing with her knickers down, caressing herself in the most intimate manner possible until the pleasure of her first orgasm overcame her.

Of course Toni was not entirely innocent of the facts of life. She had learnt about sex from discussions in the dormitory at school. But she had never been able to understand the attraction of it. To her, having a man's penis penetrate her had seemed a disgusting idea. She had always thought of sex as something a woman had to endure if she wanted marriage and a family. At the time, Toni had vowed to have neither and

14

to remain celebrate. Now her mind was in turmoil. What had it been about the pictures that had excited her so? What had caused her to behave in such a wanton manner? Certainly she had been experiencing strange stirrings in her body of late, but none that had suggested she would masturbate to orgasm as she had done.

And how sweet that orgasm had been. Like nothing Toni had ever imagined. The response of her body to her own caresses had been extraordinary, as if it had taken over from her and had exerted a will of its own. The idea of being out of control frightened her, yet still she couldn't forget the gasping pleasure she had experienced in the room.

Toni drifted off at last into a troubled sleep haunted by dreams in which young men approached her naked, their huge cocks prodding at her body as she lay, stretched out on her bed, somehow unable to escape from their insistent probing.

She overslept and was very nearly late for breakfast. Her uncle frowned as she dashed into the room on the stroke of eight o'clock.

'Good morning Uncle Carl,' she said breathlessly.

He grunted his reply.

'Good morning Aunt Gwendolyn.'

'Sit down girl. Simmonds, you may serve the porrige.'

Toni sat quietly, spooning down her porrige, trying not to catch the eyes of her relatives. She hated meal times, where the pair of them seldom spoke, and was always glad to be excused.

'You look flushed, Antonia,' said her aunt suddenly. 'What have you been doing?'

The heat rushed to Toni's cheeks.

'Nothing Aunt Gwendolyn'

'Then why has your face gone so red?'

'I don't know, Aunt.'

Her uncle sniffed. 'Girl does too much reading if you ask me. Gives her strange ideas.'

The conversation ended there, much to Toni's relief, and

the rest of the meal was completed in the customary silence. Afterwards, Toni went out into the garden and sat down in her favourite spot, an old garden seat screened from the house by a high hedge. She had been shaken by her aunt's words. What if she suspected? What if she knew of the room, and guessed that Toni had been there? But she shook her head. She couldn't possibly know. There was no way that her uncle and aunt would allow those magazines in their house. Nevertheless she vowed not to go back to the room again, and to stay above stairs from now on.

Toni's resolve lasted all of three days. Days in which her obsession with the room grew until she could think of nothing else. During the afternoons she would prowl about the house or stand, staring at the flight of stairs that led down to the kitchen, quite unable to relax as she thought of what was down there. On the third day her resistance crumbled, and she knew she must return to the room.

As usual the house was silent that afternoon as she crept down and opened the door to the kitchen. She made her way silently along the little corridor, her ears straining to detect the sound of another presence. All was silent. Her heart pounding she reached for the peg, pulled it out and twisted it and the door clicked open.

She switched on the light and closed the door behind her. At once she turned to the magazine rack and pulled one from the shelf, flicking through the pages. The photos were all of young, naked women posing, but they weren't what Toni was seeking. She glanced at two more, then picked up a third.

Once again, Toni received a shock.

The first picture depicted, not one girl, but two. The pair wore skimpy underwear and stood, facing the camera, their arms wrapped about one another. On the next page they were kissing. But this was not the peck of a pair of friends. This kiss was one of passion, like those she had seen at the cinema between man and woman. Toni shook her head, confused at the sight.

The next picture confused her even more. One of the girls had divested herself of her bra, and the other was kissing her breast, her lips over her nipple.

As Toni read on, so the pictures became more and more astounding. Both girls stripped naked and began the most intimate encounter imaginable, kissing, fondling and caressing one another with a passion that transfixed the young reader.

But it wasn't until she saw the girl licking her partner's vagina that Toni's hand reached for her crotch again.

This time she knew she would bring herself to orgasm, and she didn't want to rush it. It occurred to her that it would be good to do it without her dress. Automatically she looked about herself, then she reached for the buttons at the neck. She undid them one by one, then let the garment slide from her, stepping from it and laying it carefully on the bench.

She turned to face one of the mirrors, letting her eyes drift down the smooth curves of her body. Her underwear was as drab as her dress, the pants coming up almost to her waist, the bra fully covering her breasts. Yet still she felt excited by her own reflection, and her finger rubbed over the swell of her mound.

She reached for the waistband of the pants, hooking her thumbs inside. She hesitated for a second, still staring at her reflection, then pulled them down, sliding them over her thighs, down her legs and off. She tossed them aside and examined herself again, taking in the dark lawn of hair that covered her pubis and the furrow of her sex beneath.

She turned and went back to the bench, where the magazine lay open at a picture that depicted one of the girls stretched out on her back, her legs spread wide whilst her companion licked at her slit. She examined the girls' lovely young bodies, their full breasts and protruding nipples. Then she slipped her hand down between her legs, once again shocked at how wet she was.

She began to masturbate at once, sliding her fingers inside her as she had done before and working them back and

17

forth, trying to pace herself, though already she could feel the sense of urgency rising within her.

'They're good pictures, aren't they?'

Toni gave a little scream and swung round to where the voice had come from, slapping her hand over her pubis to cover it.

'Please don't stop on my account.'

The girl was quite young, though two or three years older than Toni. She wore a tiny miniskirt and a short blouse that was knotted below her large breasts, leaving her slim midriff bare. She had long, blonde hair that framed her attractive face. She had emerged from a cupboard set against the wall on the opposite side of the door to the magazine rack. There was a smile on her face.

Toni stepped back, the panic inside her rising. She couldn't believe she had been caught in the act. She glanced about her for a way of escape, but she had backed into the far corner, away from the door, and the girl now stood between her and it, as well as her clothes.

'So it was you, then,' went on the girl. 'I knew someone had been in here, and I guessed it had to be you. That's why I hid. I knew you'd be back eventually'

'You knew I'd been in here?'

'Of course I did, you clot. You left the light on. Besides, I could see the mags had been disturbed.'

'Oh!' Toni cursed her carelessness. What a fool she was.

'I've been waiting for you,' the girl went on. 'I knew you'd have to come back about this time of day. As soon as I saw you coming down the stairs I let myself in and hid. Now here you are.'

'I-I'm sorry. I didn't know it was private.'

'It's not really. After all the house belongs to your family, not mine. This is just a place I set aside. I thought nobody knew about it.'

'I'd better go,' said Toni, edging toward the door.

'No don't. Besides, you hadn't finished.' The girl picked

18

up the magazine from the bench. 'Hmm lesbo stuff eh? You into that kind of thing?'

'I don't understand.'

'Lesbo. Girl on girl. You know.'

'I've never seen anything like it before.'

The girl eyed her curiously. 'You're an odd little thing,' she mused. 'You've really never seen a lesbo mag before?'

'No. I've never seen any of them.'

'Gosh, you must have had a sheltered existence.'

'Who are you?'

The girl smiled her engaging smile again.

'Sorry. I should have introduced myself. I'm Alex. Alex Simmonds.'

'Simmonds?'

'That's right. The butler's daughter. Hi.'

She held out a hand, but Toni's right hand was covering her crotch and she didn't move.

'You don't have to cover yourself, you know,' said Alex. 'I've seen it all before.'

'I was embarrassed.'

'Because I caught you frigging yourself? What's wrong with that? I do it all the time when I haven't got a bloke.'

Toni stared at the girl. How could she be so casual about the whole thing when she, herself was mortified? The girl seemed totally unbothered about her state of undress, and was speaking as if nothing unusual had occurred.

'Could I have my pants please?' she asked.

'Aren't you going to finish what you were doing?'

Toni shook her head, her face glowing.

'You can if you want to. I don't mind. What's your name?'

'Toni.'

'The old couple. They're not your parents, are they?'

'No. They're my aunt and uncle. They're my guardians.'

'I didn't think they were your parents. And I guess your aunt must buy you all your clothes?'

'Yes.'

'It shows. Don't you ever get out to any boutiques?'

'No.'

'It's a pity. You've got a gorgeous figure now I can see it properly. With some decent gear you could really pull the guys. You ever been to bed with a bloke?'

'No.'

'That figures too. But you must be bored stiff in this place. Don't they ever let you out?'

'No. I've got no money anyhow.'

'So you come down here for your kicks.'

'I've only been down once before. I won't do it again.'

The girl shook her head. 'No. You must come again. I want you to. I'd love to have you share it.'

'It's such a strange place.'

'But it turned you on,' the girl glanced down at the magazine. 'If you've never seen any of this stuff before, what do you usually use to get yourself randy?

'To get what?'

'Randy. Turned on. You know, Get yourself going when you masturbate.'

'I don't usually masturbate.'

'But I saw you.'

Toni dropped her eyes. 'That was only the second time.'

'Wow! You really are a virgin. Come over here, Toni.'

Toni stood for a moment, then shuffled slowly across to where Alex was standing, keeping her hand clutched tightly to her crotch. Alex turned a couple of pages of the magazine.

'Is this the one you used last time?'

'Pardon?'

'The mag. Is this the one you used last time you were in here?'

'No. It was a different one. One with a man and a woman together.'

'So you swing both ways?'

'Swing?'

'You like girl on girl as well as man on man.'

'Both magazines made me feel the same way.'

'Kind of wet between the legs?'

Toni nodded. This was quite the most extraordinary conversation she had ever had, standing almost naked with this strange girl and being asked the most intimate questions. Yet the girl fascinated her. She was everything Toni was not. Smart, fashionable, streetwise. Toni felt suddenly envious of her easy-going manner. How many other girls would have reacted so casually to finding her in such a compromising position, she wondered.

'You want me to finish you off?' said Alex suddenly.

Toni stared at her. 'Finish me off?'

'Give you an orgasm. You want me to make you come?'

'You - you mean...'

'Sure. There's nothing worse than being interrupted.' Alex reached out a hand and ran it over Toni's face. 'Besides, you're so gorgeous. It'd be a real pleasure.'

Toni pulled back.

'You mustn't.'

'Why not? After all, you're still turned on, aren't you?'

'No. Listen I'd better put my clothes back on.'

'There's no hurry.' Alex moved closer to Toni, placing an arm about her body and pulling her to her. She was fully four inches taller than the petite youngster, and, as she felt the other girl's arms wrap about her, Toni felt suddenly overwhelmed by the desire to let the taller, more experienced girl take charge. When Alex lowered her face towards her own, Toni raised her head and gazed up into the girl's eyes, and when she felt the other girl's lips touch hers, she made no effort to draw back.

The first two kisses were tentative, no more than gentle pressure of lips against lips, as with any couple making their first attempt at intimacy. Then Alex began pressing down more insistently, and Toni felt the girl's mouth open against hers and a tongue begin to press its way between her lips. She tried to pull back, but Alex's arm was wrapped behind her neck, holding her close. Then her tongue was inside Toni's

21

mouth, intertwining with her own.

Toni was overwhelmed by he intimacy of the kiss. Nothing had prepared her for the exquisite sensation of another's tongue sliding against her own whilst Alex pressed her lips down hard, sending shivers of passion through Toni's body. All at once all resistance melted away and she wrapped her arms about the taller girl, pressing her body against hers, heedless of her state of undress. Alex's hand began to slide up and down her spine, her fingernails scraping lightly across the flesh, running down lower until the girl was able to cup her bare behind in her palm and squeeze the soft flesh.

Alex undid her young companion's bra in a single movement, quite taking the younger girl by surprise. Toni sprang back instantly, holding the bra to her chest with both hands.

'No!'

Alex continued to hold her.

'Why not? I just want to take that awful bra off you and see you properly.'

'Someone might come in.'

'Nobody's going to come in. Come on, Toni, ease up. You know you want to.'

'It's wrong...'

'Then why does it feel so good?'

Alex placed her hands over Toni's and began pulling them away. Toni resisted for a second, but the girl was too strong for her, and she let go. As she did so the bra fell from her, sliding down her arms, and into Alex's hands. Alex tossed it aside and held Toni at arm's length.

'Mmm they're exquisite,' she murmured. 'So firm.'

She reached out a hand and placed it over Toni's breast. Toni stood still, her arms by her side, her heart beating fast, her mind a turmoil of conflicting emotions. It felt delicious to be touched and kissed by this beautiful girl, and her body was crying out for more. But surely this was an immoral way to behave? Surely she should be resisting the way Alex was taking control of her body?

But when she felt Alex take her nipple between finger and thumb, causing it to swell and harden, it felt wonderful, and she heard herself moan softly with the sensation. And when the girl lowered her head and took the swollen nipple into her mouth it was all she could do not to cry aloud.

Alex sucked at one breast, then the other, sending spasms of excitement through the younger girl that seemed to travel straight to her crotch, renewing the warmth and wetness inside. Toni found herself taking hold of her companion's head and pulling it closer, pressing her chest forward as she revelled in the sensation of being sucked there. When Alex finally raised her head, Toni's nipples were hard and protruding, the sheen of saliva on them glistening in the room's light.

Alex placed an arm about Toni's shoulder and made her face the bench. She indicated the magazine, which still lay open there.

'Would you like that, Toni?' she asked.

Toni gazed down at the photo of the girl lying back, her legs spread whilst her companion licked at her sex, and a shudder of excitement ran through her, one that she knew Alex must feel.

She couldn't answer, but she didn't have to. Her reaction had told Alex all she needed. Taking Toni by the shoulders again she turned her so that she had her back to the bench and pushed her backwards. Toni felt the cool, hard surface of the wooden surface against her bare behind, then she was leaning back, prostrating herself until she lay prone across the bench top, her backside protruding over the edge.

When Alex placed her hands on Toni's knees and began forcing them apart she offered no resistance, her surrender total as she opened herself to her lover. She gazed down between her breasts at Alex, but the girl's eyes were fixed on the cleft that had suddenly opened between her legs, and Toni knew she could see how wet she was down there. Then Alex brought her head forward, protruding her tongue as she did so.

23

'Oh!'

When Alex's tongue touched her clitoris, Toni cried aloud, her hips suddenly thrusting forward involuntarily against the girl's face. Alex took hold of her thighs, holding them down against the bench, then went down again, licking as her solid little love bud, sending shocks of pleasure through the writhing youngster. She licked harder, closing her lips about Toni's clitoris and sucking whilst she flicked her tongue back and forth, bringing new cries from her naked partner. Then she slid her tongue lower, over the soft flesh of Toni's slit and delved into her vagina.

It was all Toni could do to stay on the bench, her body writhing back and forth, her hips jabbing forward in the most overt manner as she encouraged her lover's tongue ever deeper inside her. He backside rose clear of the bench's surface as she forced her pubis into Alex's face, urging her on as the passion overwhelmed her. It was like nothing Toni had ever imagined, her entire being concentrated on the tongue that darted in and out of her.

She raised her head once more, and caught sight of her reflection in one of the mirrors. At once she was captivated by the image of the small, naked figure, her bare breasts shaking back and forth as she pressed her open crotch against the other girl's face, splashes of wetness shining on her inner thighs.

Then, without warning, she was coming, hoarse shouts echoing about the room as the most incredible orgasm shook her frame, her backside slapping against the bench as Alex continued to lick and suck at her. At that moment Toni was totally absorbed in her own wanton enjoyment, her entire being intent only on milking every last ounce of pleasure from the tongue of the other girl.

When, at last, it was over, she slumped back onto the bench, quite exhausted by her exertions, her chest heaving as she regained her breath. Alex remained between her thighs for a moment longer, then rose to her feet and smiled down at the

24

naked, spreadeagled figure.

'See?' she said. 'I told you you'd like it.'

Chapter 3

'Move your fingers a bit lower. That's it. Oh god that's it. Circle round my clitoris. Oh yes! Oh wow Toni, you're doing great.'

Toni stared down at her friend. Alex was stretched out on a mattress in the corner of the room, quite naked, her legs wide apart whilst Toni fingered her crotch, her body writhing with excitement as the younger girl played with her. She studied Alex's figure. This was the first time that Toni had seen her without clothes, although they had been friends for a week now, and Alex had brought her to orgasm twice more since their first encounter. Today, though, Toni had nervously suggested that it was her turn, and the eagerness with which Alex had stripped off had shown her that she had made the right suggestion.

Alex had coached her all the way, showing her where to kiss, where to touch, where to fondle, and Toni had complied willingly. Now, as she prepared to taste the girl for the first time, she felt a great thrill rise within her.

The two had rapidly become friends, although their personalities were quite different, precisely opposite, in fact. Toni was quiet, shy and submissive, whilst Alex was authoritative and domineering, yet a genuine fondness had grown between them. Somehow their differing personas seemed to complement one another and further cement their friendship rather than the opposite.

They had met every day since that first afternoon. On their second encounter, Toni had been reluctant, still ashamed of her behaviour the day before, but Alex had sensed this and made no attempt to approach her. Instead they had talked.

Alex, it turned out, was the only daughter of Simmonds.

25

Her mother had left him some years ago and he had brought her up on his own. She had been allowed to live in the house by Toni's relatives under sufferance, and had always kept a very low profile, so that her very existence had been hidden from Toni. She worked in the local hotel as a barmaid in the evenings. Alex had a wealth of stories about men and about sex, and Toni found her a fascinating companion. They had taken to meeting every afternoon in the secret room, and their encounters had been a real escape for Toni.

It was on their third meeting that Alex had suggested reading some of the magazines. Toni had been reluctant, knowing the effect they had had on her previously, and sure enough she had ended up with Alex's hand down her panties bringing her to her third orgasm. Then, the day before, it had happened again.

And now here she was bringing similar pleasure to Alex. She watched the young woman stretched out before her, moaning softly as Toni pressed her fingers into her vagina. There was no doubt that Alex was an extraordinarily beautiful girl, her large breasts barely sagging despite her prone position. Toni studied the nipples, with their large areolae and thick rubbery teats. They looked very enticing indeed and, on a sudden impulse, she lowered her head and placed her mouth over one, sucking at it gently.

'Mmm that's gorgeous, Toni,' moaned Alex, pressing her chest forward. 'Suck the other one as well.'

Toni moved back and forth, sucking first one breast, then the other, enjoying the way her friend reacted to the intimate kisses. The girl's skin tasted good, and the scent of her perfume was like an aphrodisiac to Toni. She could have gone on sucking her teats all afternoon, but there was something else she wanted. She paused and Alex opened her eyes, gazing up at her.

'You want to lick me?' she asked.

'Mmm.'

'Sure?'

'Yes.'

'Well come and get me.' Alex leaned back and opened her legs still further, pressing her pubis up in an unambiguous gesture of abandon.

Toni moved down until she was crouching between Alex's legs, her fingers still moving back and forth inside her. She stared at the pink gash between her thighs, noting the wetness that had seeped from deep inside her lovely friend. Then she slowly leaned forward, spreading the girl's sex lips with her fingers. As she came closer the scent of female arousal filled her nostrils, and a new thrill coursed through her. Tentatively she protruded her tongue and licked at her friend's clitoris. Immediately a groan issued from the girl's lips. Spurred on by this, Toni licked harder, making the muscles of Alex's sex contract as she worked her tongue back and forth over the hard bud of flesh.

'That's great, Toni,' gasped Alex. 'Now put it inside me.'

Slowly Alex moved her tongue lower, sliding it down the girl's nether lips, feeling them twitch as she did so. She began to lick up and down Alex's slit, relishing the taste of her excitement. Then she found the entrance to her vagina and pressed her tongue hard against it, penetrating the moaning girl and making her sex convulse with arousal. Spurred on by this reaction she began licking ever deeper into her friend's sex, wringing cries of passion from her as each push brought her to new peaks.

Alex came with a gasp, pressing her crotch up into Toni's face as her orgasm shook her. For Toni it was fascinating to feel the emotion in the girl as her climax overcame her, and she kept her tongue firmly buried in her friend's furrow until the spasms ceased and she lay back, her breasts rising and falling as she regained her breath.

'That was wonderful, Toni,' she said. 'You did really well.'

Toni blushed. 'I just thought it was time you had some pleasure.'

Alex pulled her down and kissed her on the lips.

'Thanks.'

Suddenly embarrassed, Toni rose and walked away, crossing the room to the wall that was hung with chains. She took one in her hand. It was strong, like a dog chain, and it felt cold and hard under her fingers.

'Alex, what are the chains for?' she asked suddenly.

The other girl rose and moved to where she was standing.

'Bondage,' she said. 'Maybe a bit of S and M.'

'S and M? What's that?'

Alex ruffled her hair. 'I never cease to marvel at how innocent you are, Toni.'

Toni glanced at her friend's naked body.

'Well I'm not going to stay innocent for long with you around,' she said. 'Tell me what it's for.'

'It's for people who get their kicks from being tied up,' she said. 'And maybe a bit of whipping.'

'Whipping?'

'Certainly.' Alex ran a hand down Toni's back and closed it over her behind. 'You ever fancy having that pretty little backside whipped, Toni?'

The words sent a shiver down Toni's spine. 'I... I don't know.'

Alex stared at her strangely. 'Seriously?'

'I've never thought about it before.'

'And now you have thought about it?'

'I don't know. Do you like it?'

'I like doing the whipping. But it's guys I get to whip. I've always fancied whipping a girl though.'

'It's a bit, well, kinky isn't it?'

I guess so. But what's wrong with that? We only live once, you know. I reckon you should always give something a go if it appeals.'

'I suppose you're right.'

'And does being whipped appeal?'

'It sounds... Well, exciting'

Alex looked Toni in the eyes. 'Hey, Toni, do you really

28

want to try it?'

'I'm not sure.'

'I'd really like to do it to you.'

'Whip me?'

'Yes.' There was an air of excitement about Alex that Toni had not seen before.

'Would I be tied up?'

'That's right.'

'What would I be whipped with?'

'A horsewhip. Or a cane. Listen, Toni does the idea really turn you on?'

'I think it does.' Toni had no idea why it should be, but her mind was suddenly filled with the image of herself chained naked to the wall whilst her backside was whipped, and the thrill it gave her was totally unexpected.

'Tomorrow, then,' said Alex. 'We'll do it tomorrow.'

'Hang on, Alex. I'm not sure.'

'I am.'

The following afternoon it was a very nervous Toni who made her way down the stairs to the kitchen. She had scarcely slept the night before, her mind filled with the prospect of what Alex had suggested. Now, as she pulled at the hanger and heard the door click, her heart began pounding all the harder.

She pushed open the door and stepped inside, closing it behind her. Then she turned and stopped short.

Alex was standing in the centre of the room, holding a thin whip in her hand. She wore a black leotard made of shiny leather that hugged her curves like a second skin, pressing her breasts upwards so that an almost obscene area of cleavage was on display. Her legs were encased in black fishnet tights and long boots that came almost to the knee. The leotard was cut so high that her thighs were uncovered to her waist, no more than a thin strip of leather covering her crotch. She wore black gloves on her hands and a black peaked cap was placed jauntily on her head. She stood, hands on hips, an arrogant smile on her face.

'So, you finally got here.'

'I'm not late, am I Alex?'

Crack!

Alex brought the end of the whip down against the side of her boot, the sound making Toni jump.

'You will call me Mistress, young slave.'

Toni realised that Alex was playing a game, and that she was expected to join in. All at once the situation excited her. There was something intensely arousing about the sight of Alex in her dominatrix costume, and about the way she was being called on to submit, and she dropped into her part at once.

'Yes Mistress.'

'That's better. Now, you are here for punishment. Do you understand?'

'Yes Mistress.'

'Stand over by the wall, facing me. Now!'

There was a genuine edge of authority in the command, and Toni hurried to obey, scuttling across and taking up her position.

'Hands behind your head. Legs apart.'

Toni did as she was told.

Alex strolled across and looked her up and down.

'Strip, slave,' she commanded. 'Show me what you've got.'

Toni hesitated for a moment, and once again Alex cracked the whip down against her boot.

'Move!' she barked.

At once Toni began to undress, fumbling with the buttons of her dress, her nervousness and excitement combining to make her suddenly clumsy.

She pulled the dress over her head and Alex snatched it from her, tossing it into the corner.

'The bra and pants,' she ordered. 'Get them off.'

Toni felt genuinely aroused as she reached to undo her bra. Somehow, Alex's domineering manner was kindling a desire within her that she hadn't previously been aware of. It was a desire to submit, to let another person take control of her. She shivered slightly as she handed first her bra, then her panties to the leather clad beauty, then took up her submissive stance again, hands behind her head, legs apart, revealing all her charms to the other girl.

Alex began to walk round her, inspecting her naked flesh. She reached out the whip and teased Toni's nipple, making it pucker to hardness at once. She smiled.

'Little slave is getting turned on is she?'

Toni said nothing, then jumped as the whip was brought down stingingly on her thigh.

'Answer me.'

'Yes Mistress.'

'That's better. What a pretty little body you have, slave. But how much prettier it will be when it's striped with the whip. Don't you agree?'

Toni shivered. 'Yes Mistress.'

'Good. Now turn and face the wall.'

Toni turned, and found herself facing one of the mirrors that lined the wall of the secret room. She barely had time to register this, however, before she felt her wrists grabbed and the cold bite of metal as manacles were closed about her wrists, forcing her arms above her head. Then Alex dropped to her knees and snapped a pair of shackles onto Toni's ankles. It had all happened so fast that Toni barely had time to register what was happening to her. Now, as she tugged at her bonds, she realised she was helpless, and a strange feeling of anticipation ran through her as she felt Alex tug down on the ends of the chains, dragging her arms up higher with every pull.

Alex continued to pull at the end of Toni's chains until her arms were at full stretch above her. Then she shifted her attention to the shackles on her ankles, tightening these so that her legs were forced wide apart.

31

By the time she had finished, Toni's body was in a state of tension, her arms held high above her, the muscles taut. She gazed at her reflection, seeing the way her breasts were stretched almost oval, and the overt way her sex was displayed. For the first time she understood the purpose of the mirrors. They were there to allow her to see her own punishment and to show her how she looked to her punisher. Behind her was another mirror that reflected her rear view, and she gazed at the white, rounded globes of her behind, so perfectly presented for what was to come.

All at once she heard a swishing sound, and she turned to see Alex taking some practice strokes. She saw how the whip bent back as it sailed through the air, and a knot formed in the pit of her stomach as she contemplated the leather landing on her bare flesh.

At that moment she felt her nerve go. What had seemed an exciting idea suddenly became a rather frightening fact. The reality of allowing the whip to kiss her bare flesh was upon her, and the prospect filled her with doubt.

Whether Alex had sensed her reluctance, or whether she intended to gag her captive anyhow, Toni didn't know. What she did know was that, as she opened her mouth to protest, a large rubber ball was forced between her lips and a strap placed about her head.

'Mmmf' Toni's protest was stifled to an incomprehensible mumble as Alex tightened the strap. She shook her head back and forth to try to dislodge the gag, but it was hopeless. Once more she gazed at her reflection, and realised that she was entirely in Alex's power.

'Right, little slave,' said Alex. 'That should stop you screaming the place down. Now let's see how you react to a taste of the whip.'

Toni braced herself as best she could as she felt the cool leather tap against the flesh of her backside. Then it was pulled away and she heard the swish of the whip descending.

Swish! Whack!

The first blow landed across her buttocks, the whip landing with a loud crack that echoed about the room. For a second Toni felt nothing, then a terrible stinging pain enveloped her, and she cried out into her gag. She looked across at the mirror behind her and saw a thin white stripe across her behind. Even as she watched it began darkening to red.

Swish! Whack!

A second blow fell, every bit as hard as the first, the leather cutting into her pale skin and bringing a fresh cry from the helpless captive. Already she could feel the tears welling up in her eyes, but her cries for mercy were incomprehensible as Alex raised her arm again.

Swish! Whack!
Swish! Whack!
Swish! Whack!

The whip cracked down again, and again, and again, each stroke laying a fresh stripe across Toni's lovely behind. She was moving now, writhing in her chains in a vain effort to avoid the terrible blows. The pain was awful, like the stinging of a thousand wasps, and a thin sheen of sweat had broken out on Toni's body as the punishment continued.

Swish! Whack!
Swish! Whack!
Swish! Whack!

Again and again the leather cracked against her unprotected skin. She tried to twist and turn, but her bonds were too tight, so that every blow found its target, making her buttocks burn with pain.

Swish! Whack!
Swish! Whack!
Swish! Whack!

The whipping went on for another five minutes, a steady stream of stokes cutting into her bare flesh. Then, unexpectedly, the beating stopped, and Toni hung in her chains, panting for breath, the tears coursing down her cheeks. She turned to see Alex staring at her, an expression of delight in her eyes as she took in her captive's naked body. Then she felt the whip again, but this time it was being pressed between her legs, the rough leather running along her slit and chafing hard against her clitoris.

Toni gave a gasp. All at once she was more aroused than she had ever been. The sensation of the leather rubbing against her love bud was the most delicious thing imaginable, and the pain was momentarily forgotten as she revelled in the coarseness of the whip's surface.

Alex worked the whip back and forth, watching Toni's expression in the mirror as she pleasured her. She manipulated it expertly, bringing Toni close to her peak, then withdrawing it once more. The captive gave a little moan of frustration, wanting desperately to be touched there again. Instead Alex drew back her arm.

Swish! Whack!

She brought the weapon down on her young friend's behind once again, the shock of the blow shaking Toni's small body.

But now things were strangely different for the youngster. This time the pain seemed insignificant compared to the burning heat between her legs. In fact, as Alex whipped her again, she felt her arousal increase, and she found herself thrusting her hips forward in a lewd dance of lust, wanting Alex to excite her clitoris again, trying to show her how aroused she was.

Swish! Whack!
Swish! Whack!
Swish! Whack!

If Alex sensed the youngster's desires, she gave no sign. Instead she concentrated on whipping her young slave, blow after blow falling onto her naked flesh. Toni's behind was agony now, but she scarcely cared. For a truth had dawned upon her that she had barely suspected.

The beating was turning her on.

She stared at the image in front of her, the naked, chained

34

gagged girl hanging helpless whilst the leather-clad vixen beat her behind, and she suddenly felt a wetness in her crotch such as she had never felt before. She had suspected for a while that her natural propensity was toward submissiveness, but she had never dreamed to what extent she could be aroused by it. Now, as the blows rained down on her throbbing backside, she saw for the first time how such treatment could excite her, and she bit hard on the ball gag as she felt the desires inside her increase.

All at once she realised that the punishment had ceased. She glanced at the image in the mirror behind her. Her entire backside was glowing red, with more stripes down the back of her legs and across her back. She caught Alex's eye. The girl was breathing heavily with the exertion of the beating, her gaze fixed on Toni's body. More than anything now, Toni wanted an orgasm, and she thrust her backside back at her punisher, moaning behind her gag.

A slight smile spread across Alex's face, and she reached out with the whip, running it gently up the inside of Toni's thigh. The touch made Toni's body jump, and she tried to spread her legs wider, inviting Alex to touch her at the centre of her desires. But Alex wasn't to be hurried, stroking the whip slowly up her creamy flesh, stopping just short of the pink sex lips that shone with moisture under the harsh lights of the room.

Then, at last, she moved it higher, and a shudder ran through Toni's body as the rough leather found her clitoris once again. Alex ran it back and forth over the swollen little bud, bringing new moans from her captive. Then she began sawing the weapon to and fro inside the furrow of Toni's sex, leaving a glistening trail of wetness across its surface as she frigged the gasping youngster.

Toni came almost at once, her helpless body shaking back and forth as her orgasm overcame her. As she did so, Alex pressed all the more on her slit, bringing new waves of pleasure to the naked captive as she rocked back and forth in her chains, trying to grind down against the whip still harder, despite the fact that her chains prevented it.

It was a wonderful orgasm that completely overwhelmed the youngster, and Alex continued to pleasure her until her body was still, and her muffled moans had subsided. Only then did she withdraw the whip, holding it up for Toni to see the moisture that coated it.

Alex shook her head.

'Wow, Toni,' she said quietly. 'I've seen guys who enjoy the whip before, but I've never seen anyone come like you just did. You're a natural born slave.'

Chapter 4

Toni crept quietly down the stairs that ran down to the kitchen. As always in the afternoons, it was deserted. She almost ran through to the corridor, and her heart leapt when she saw the small piece of paper that was stuck on the door of the secret room. It bore a motif, a picture of a chain and whip intertwined. The girl gave a sigh of relief. It meant that Alex was in the room.

The two girls had designed the device between them as a kind of trade mark. Toni was something of an expert with the pen, and Alex had been impressed with the result.

'That'll be our badge of membership,' she had said.

'Membership of what?'

'I don't know. What about `The Whipcord Club?'

'How many members has this club got?'

Alex had giggled. 'Just two at the moment. It's a very exclusive club you know.'

'The Whipcord Club it is, then. We'll both carry a card with the mark on it, and whenever we're in the room we'll post it outside so that the other can see.'

'That's a great idea. It'll be our secret sign.'

That had been five days ago, and Toni hadn't seen Alex

since, though she had made her way down the kitchen stairs every afternoon and waited in the room. Now, though, her patience had been rewarded. Alex was in, and she fumbled excitedly with the catch to admit herself.

She fell into Alex's arms almost before she had the door closed, and the pair hugged one another.

'Alex, where have you been?' gasped Toni.

'I had to work afternoons at the pub,' said her friend. The regular barmaid was off sick. I wanted to get a message to you.'

'And I'd thought you'd forgotten me.'

'No danger of that. How's your backside?'

'Still a bit sore. But it's a nice kind of sore.'

'You really enjoyed that, didn't you?'

Toni blushed. 'I don't know why.' She said. 'It just seemed such a thrill, that's all.'

'And you've got plenty to learn yet.'

'What kind of things?'

'Men for a start.'

'I'm not sure I need men now that I've found you.'

'You have to try one, first,' said Alex.

'Like who?'

'Like John.'

'Who's John?'

'A friend. He'll be here soon.'

Toni stared at the girl.

'Here? You mean in this room?'

'That's right.'

'But this is out private place. Why did you ask someone else here. I wanted to...'

Toni's voice trailed away as she realised what she was about to say.

'You wanted to what?'

'Nothing.' Toni felt the blood rush to her face.

Alex moved closer and put an arm around her friend.

'Tell me what you wanted to do.'

'You know. What we usually do.'

'You could do it with John.'

Toni drew back. 'Alex!'

'What's the problem? You said you wanted to learn more.'

'But with a man!'

'That's the way you're supposed to do it if you remember rightly,' laughed Alex. 'John's as good a guy as any to start with.'

'But I don't even know him.'

'You didn't know me until a couple of weeks ago. Now look at us.'

'That's different.'

'Why is it different?' insisted Alex. 'We were strangers, now we're lovers. Now that you've got a taste for it, I just think you should try the real thing.'

'I'm not sure. Who is John?'

'He's an old friend. And an occasional lover. You'll like him.'

'Well... I'll tell you what. I'll meet him, but I'm not promising anything more than that.'

'Okay. That suits me.'

'Wait!' Toni's face suddenly fell. 'I can't meet him dressed like this. He'll think I'm some kind of dowdy old maid. Look at this awful dress I'm wearing.'

Alex laughed. 'I'd thought of that,' she said. 'Come over here.'

She led Toni across to one of the cupboards that lined the walls of the room and opened it. There, hanging inside, was a small, black dress.

Toni gasped. 'Wow, Alex, that's gorgeous.' Then her face clouded. 'But will it fit me? You're much bigger than me.'

'It'll fit fine. I bought it years ago when I was much more like your size. It's been at the back of my wardrobe for ages. As soon as I saw it I knew it would be you. Here, try it.'

She took the dress from the rail and handed it to Toni. As she took it, the girl noted that there was a black bra and panties hooked over the hanger.

'Underwear too?'

'We've got to get the full effect,' said her friend. 'No sense doing these things by halves. Now get those things off.'

Toni unzipped her dress and let it fall to the floor. Then she stripped off her underwear and picked up the black panties. They were very small indeed, the front panel being made of a transparent lace so that when she pulled them on her pubic hair was clearly visible through them. The bra was no less brief, the cups lifting her pretty young breasts, barely covering the brown rings of her areolae as she fastened it behind her.

She pulled the dress over her head. It was made of a tight, stretchy material that hugged the curves of her body. The hem came down to only just below her crotch, and the neckline plunged low, revealing a wide expanse of cleavage. She turned to the mirror, eyeing herself critically.

'You don't think it's a bit tarty?' she asked anxiously.

Alex laughed. 'Make your mind up Toni. Do you want to look sexy or not?'

Toni smiled. 'I guess you're right. It's just that...'

She was interrupted by a rap on the door. She turned to Alex, suddenly very nervous, but her friend seemed completely relaxed.

'That'll be him,' she said. 'Better let him in.'

'What, me?'

'Sure. Come on, Toni, don't be scared.'

Feeling suddenly very conspicuous in her outfit, Toni crossed to the door. She placed a hand on the handle, then clanced back anxiously to Alex.

'Go on.'

She pulled the door open a crack and glanced round it. On the other side stood a man. He was in is mid-twenties, with short, dark hair . His face was pleasant, without being classically handsome, and he smiled at her.

39

'Hi. You must be Toni.'

Toni felt her face redden as his eyes passed over her.

'That's right,' she said. 'And you must be John.'

'Got it in one. Aren't you going to ask me in?'

'Of course.'

Toni stood aside and allowed the young man to enter. He was quite tall, and as he passed he seemed to dwarf her petite figure, so that she found herself wishing Alex had brought a pair of high heels as well as the dress.

To Toni's surprise, Alex had produced a bottle of red wine from somewhere and was pouring three glasses. As she and John approached she handed them one each.

'Here's to relationships,' she said, raising her glass.

Toni took a sip of the wine. It was full and fruity, and she rolled it about her mouth, savouring the taste before swallowing it.

'What do you think?' said Alex.

'It's nice,' replied Toni, and John nodded his agreement.

They began to chat, small talk at first. Toni found their new companion amusing and easy to talk to. She sat down beside him on the bench and was soon giggling at his jokes.

Alex had laid some of the magazines out where they were sitting, and she suddenly picked one up, turning to a picture of a naked woman sucking hard at her partner's penis.

'What do you reckon to his cock?' she asked Toni.

The youngster was taken aback, and her face glowed as she glanced down at the picture.

'I...er... It's very nice,' she said quietly.

'That's what you said about the wine,' giggled Alex.

'Well that's nice too,' said Toni, slightly nonplussed.

'Which one would you rather have in your mouth?'

'I... I'm not sure I...'

Alex exploded with mirth. 'I'm sorry, Toni. I didn't mean to embarrass you.'

Toni glared at her. 'I'm not embarrassed,' she insisted.

'Yes you are. Your face went bright red the moment I

40

mentioned his cock.'

'I'm not,' insisted Toni.

'Then would you like to see John's cock?'

Toni stared at her friend. Alex and John were both looking at her with amused grins.

'Stop teasing me.'

'We're not teasing you. Don't you want to see John's cock?'
Alex was stroking the front of the man's jeans, and Toni could
already see a bulge there. Now, as she watched, her friend
reached for his fly and began sliding the zip down.

John gave a little grunt of pleasure as the girl reached inside, her fingers closing over the thin material of his briefs.
Toni could see the long curve of his penis as it strained against
the material, and she felt a sudden surge of excitement inside
her as she watched her friend run her fingers over its length.

'I think John's pleased to see you,' she said. 'Come and
feel how hard he is.'

Toni went to step back, but Alex grabbed hold of her wrist,
pulling her closer. The young beauty tried to resist, but her
friend was insistent, and eventually she allowed her hand to
be placed over the bulge at John's crotch.

At once she was struck by how hard and hot he felt down
there. She ran her fingers down the length of his shaft, fascinated by the feel of his manhood. When Alex let go of her
wrist she made no attempt to withdraw, her fingers squeezing
the solid flesh.

'Take it out,' urged Alex.

Toni glanced up into John's eyes, and he gave a little nod.
She turned back to his crotch. Then, slowly, she mover her
hand up to his waistband.

She hooked her fingers under it, feeling the thick wiry
pubic hair underneath. Then she began to tug gently at it, her
eyes fixed on his bulge. As she did so it suddenly sprang to
attention, and Toni found herself staring, for the first time, at
a rampant male organ.

'Go ahead, Toni,' urged Alex. 'Feel it.'

41

Toni reached out a tentative hand towards John's tool. She ran her fingers gently up its length, feeling the roughness of the veins that stood out from it. As she touched it, it twitched, and she saw the tight sac of his scrotum contract. She wrapped her fingers about his shaft, amazed at how hard and thick it was, drawing the skin back and revealing the smooth, shiny helmet beneath. A bead of moisture shone on the tip.

'Taste it, Toni,' said Alex. 'Suck his cock.'

Toni looked up into John's eyes, and the man nodded. 'Go ahead, Toni,' he said. 'Suck me.'

Slowly, her eyes fixed on John's erection, Toni slid from the bench and dropped down onto her knees, still grasping his shaft. She moved her head forward, her nostrils catching the musky aroma of John's arousal. For a second she hesitated as a sudden realisation of what she was doing struck her. Here she was, about to take this man's cock into her mouth. She, little virgin Toni, up until a few days before a complete stranger to the emotions that were rising up inside her. Then she moved her head forward and opened her lips, took him into her mouth

He tasted oddly bitter, and she sucked at him, running her tongue over his glans and reaching for his balls, cupping them in her palm and caressing them gently. As she did so she looked up into his eyes. John's face was a mask of concentration, his head thrown back, his mouth slightly open. He moved his hips forward, pressing his thick member deeper into her mouth and she responded by sucking still harder, her fist working its way gently up and down as she did so.

So intent was Toni on fellating the man, that she didn't notice Alex rise to her feet and move round behind her. It wasn't until she felt the girl's hands sliding up the backs of her legs, caressing the smooth flesh there, that she became aware of her presence. She gave a stifled moan, shuffling her knees backwards and pressing her backside back against her friend whilst continuing to suck greedily at John's knob.

Alex moved her fingers higher, slipping them through the

42

legs of Toni's panties and running them along her slit. Toni felt the muscles inside her contract, forcing the moisture within her onto the lips of her sex as she responded to the other girl's touch. She was becoming more and more aroused by the second, the heat in her belly increasing as she sucked hard at John's cock.

Alex pulled down Toni's panties in a single movement, lowering them to her knees. Then her fingers were back at work again, delving into her honeypot and bringing new gasps of excitement from the girl.

'She's wet enough, John.'

Toni heard the words, but it was a few moments before their meaning sunk in. It wasn't until John took hold of her face in his hands and lifted it from his stiff knob that she realised what was happening. Then she felt herself being lifted and turned, then pressed back against the bench.

'No,' she protested as Alex pinned her back against the hard, wooden surface, at the same time pulling off her pants and tossing them aside. But it was already too late. John was standing between her thighs, pressing her knees apart and lifting her skirt up to her waist, revealing the dark thatch that covered her pubic mound and the pink gash below.

Alex moved round behind her, immobilising her shoulders against the bench whilst John took hold of his erection and guided it towards her burning sex. Toni's mind was a whirl of confusion. On the one hand she was aching for relief from the heat within her. On the other she knew that what she was doing was contrary to everything she had been taught about proper behaviour.

Then she felt the stiff heat of John's cock press against her swollen clitoris, and she knew she must surrender to him.

He slipped into her in a single movement, his rampant organ filling her and bringing a cry from her lips. She had expected pain, this being her first time, but instead felt nothing but pleasure as he pressed home, stretching the walls of her tight vagina.

43

Toni could scarcely believe what was happening to her as John deflowered her with strong even strokes, his shining cock pumping back and forth inside her as he took his pleasure. She had never imagined that sex with a man could be like this. Compared to Alex's fingers, his cock felt exquisite, each stroke bringing new peaks of pleasure to her as she pressed her thighs up at him, urging him on, her backside slapping against the surface of the bench with every thrust. She raised her eyes to look at Alex who, no longer needing to hold her down, slid her hands down inside her bra and began to fondle her breasts, the touch of her soft fingers like electric shocks running through Toni's stiff nipples.

All at once she felt John stiffen, and she gazed down at him. His eyes were tight shut as he thrust his hips against hers, the thrusts turning to jabs as the tension in him increased.

Then he was coming, pumping spurt after spurt of hot semen deep into Toni's vagina. Toni screamed aloud, prompting Alex to slap a hand across her mouth to stifle her cries as an extraordinary orgasm shook her lovely young body from head to toe. John continued to thrust hard into her, his swollen manhood twitching as it delivered its load, each new jet of spunk bringing fresh cries from the wanton youngster.

Then he was slowing, the flow of semen gradually easing as his passion began to ebb. Toni continued to press her hips up at him, milking him of every drop of his seed, until she sensed that he was spent. Only then did she relax, gradually lowering her backside onto the hard wooden surface, her cries dying to gasps as she came down.

John withdrew slowly, his long cock sliding easily from her, and for the first time the youngster had the sensation of his semen gently seeping from her slit. She stared up into the eyes of Alex, who was still leaning over her, massaging her breasts, a slight smile on her lips.

'See?' she said. 'Nothing like the real thing.'

And she lowered her lips onto Toni's.

Chapter 5

Toni tugged at the bonds that held her arms stretched high above her head, trying in vain to find some relief from the stiffness in her joints as she twisted her naked body from side to side. She glanced across at the mirror opposite her on the wall. What she saw was a lovely young girl, her limbs forcibly spreadeagled into an X-shape by the cruel ropes that held her to the frame, her mouth forced open by a black leather ball-gag that left her incapable of speech. Her gaze travelled down her body, taking in the tension in her limbs, her muscles taut, her young breasts stretched almost oval by her bondage. She glanced down at her sex, remarking on the way the lips had been shaved of all hair, leaving only the neat, dark triangle that covered her pubic mound.

She remembered the day Alex had shaved her, stretching her out on the bench and rubbing the foam into her soft nether flesh before scraping the long, cold razor over it. She remembered too how John had reacted to the sight of her bare cunt lips, bending her forward over the bench and fucking her then and there.

She wondered how long she had been held like this, her body strung up and helpless. It seemed like hours, though she knew it must be less. Alex had waylaid her the moment she had walked into the room, ordering her to strip naked, then placing her in this cruel, painful bondage. Toni had expected a whipping, or possibly a session with a dildo. Instead Alex had simply checked her bonds and then left her alone, her mind filled with erotic thoughts, her sex wet with unfulfilled anticipation.

Her mind went back over the past few weeks and she considered how radically her life had changed since meeting Alex. Then she had been bored and lonely, with nothing whatever to look forward to. Now she simply lived for the afternoons, when she would hurry down to the secret room, hoping against hope to find the whip and chain motif on the door. When she saw it, her heart would leap, and she would fumble eagerly with the catch, anxious to discover what Alex had in mind for the afternoon.

Some days John would be there, and Alex would coach her in giving him pleasure, teaching her how to keep him aroused without making him come too soon, showing her where to kiss and suck him and instructing her in the control necessary to massage his cock using the muscles inside her vagina. Each session would end with Toni gulping down his spunk, or experiencing the joy of an orgasm as he exploded deep inside her.

When John wasn't there, Alex would sometimes bring Toni off herself using her tongue or one of the myriad sex toys in the cabinets. Sometimes they would simply lie naked together, leafing through the magazines and masturbating both themselves and one another. Whatever they did, Toni would find herself feeling more alive than she could ever remember as she discovered the joys of her own sexuality.

Today was the first time she had been tied up, though, since that memorable occasion when Alex had whipped her, and the sensation of the bondage had immediately brought back to her the extraordinary excitement of that afternoon. She wondered what it was about being helpless and vulnerable that turned her on so. Even now, after all this time hanging from the wooden frame to which she had been tied, her ardour was undiminished, and the desire to touch herself between her legs was almost overwhelming.

Suddenly she heard the sound of the latch on the door, and she looked up, her stomach knotting as she contemplated the sight she must make. For a second she almost panicked. What if it wasn't Alex? What if someone else had discovered the room? What on earth would they think to find her naked and suspended as she was?

Toni gave a sigh of relief as she saw Alex's familiar face at the door. Her relief soon changed to shock, though, when she realised that there was somebody with her.

46

It was a man, of a similar age to John. Though much leaner and with his dark hair tied back in a ponytail. He had been speaking to Alex as she opened the door, but at the sight of Toni he stopped in mid-sentence, his mouth agape.

'Hi, Toni,' said Alex. 'Miss me?' She spoke as if it was the most natural thing in the world to find her friend naked and bound as she was.

'Mmmf' mumbled Toni.

'This is Gerry, by the way,' Alex went on. 'He's another mate from the pub.'

Clearly Gerry had had no idea what he would find in the secret room, and he stared at Toni's naked body with amazement whilst the youngster's face glowed scarlet. She couldn't believe that Alex was allowing her to be displayed in this way. It was the most humiliating thing that had ever happened to her.

And yet...

And yet the sensation of having Gerry's eyes on her bare breasts and sex was arousing her more than she could believe possible. There was something about being naked before him. Something that was kindling quite unexpected desires within her, so that it was all she could do to keep her hips still as she imagined the sight that her bare crotch must make.

'John and I have been introducing Toni to the pleasures of fucking,' said Alex, her voice still matter-of-fact. 'She's got a bit of a propensity for the whip, you know. I thought you might like to watch. That's okay, isn't it Toni?'

Toni glared at her, unable to reply.

'I'll tell you what, Gerry,' said the girl. 'Why not have a look in that cabinet over there for a short horse whip?'

The man stared at Alex for a second, then shook his head and walked across to the cabinet. Alex approached her captive. Running a hand gently over her breast, she pulled the gag from her mouth.

'What on earth do you think you're doing, Alex?' whispered the hapless captive.

47

'I just brought Gerry along to watch,' replied her friend. 'I thought you might enjoy it.'

'Enjoy it? But I've never met him before. And now he's seen, well, everything.'

'And very nice it is too. Did you notice the way his jeans are bulging? I reckon he approves.'

'But Alex. I'm stark naked.'

Alex grinned. 'I know. And by the look of you, you're enjoying every second.'

'Don't be silly. It's terribly embarrassing. Please let me go, Alex.'

Alex slipped a hand down over Toni's stomach, and her finger probed between her legs, finding the hard little nut of her clitoris. She rubbed it, bringing a gasp from her young captive.

'You feel pretty aroused to me,' she said. 'Don't tell me this doesn't turn you on, Toni. Your nipples are stiff as hell. I think being seen by Gerry is giving you a real thrill. You're a bit of an exhibitionist on the side, aren't you?'

Toni dropped her eyes. She glanced across at Gerry, who was still rooting through the contents of the cabinet, though she guessed he was staying out of the way in deference to their conversation.

'I'm just going to put a few strokes across your pretty backside,' went on Alex as she continued to stimulate Toni's bud. 'Gerry won't even touch you.'

'But what must he think of me?'

'He'll think you're bloody sexy I guess. At least that's what I think. Now that's enough chat'

And with that, she pushed the gag back into Toni's mouth and tightened the strap once more. Then her hand went back to Toni's crotch. Toni gave a muffled groan as her friend slipped a finger into her again. Gerry had turned round now and was watching them, a short whip clutched in his fingers. Toni glanced in the mirror, seeing how her firm young breasts jutted out from her chest, the nipples standing out like solid knobs, and a shiver of excitement ran through her. Alex was right, it was thrilling to be watched. When Gerry crossed the room to join them once more, she found herself thrusting her hips forward, as if trying to draw his attention to the wetness between her legs.

Gerry handed the whip to Alex. It wasn't very long, but it was extremely thin, so that it bowed back as she swished it through the air.

'I'm going to give Toni ten strokes,' announced Alex. 'I think you'll like the way the stripes decorate that pretty behind.'

Toni was unable to reply, but the tremor that passed through her body, making her breasts quiver deliciously, was not one of fear.

She watched as Gerry sat down behind her, his eyes fixed on the pale swell of her bottom. Her heart was beating fast in anticipation of the whipping she was about to receive, but it wasn't fear that made the adrenalin flow now, it was excitement. She braced herself as Alex tapped the cane against her soft flesh.

Swish! Whack!

The whip came down hard across her behind, stinging dreadfully as the thin leather bit into her unprotected skin. In the mirror behind her she saw the quickly-darkening stripe that had been laid across her backside.

Swish! Whack!

Down came the whip again, laying a stripe just above the first, the pain searing through Toni's helpless body.

Swish! Whack!
Swish! Whack!

Alex was setting about her task with gusto, each blow sending a spear of agony through Toni's body so that the tears flowed from her eyes as he body swayed back and forth in its bondage.

Swish! Whack!
Swish! Whack!

Through her tears, Toni could see Gerry watching her punishment. His crotch was bulging even more, now, and he was running his hand up and down over the swelling. The thought of his rampant cock just beneath the material sent a new surge of lust through the young girl's body, and suddenly she longed to have him inside her, fucking her hard.

Swish! Whack!

Swish! Whack!

Two more stripes were laid across Toni's smooth skin, these ones falling across the back of her legs just below the swell of her backside. Her body was jumping now, like some uncontrolled marionette bouncing on its strings as she tried in vain to dodge the blows. Yet, mixed with the pain, there was the thrill of arousal, the sensation of the whip cutting into her bringing an inexplicable excitement that caused her sex lips to convulse involuntarily, in the way Alex had taught her to stimulate a man's cock.

Swish! Whack!

Swish! Whack!

The final two blows fell with undiminished force, rocking her naked body forward as they found fresh areas of her behind to decorate with thin, cruel stripes. Toni was sobbing now, her whole person shaking. Yet her arousal was more apparent than ever, the wetness in her crotch escaping onto her thighs as the muscles inside her contracted.

She raised her head, aware that her cheeks were streaming with tears, and stared into Alex's eyes. Her friend reached up and brushed the tears aside, then kissed her on the cheek.

'Was that good?' she asked.

'Mmmf.'

'It was supposed to get you aroused. That's what you like isn't it?'

'Come here Gerry.' Alex beckoned to the man. As he rose to his feet and walked across, his erection became even more obvious, pressing the front of his jeans forward.

'Looks like Gerry enjoyed it too,' said Alex, smiling.

50

'Maybe we should give him some relief.'

Gerry stood just in front of Toni, his eyes fixed on her nakedness, watching the way her breasts rose and fell as she struggled to regain her breath after the beating. For Toni it was more arousing than ever to have his eyes upon her, and once more she found herself thrusting her hips forward as if offering her sex to him.

Alex dropped to her knees and reached for his fly. Toni looked on, transfixed as she slid down his zip and reached inside, pulling out the man's erection. His cock was long and thick, possibly even larger than John's, and Toni found herself suddenly racked with jealousy as she watched her friend run her fingers up and down its length. All at once she wanted Gerry's cock more than anything else. She wanted to stroke it, to suck it, to feel his balls as they expanded and contracted inside their tight sack. But most of all she wanted it inside her, thrusting hard into her sex, bringing her the relief that she now craved. Instead she could only watch as Alex took it into her mouth.

Toni had never known such frustration. The fire in her backside was almost forgotten compared to the burning need in her cunt as she watched Alex fellate Gerry. She moaned aloud with desire, but her friend paid no attention, her head bobbing up and down as the length of Gerry's erection slid in and out of her mouth. Toni looked into Gerry's face, seeing how his eyes roved over her breasts and sex. It was she that was turning him on. She that had brought about his arousal in the first place. Yet she was forced to spectate, her naked body providing the stimulus, yet no more a part of the action than one of the pictures in Alex's magazines.

All at once, Alex sat back on her heels, her fingers still working up and down Gerry's shaft. For a moment Toni thought she had finished with Gerry and was about to let him fuck her. Then she saw with dismay the look of tense concentration on the man's face, and she knew it was too late for that.

51

He came suddenly, a great jet of semen spurting from the end of his cock, describing an arc through the air as it flew into Alex's open mouth. A second gob of white fluid leapt from him, then a third and forth. Alex knelt in front of him, her mouth wide, ensuring that Toni got a grandstand view of his climax.

He went on coming, some of his semen splashing onto Alex's cheeks and chin as she held her face up to him. Only when the final dribble had escaped did she release his twitching organ.

Alex rose to her feet in front of Toni, her mouth open so that the tethered girl could see the white fluid swimming in there. Then she pulled away the gag once more and, wrapping an arm about Toni's neck, pulled her face toward her own. As their lips met, Toni's mouth opened and Gerry's spunk flowed onto her tongue. In her high state of sexual arousal, the taste of his seed renewed the girl's passion, and she swallowed it down eagerly, her tongue licking about the crevices in Alex's mouth in search of every drop.

The kiss was long and passionate, and when Alex pulled back her mouth, Toni's face was smeared with the fluid and she was positively gasping with passion. She thrust her hips forward against her friend's body, willing her to touch her between the legs. But Alex just smiled and stood back, leaving Toni groaning with frustration.

Alex took Gerry by the hand, and led him toward the door.

'Wait,' cried Toni. 'Where are you going?'

'I'm just taking Gerry home,' replied Alex.

'But what about me? You can't leave me like this. I need...' Toni's voice trailed away.

'Need what?'

'You know.'

'This is a new phase of your training, Toni,' said her friend. 'It's called frustration. See you later.'

And with that she took the young man through the door and closed it behind her, leaving Toni to gaze after them in dismay.

Chapter 6

'Do you think we've done enough food?'

Toni stood, surveying the table on which were arrayed plates of sandwiches, sausage rolls, vol-au-vents and other items of food. Beside them were numerous bottles of wine and cans of beer.

'Yeah, it'll be fine,' replied Alex, placing a stack of paper plates on the table. 'After all, if they want anything else, they can always eat us.'

Toni felt her face redden. 'Do you really think we should go through with this?' she asked.

'Of course. That's the idea. Any fool can throw a party with booze and a few nibbles. It takes a bit more to lay on a cabaret, though.'

'It's just that I'm nervous.'

Alex took the youngster's hand. 'Of course you are. I am a bit myself. But think how much fun it'll be!'

Toni smiled. 'Yeah,' she said.

The party had been Alex's idea. John had announced that his birthday was close, and the two girls had got together to decide how to celebrate it. Alex had obtained the drink cheaply from the pub, and she and Toni had worked together in the small kitchen that was part of the butler's quarters preparing the food.

The real bonus had come when Uncle Carl and Aunt Gwendolyn had announced that they were going out for the evening. It was most unusual for them to go anywhere, but on this occasion they had been given tickets for the opera by a friend and had decided to go. Toni had been hardly able to believe her luck when they had announced it. It gave her the perfect opportunity to hold the party, and she had rushed down to tell Alex as soon as she was able.

The cabaret, too, had been Alex's brainchild. At first Toni had been shocked by the suggestion that they do a striptease for their guests, but Alex had quickly persuaded her, and the more she thought about it, the more she found herself excited by the prospect of flaunting her body in front of a number of men.

Once they had agreed on the idea, Alex had set about making preparations, getting their costumes together and finding some appropriate music. They had practised together in the afternoons until they were both familiar with the music and the moves they would make. And now they were ready to go.

Alex glanced at the clock. 'They should be here any time.'

'Remind me who's coming.'

'Well there's John, of course. And Gerry. Then there's Len and Frank. They're both regulars in the pub. And Peter, the part-time barman.'

'Five men, and just the two of us. Aren't you a bit scared?'

'What's to be scared of?'

'Well... What we're going to do.'

Alex looked at her. 'You're not chickening out are you, Toni?'

'No. Not as long as you're with me.'

Alex took her hand. 'I'll be with you,' she said, smiling.

At that moment, a knock sounded at the door, the noise making Toni jump. Alex noticed her reaction.

'My, you are nervous tonight,' she said. 'Go and open the door.'

Toni crossed the room and placed a hand on the handle. She took a deep breath, then turned it. There were two young men standing outside. One was tall, his hair cut extremely short, a gold earring hanging from his right ear. The other was shorter, his hair combed back. Both looked to be in their mid twenties, and both eyed Toni with interest. She was wearing the black dress she had worn when she met John, and she suddenly felt very conspicuous as the pair ran their eyes up and down her body.

'I'm Len,' said the taller man. 'This is Frank. We're not early, are we?'

'No.' Toni's throat was dry, and the word came out like a croak. She coughed. 'No,' she said again. 'Come on in.'

The pair entered.

'Hi Len, hi Frank,' said Alex.

'Hi Alex.'

'This is my friend Toni.'

'Hi Toni.'

'Hello.'

Toni held out her hand, then wished she hadn't, feeling very stiff and formal as the pair shook it. Alex laughed at her discomfort.

'Don't mind Toni,' she said to the men. 'She's just a bit shy. You'll find her very friendly once she gets going.'

Toni glared at her friend, then turned to the men.

'Like a drink Frank, Len?'

'Beer please.'

She opened two cans and handed them one each. Then she poured two glasses of wine and gave one to Alex. She drank her own down rather too quickly, and dissolved into a coughing fit. Alex took her glass from her and slapped her on the back.

'Calm down, Toni,' she said.

'I'm sorry,' spluttered the youngster.

At that moment there was another knock at the door. This time Alex answered it whilst the embarrassed Toni composed herself. It was John and Gerry, accompanied by another man who was introduced to her as Peter.

More drinks were poured and Alex put on some music. Soon the drinks and Alex's calm amiability began to melt the ice, and the five men and two girls chatted more easily. Toni had a second glass of wine, enjoying the warm feeling it brought to her. Then John suggested a dance, so they turned up the music and soon she found herself pressed against his strong body as they drifted about the floor.

The party had been going for more than an hour when Alex took Toni to one side.

'I reckon it must be nearly cabaret time,' she smiled.

Toni felt a tight knot forming in her stomach.

'We're going to do it, then?'

'Of course. Come on, Toni, after all those rehearsals.'

Toni smiled nervously. 'Yes, you're right,' she said. 'Let's go and get changed.'

Alex turned down the music for a moment.

'Listen guys,' she said. 'We've got a little surprise for you. Just wait here, we'll be back in a minute.

The pair slipped out of the room and made their way to Alex's room, where their outfits were laid out. Within ten minutes they were ready and heading back to the party.

The men looked up in anticipation as the two lovely girls entered the room. Both wore long cloaks fastened at the neck, so that it was impossible to see what they wore underneath. Toni looked round at their faces, trying not to betray her nervousness, though her heart was hammering so hard that she felt sure it must be audible to them. She looked at her friend, who seemed perfectly calm. She could scarcely believe what they were about to do.

Alex made the men sit on a low bench facing the far wall whilst Toni set up the lighting, training a number of spotlights on that end and dimming the lights at the other. Then she changed the CD and turned up the volume.

'You ready then?' whispered Alex.

'As ready as I'll ever be.'

'Then let's do it.'

The music started slow and orchestral, the notes swirling about the room as the two girls got together in the centre of the makeshift stage. As the sound increased they each reached for the drawstring at the other's neck and pulled it undone. The cloaks fell away, and a series of wolf whistles sounded from the men as they saw how the pair were dressed.

56

Alex's outfit was denim. She wore a tight pair of hot pants that hugged the curves of her behind beautifully. The waistcoat was tiny, joined across the front by a narrow chain so that it was obvious to all that she wore no bra, her breasts pressing the material forward. On her head was a denim cap, set at a jaunty angle and her lower legs were encased in shiny black boots that came up almost to her knees.

Toni's outfit was in contrast to her friend's. She wore a red dress made of a silky material that was so short that it didn't even cover her crotch, leaving her brief red panties visible to all. The neckline of the dress plunged to her waist forming a deep vee, the tight material pressed hard against her breasts so that her hard nipples were clearly outlined. She wore black fishnet stockings on her legs held up by a garter belt and suspenders that left at least four inches of creamy thigh visible above them. On her feet were red stilettos.

The two girls stood side by side, smiling at the whistles and catcalls from the men. Then the music changed to a throbbing disco beat, and they dropped into their dance.

For the first few minutes the pair simply shimmered about the floor, their lithe young bodies twisting and swaying to the music. Toni found herself instantly absorbed in the dance, and for the moment all else was forgotten as she moved with the rhythm.

The tempo changed again and the pair turned to face one another, moving close and letting their breasts brush together. As they did so, Toni reached up and flicked undone the chain across the front of Alex's waistcoat whilst at the same time Alex placed an arm behind her friend's neck and unhooked her dress.

As they swung round to face the audience again, Toni felt the front of her dress fall away, and all at once her breasts were bare, much to the delight of the watching men, who shouted their approval. She glanced across at one of the ubiquitous mirrors, momentarily studying her reflection, noting the way her breasts quivered deliciously with every step, the

57

nipples hard and protruding. She glanced across at Alex. The girl had discarded the waistcoat so that she too was naked from the waist up, the pale flesh of her breasts accentuating the dark brown of her teats.

The dance went on, and Toni found herself enjoying it more with every second. There was something about the rapt attention of the men that gave her a real boost. She would never have believed it possible that baring her body to a group of males would turn her on, but right now she was more aroused than she had ever been, and she found herself laughing aloud at the lewd comments from her audience.

Once again a musical cue made her turn to her partner. This time, as she undid the button on the front of Alex's shorts, her friend slid down the zip that ran from her waist down the back of the skirt. The garment fell away, leaving her clad only in pants, stockings and suspenders. She kicked it aside, dropping to her knees in front of Alex and easing the tight shorts down over her thighs and off.

She remained where she was for a few seconds, running her fingers up the smooth flesh of Alex's inner thighs, allowing them to brush against her friend's crotch and to trace the outline of the slit beneath. Alex simply stood there, her hips swaying from side to side as her friend felt her body. Then she took hold of Toni's hands and pulled her to her feet, and they were dancing again.

The men sat, their eyes fixed on the two young beauties as they swayed to the music, their near-naked bodies moving in perfect unison about the makeshift stage. To Toni, their gazes were almost like a physical caress that spurred her to flaunt her body even more. She glanced across and caught Alex's eye, recognising the same sense of excitement in her friend as the girl winked at her.

The two moved together just in front of their audience. Then, standing shoulder to shoulder, they began to shake their breasts from side to side leaning forward so that their succulent mammaries were just in front of the faces of the delighted men. Toni reached up and took hold of her lovely orbs, pressing them forward as if offering them to the men, her stiff nipples only inches from their mouths. For a second she hoped one of them would lean forward and suck her swollen teats, then her arm was taken by Alex, who pulled her back against her and began to stroke her breasts from behind, her fingers squeezing and caressing the soft flesh.

Toni leaned back against her friend, loving the way she was touching her so intimately. She rested her head on the other girl's shoulder, turning her face round and kissing her on the lips. The men were whistling again now, and Toni knew what it was that they wanted. Alex knew too, for Toni suddenly felt her friend's hands leave her breasts and begin sliding down her body to the brief red panties that were her only concession to modesty before the watching men.

Alex's hand ran over her stomach, then slipped under the elastic of her briefs. Toni gave a stifled gasp as she felt her friend's fingers run down over her pubic hair and slide between her legs. She knew she was wet down there, and that Alex would feel the lubrication that coated her sex lips, as well as the hard nut of her clitoris, and she moaned quietly as the woman rubbed against it, sending shocks of excitement through her body. She glanced down at the men. She could tell by their faces that they sensed her arousal. She imagined their cocks straining against their pants as they watched, and she suddenly wanted to bare all to them and to abandon herself to the passion that was overwhelming her. Even as these ideas filled her head, she felt Alex slide her fingers out of her vagina and slip her thumbs under her waistband.

'Spread your legs,' she whispered in Tony's ear. 'Show them what you've got, Toni, you sexy slut.'

To Toni's surprise, far from being offended by her friend's remark, the words sent a new shiver of passion through her. She glanced across at her reflection, noting the way her body was writhing against Alex's almost as if it's gyrations were beyond her control. She was acting like a slut, she couldn't

59

deny it, but nor could she deny the intense excitement she felt as she leant back and spread her legs wide, pressing her pubis forward toward the watching men.

Alex began to ease the pants down over Toni's hips, revealing the dark triangle of pubic thatch that the wanton youngster had trimmed so assiduously earlier that day. She moved them lower, so that Toni's slit was almost uncovered. Then Toni realised that, with her legs spread as they were, her friend wouldn't be able to remove the briefs. She would have to close her thighs again, thus diminishing the effect of the loss of her final scrap of cover.

She needn't have worried. In a sudden, unexpected movement, Alex took hold of the flimsy garment and simply ripped it in two, the thin lace coming apart like paper in her hands, leaving Toni's crotch quite bare. The lovely youngster gave a gasp of surprise as she realised that, apart from the stockings and suspenders, she was now completely nude, her gaping sex on clear view to the five men watching.

Her embarrassment increased as she felt Alex's fingers slide up her thigh and slip into her vagina once more, this time in full view of those watching. She delved deep into Toni's love-hole, bringing new gasps of passion from the youngster, who pressed her hips down against her probing fingers, suddenly overcome with lustful desire. Alex continued to finger her, holding Toni's naked body against her own, one hand kneading her breasts, the other stimulating her wet crotch, whilst all the time the two beauties swayed back and forth to the music.

All at once Alex released Toni and, grasping her by the shoulders, turned her round so that she stood with her back to those watching, giving them a perfect view of her bare behind. She took hold of Toni's hands and placed them on her own hips. Then she looked her in the eye. Toni knew at once what was required of her, and she dropped to her knees, as if worshipping the taller woman. Her hands moved down to take hold of her panties, then she paused, watching as Alex's hips moved with the rhythm of the beat. From behind her the wolf-whistles told her that the men were growing impatient, and she slipped the flimsy pants down about an inch, uncovering a tuft of fair pubic curls as she did so.

The music swelled and Alex's hips swayed back and forth, her firm breasts bouncing with the rhythm in a way that fascinated Toni as she knew it must the men. All at once she wanted to taste her friend's arousal. She gripped the flimsy knickers once more and pulled them down, over the girl's thighs and off in a single movement as the men's cheers rang in her ears. Then she raised her head and, forcing Alex's thighs apart, licked at her bare slit, tasting the juices that were seeping from it and bringing a moan from the woman dancing before her.

Toni delved her tongue deep into Alex's honeypot, her fingers gripping her friend's buttocks as she licked greedily at her, seeking out her clitoris and sucking at it, her tongue flicking back and forth over the hard little knob of flesh.

Alex stood, her head flung back, her hips pressing forward, grinding her crotch hard against her friend's tongue, clearly extraordinarily aroused by the licking she was receiving. Toni had almost forgotten the music, so absorbed was she in pleasuring the other woman. Then the tempo suddenly changed she was reminded of it once more as Alex suddenly took hold of her shoulders and pulled her up to stand in front of her.

For a few moments the two naked girls danced face-to face. Toni felt her nipples brush against Alex's warm, smooth flesh, the hard, brown knobs stiffening still further. Then Alex grabbed her and turned her to face the men once more, before pulling her backwards and laying her on the ground on her back. Toni spread her legs, offering the men the most intimate view possible of her most private place. She raised her head and peered between the twin mounds of her breasts. All eyes were fixed on her crotch, and she felt her sex lips contract in an involuntary movement that was not lost on those watching.

She glanced up at Alex, who was dropping to her knees behind her. The woman leaned forward and planted a kiss on Ton's lips, her breasts dangling deliciously. Then she began moving forward over Toni's body on all fours, making her way slowly toward the centre of the girl's desires.

When Toni felt Alex's tongue brush against her slit she almost came then and there, her hips jerking upwards as the firm, probing muscle worked its way back and forth over her clitoris. She glanced up. There, directly over her face, was Alex's gaping vagina, traces of love juice and saliva streaked across her inner thigh. Toni grasped her, raising her head and placing her lips over the warm moistness of Alex's sex, licking and sucking it with undisguised relish.

The two girls were locked together, licking hard at one another, their bodies convulsing as muffled moans escaped from them. Toni was on fire with lust now, and she knew Alex was the same. They began rolling about on the floor, first one backside, then the other raised in the air, pumping down against the greedy, slurping lips of the other, both oblivious to the extraordinary sight they made as they thrashed about together.

They came simultaneously, their moans turning to stifled cries as they thrust their crotches hard against one another's mouths. Toni was completely lost in the sheer pleasure of her climax, relishing the taste of her friend's arousal as the warm liquid flowed anew into her open mouth.

Their orgasms continued for a full minute before Toni sensed her friend begin to relax. She did the same, the urgency of her licking decreasing as she lapped up the last of Alex's juices. Then, at last, she dropped her head back and the pair rolled apart, both lying on their backs, their legs spread, their young breasts rising and falling as the excited applause of the men rang in their ears.

Chapter 7

Toni propped herself up on one elbow and gazed down at her body. Her thighs were streaked with wetness, a mixture of saliva and of the love juices that had leaked from her during the extraordinary show. She glanced across at Alex, who was still lying flat on the floor. She could scarcely believe what they had done. The act had been rehearsed as a simple strip-tease, with perhaps a little heavy petting at the end. She had never for a moment thought that they might end up in such an intimate clinch, and she certainly hadn't expected so public an orgasm. And yet it had been the most extraordinarily exciting thing she had ever experienced, and she had been totally turned on, all the more so by the fact that they had been watched throughout the whole performance. Even now, as she pulled herself slowly to her feet, she knew that the men's eyes were fixed on her breasts and crotch, and the thought of it sent a tremor of excitement through her.

She moved to where Alex was lying and gazed down at her. The older girl smiled.

'That was quite something. I could do with a drink.'

'I'll get you one.'

Toni walked across to the drinks table and poured out two large glasses of wine. Then she returned to her friend, who was on her feet now, and handed one to her.

'Here's to drunkenness and debauchery,' said Alex, clinking her glass against Toni's.

'Drunkenness and debauchery,' smiled Toni, and drank down her wine.

She looked across to the discarded clothes. 'I suppose we'd better get dressed,' she said.

At that moment, though, she felt strong arms surround her waist from behind. She turned to find Len facing her.

'Care to dance?'

'I'd better get dressed first.'

'I prefer you like that.'

'Yes but...'

'Don't get dressed yet.'

Toni turned to Alex, who smiled.

'Go on, Toni,' she said. 'After all, it is a party. And you do have a gorgeous body.'

Len placed an arm about her and pulled her close. 'Let's dance.'

It was a slow number, and Toni fell easily into the rhythm, allowing Len to hold her close, enjoying the sensation of having her naked young body pressed against his strong frame. He held her about the waist whilst she wrapped her arms around his neck. Her small stature meant she had to stretch up to him, but she liked the feeling of having his tall, powerful physique towering over her.

It felt odd to be dancing naked with him, and at first she didn't meet his eyes with her own, preferring to bury her face in his chest, momentarily embarrassed by her lasciviousness. She glanced across at Alex, who had retrieved her cloak and fastened it at the neck, though it provided scant cover for her, hanging open at the front so that one of her breasts was uncovered. She seemed careless of the fact, though, and was chatting amiably with the other men whilst sipping her drink.

Toni felt Len's hands begin to slide down her body, taking hold of the firm roundness of her buttocks and squeezing them, his large, strong hands closing about the flesh and kneading it. She made no complaint as he did so, simply pressing her body closer to his, trying to resist the temptation to thrust her hips against his jeans as his touch began to kindle base emotions within her.

He became bolder, sliding a finger down between her legs from behind and running it lightly along her slit. Toni bit her lip in an effort to suppress a groan of pleasure as he touched her there, the finger moving back and forth, barely penetrating her.

She looked up at him.

'You mustn't,' she whispered.

64

'Mustn't what?'

'You mustn't touch me there. People can see.'

'Let them see. You like being watched. I could tell whilst you were dancing.'

Toni blushed. 'That was just an act.

'Some act. Your orgasm was real, wasn't it?'

'Yes but...'

'Well then.'

He shifted his other arm from her buttocks and ran it up her flank, sliding it round and closing it over her breast. Immediately the nipple hardened, sending a shudder of pleasure down through Toni's body.

'Christ, you're making me hard,' he whispered. 'You want to see?'

Toni looked up at him. She did want to see. She could already feel the solid lump at his groin pressing against her, and she could imagine his penis straining against his fly as he touched her up.

He smiled, and she knew he could see the desire in her eyes.

'Go ahead,' he said. 'Take it out.'

Toni glanced behind her. The other men seemed to be absorbed in their conversation with Alex, who was holding forth, laughing aloud with them, apparently oblivious to the passions of the pair on the dance floor.

Slowly she removed her hands from Len's neck and felt down between his legs. He was, indeed, hard down there and she ran her hand over the swelling, squeezing it between her fingers. He thrust his hips forward against her hands, urging her on, and she knew she wanted to feel him properly.

She reached for his zip, pulling it down, then slipped her hand into his jeans. With a shock she realised that he wasn't wearing any underpants, and that it was the warm, bare flesh of his rod that she could feel inside. She ran her hand up and down its length. The end was circumcised, bulbous and smooth, and he drew his breath in sharply as her fingers ran over it.

'How does it feel?' he asked.

'Hard,' she whispered.

'Wouldn't you like to taste it, like you tasted Alex?'

'What, here?'

'You licked Alex's cunt here, in front of all of us. Why not suck my cock?'

'Couldn't we go somewhere?'

'I'd rather do it here.'

Once again, Toni glanced round at the others, but nobody seemed to be paying her and Len much attention. She closed her hand about his shaft and eased it from his jeans until it stood erect, pressing into her belly, the tip a deep purple colour.

Slowly she lowered her body, dropping to one knee, then the other. She gazed at the thick erection that stood just in front of her face, bobbing occasionally as it twitched. Then she leaned forward, opening her mouth and taking it inside.

It was only the second penis that Toni had ever tasted, and she relished the scent and bitter taste of his maleness as she sucked at it enthusiastically, moving her head back and forth as she allowed him to fuck her pretty face, her breasts shaking with every movement.

It was a lovely cock, the shaft thicker than John's, the bulbous end filling her mouth. She grasped his balls, caressing them lovingly, concentrating hard on bringing him pleasure, her own desires momentarily forgotten as she relished his solid maleness.

All at once she felt a hand on her behind, and she swung round in astonishment, momentarily abandoning the rod she had been devouring so greedily. There, behind her, was Frank, Len's friend, and he was down on his knees, running his hands over the soft globes of her backside. She made as if to protest, but suddenly her face was grabbed and pulled round and she found Len's cock being thrust into her mouth once again. Even as she began to suck at him once more, she felt Frank's fingers creeping down the crack of her behind and on toward

66

the very centre of her desires. She wanted to close her legs, and to deny him the access he sought, but when she felt his finger brush against her slit, her whole body shuddered with desire, and instead found herself raising her bottom and pressing it backward, encouraging him to feel her up.

He slipped a finger into her vagina, bringing a delicious sensation to the young girl as he twisted it round inside her, his thumb working down to her clitoris and rubbing hard against it, each movement bringing her to new heights as the fire in her belly was rekindled. His other hand came round her and grasped hold of her breast, kneading the soft flesh. Toni's body was tingling with desire now, so that it was all she could do to concentrate on the massive erection that was thrusting hard into her open mouth.

Suddenly she felt another, softer hand on her shoulder, and she glanced up to see Alex standing over her, still naked beneath the cloak. She ran her fingers through Toni's hair as the youngster fellated her friend.

'Ready to try something new, little apprentice?' she asked.

Lisa had no way of answering, but she didn't need to. Alex touched Len on the arm and whispered something in his ear. The man gave a grin and a nod, and Toni suddenly felt him backing away from her. She shuffled forward on her knees, keeping her lips locked about his erection. Alex guided them to a low couch, where Len slowly sat down, his thick, pink cock still standing proudly from his fly. Toni set to work again, crouched on all fours between his legs, her breasts dangling as she worked her head up and down. Almost at once she felt strong male fingers moving up her inner thighs and she knew Frank was back.

He began fingering her vagina again, making the wetness flow anew as he worked two digits back and forth inside her. Then she heard a sudden grunt from him and she released her mouthful of male for a moment, gazing back behind her. Alex had undone Frank's trousers and had released his cock, which was as hard and erect as Len's. Her fist was closed about its stem and she was working the foreskin back and forth with easy strokes. Toni watched her masturbate him for a few moments, then returned to Len's cock with renewed vigour, slurping hard at his meaty length, the saliva running down his shaft and into his thick, dark mat of pubic hair.

All at once, Frank's fingers left her sex, and she gave a little moan of disappointment. Moments later she was gasping with surprise as something else touched her down there in the most intimate place, something hotter and thicker than a man's finger. Something that began pressing hard against the moist entrance to her vagina.

With a shock, Toni realised that Frank was about to fuck her, even as she was fellating Len. Her immediate reaction was one of indignation. How dare they presume to use her body in so intimate a manner without even asking? Surely nobody could expect her to take on two men simultaneously? Then she felt Frank penetrate her, and all at once the delicious sensation of having a thick cock pumping back and forth inside her drove all thought of protest from her mind. Instead she spread her legs wider to accommodate his thick organ. She glanced up at Alex, who was sitting back, watching with satisfaction as her young protege was doubly fucked. Behind her the other three men also had their eyes fixed on the threesome, broad grins on their faces as they witnessed the youngster's ravishment, and once again Toni felt a fresh thrill of excitement at the thought of the spectacle she must be presenting, giving herself so freely.

Frank was fucking her in earnest now, his belly slapping against her backside as he pumped back and forth. The sensation of his stiff erection sliding over the walls of her sex was extraordinary, and already she could feel another orgasm building inside her as he shook her pretty young body with his thrusts. She could sense a new urgency in Len, too. There was a sudden stiffness about his movements as he jabbed his hips forward, his face a study in concentration.

Len came with a gasp, his thick, hot semen flowing into

her mouth, almost taking her by surprise as it shot from the end of his cock. Lisa had never had a man come in her mouth before, and the sensation was an extraordinary one. She gulped down the viscous fluid, still sucking hard as he released yet more into her willing mouth. She felt some leak from her lips and dribble down her chin as she struggled to keep pace with the rate at which he was pumping it into her.

She was just sucking the last vestiges from the end of his organ when another flood suddenly filled her. This time it was her vagina that received spurt after spurt of hot come as Frank released his load into her, his hips thrusting hard against her as the passion of his orgasm overtook him. That was enough for Lisa, and she let herself go, a delicious orgasm shaking her lovely young body, her cries echoing about the room as she found release for the second time that evening.

Frank continued to pump his hips against hers until the last drop of his spunk had escaped from him, then he pulled out, rising to his feet and tucking his cock back into his trousers. Len, too, withdrew, allowing her to lick the sperm from around her lips and swallow it down. Toni rose slowly to her feet., staggering slightly as she did so. She felt a mess, her hair dishevelled, her thighs splattered with semen.

'I think I need a shower,' she said to Alex, who had watched the whole performance.

'One more thing beforehand,' said Alex.

'What now? Isn't taking two guys enough?'

Alex laughed. 'Yeah, for any normal chick. But you're something special, Toni, and this is a special evening.'

'Go on then,' said Toni resignedly. 'What's the idea?'

'Peter would like to tit-fuck you.'

'What?'

'He wants to come between your tits.'

Toni looked across at Peter, who was standing behind Alex looking slightly embarrassed. 'I've never heard of that before,' she said.

'Then you're in for a treat.'

Toni looked at her. 'You really want me to?'

'Yes.'

'Well... All right then. What do I do?'

Alex kissed her on the lips. 'Great, Toni,' she exclaimed. 'I'll tell you what, I'll get him started. Then I'll get a bottle of bubbly to celebrate. I've got one in the flat chilling.'

'It's a deal,' said Lisa. She was relieved that Alex was, at last, joining in the sex. She was afraid that she would end up the only action available to the men that evening. Not that she wasn't enjoying herself. She had never felt so aroused in her life, and the prospect of a tit-fuck fascinated her more than she cared to admit. She settled herself on the couch and watched as her friend pressed Peter down beside her and began undoing his fly.

Alex dragged his jeans off in a single movement, leaving his penis standing vertically from his groin. Toni couldn't take her eyes from his long, curved manhood, the foreskin drawn slightly back so that she could see the way his glans gleamed with his secretions. At once she felt her desires return as Alex leaned forward and took him in her mouth.

Alex fellated Peter expertly, her lips sliding up and down the length of his organ whilst her hands caressed his balls and worked his foreskin back and forth. Peter was clearly loving every second, his face a picture of enjoyment as she moved her head back and forth, the loud sucking noise the only sound as, once again, the men looked on with undisguised interest.

Alex went on for a good five minutes, during which time the tension in Peter's face increased with every stroke. At last she sat back to admire his stiff pole, which shone with her saliva, its length twitching rhythmically, betraying how strong was his arousal.

'Right, Toni,' said Alex. 'I think he's ready for you. Lie on the floor.'

Alex dropped down to her knees, then prostrated herself on her back, aware of the trickle of sperm that escaped from her vagina and trickled down onto the floor as she did so .

70

She gazed up at Peter, who also fell to his knees, then straddled her, his cock as hard as ever.

He moved forward, up her body, until his shaft was lying between her breasts.

'Push your tits together,' said Alex. 'So that they trap his cock.'

Toni did what she was told, grasping hold of her firm young globes and squeezing them about Peter's shaft. At the same time, her fingers moved to her nipples and she started to play with them, rubbing the firm knobs of flesh back and forth.

Peter began to move, his hips pumping back and forth as he tit-fucked the beautiful young girl beneath him. To Toni, the sensation was extraordinary as she gazed down, seeing his glans move in and out between her breasts. There was something inexplicably exciting about having a stiff dick between her lovely orbs, and Peter's own excitement transmitted itself to her as he thrust himself against her naked body.

Alex bent down and kissed Toni's cheek.

'I'll go and get the bubbly,' she whispered. 'You're doing great.'

Toni watched as she crossed the room and slipped out the door, leaving it slightly ajar. Then she turned her attention back to Peter, who's tempo was rapidly increasing as his passion rose.

He came suddenly, his cock spitting great gobs of semen onto her neck and chin. She lifted her face, opening her mouth so as to catch the jets of spunk that flew from him, loving the way the hot fluid squirted out with such force and splashed against her face and tongue.

She held her breasts about his cock until the last dribble escaped and ran down into her cleavage. Then she let her head fall back and gazed up into his eyes.

He rose, a drop of white fluid still hanging from the end of his knob. As he did so, Toni became aware of another figure standing behind him, a tall man dressed in a dark suit. For a second she wondered if she was to be fucked again before she was allowed her glass of champagne and a shower. Then her eyes fell on the man's face, and a cold fear suddenly gripped her.

'Uncle Carl!' she gasped.

Chapter 8

The next few minutes were, for Toni, a complete blur. She remembered being hauled bodily to her feet by her uncle, and then his voice roaring at the men. She remembered poor Peter, struggling to pull his trousers back on as he was ejected by her uncle, the others fleeing before him. Then there was the terrible anger in her uncle's eyes as he turned back to her.

She had tried to cover herself, one hand clutched to her crotch whilst she wrapped an arm across her breasts in a desperate attempt to hide her nakedness. He had approached her with a look of thunder on his face.

'What the hell do you think you're doing?' he shouted.

Toni could do nothing more than stare at him, her legs feeling like jelly. It was the nearest she had ever heard him come to swearing, and the words had genuinely shocked her.

'Well?' he roared. 'Answer me girl!'

'I... It was a party,' she stammered.

'A party? What kind of a party is it where a girl is stark naked? Just look at you.'

'We were just having fun.'

'Having fun? You filthy little whore.' He drew back his arm as if to strike her, and Toni cowered away.

He lowered his arm. 'No,' he said. 'We'll punish you properly. You'll come upstairs with me.'

At that moment a face appeared behind him, peering round the door, and for the first time Toni realised that Alex had not been in the room when her uncle had burst in. She must have been still getting the champagne. Now, as she stared at Toni, the alarmed girl shook her head urgently.

72

'No, go away,' she said.

'I'll do no such thing,' said her uncle, clearly unaware of Alex's presence. 'Come on, upstairs!'

He grabbed hold of Toni's arm, and began to pull her toward the door. To her intense relief, Toni saw that Alex had finally realised what was happening and had withdrawn, so that the doorway was now empty.

Toni's uncle was a strong man, and his fingers dug into her arms as he dragged her out the door and through the kitchen.

'My clothes,' she gasped, but he simply gripped her the harder.

'You should have thought of that before you started flaunting yourself. I'm just glad that we decided to return early. Heaven knows what you would have been up to if we'd been out any later.'

He took her up the stairs and along the hallway toward the drawing room. Toni could see a light shining from the door as they approached, so she knew her Aunt Gwendolyn would be in there. She hung back once more as they came closer, afraid to face the woman, but her uncle did not slacken his grip.

'Did you find out what all the noise was Carl? I was just saying...'

Her aunt's voice broke off as he came into view with the naked youngster in tow.

'What on earth...'

Toni's face was bright scarlet as her uncle brought her into the room. She was still trying to cover her private parts with her hands, but it wasn't easy. Then she gave a gasp of dismay. Her aunt was not alone. There was a third person in the room.

Toni stared at the woman. She was tall and heavily built, with a body that reminded her of the Russian shotputters she had seen at athletics meetings on television. Her face was ugly, almost frog-like, and her grey hair was worn in a severe bun on her head. She wore a dark, shapeless dress that came

73

to her knees. She regarded the naked girl with a look that sent a pang of genuine fear through her.

'What on earth is going on, Carl,?' asked Aunt Gwendolyn. 'And where are Antonia's clothes? Good god, girl, have you no shame? Go and get something on!'

'No, wait,' ordered Uncle Carl. 'Stay where you are. You've got some explaining to do, young lady.'

Toni stood, her shoulders hunched forward, an arm wrapped across her breasts covering her nipples, her other hand clutched to her crotch, her eyes cast down.

Uncle Carl explained the scene he had come across in the secret room. As he did so, Aunt Gwendolyn's jaw dropped further and further.

'He was astride her?' she said incredulously.

'With his penis between her breasts. He was ejaculating on her when I entered.'

'And was she trying to stop him?'

'On the contrary. She seemed to be enjoying it. She had her mouth open and some of his ejaculate went into it.'

'But that's disgusting.'

Uncle Carl turned to confront Toni.

'Now, young lady,' he said. 'Who were those men?'

'Nobody,' mumbled Toni.

'You must know who they were.'

'They live in the village. I don't know their names.'

'You don't know them? Yet you were naked. And you allowed the man to do that?' asked Aunt Gwendolyn.

'I fear it is worse than that,' said her uncle. 'Take your hand away from between your legs girl.'

'But I...'

'Do it!'

Slowly Toni removed her hand from her crotch, revealing the sperm that still leaked from her vagina and was evident on her thighs.

'Look at that,' exclaimed her uncle. 'She's had intercourse with one of them.'

74

'Or possibly more,' sniffed her aunt. 'Who set up this disgusting get-together?'

'I did,' said Toni quietly. She was determined to protect Alex, only too aware that, should her guardians become aware of her role in the affair, her friend would be ejected from the house and her father might even lose his job. She only hoped that Alex would have the good sense to be, even now, removing the magazines and whatever else she could from the room before either her uncle or aunt went back.

'You set it up? On your own? How did you know those men?'

'I... I met them in the village.'

'When?'

'In the afternoons. Whilst you were resting. I've been walking into the village. They suggested the party. They brought some drink and some records. It was just meant to be a bit of fun.'

'A bit of fun? Acting like some common whore? They weren't paying you were they?'

'No. It wasn't like that.'

Her uncle shook his head. 'To think we took you in under our own roof, and you repay us by acting like some gutter slut.'

'I wasn't...'

'Silence! You will have to leave this house, of course, though where you will go I don't know. If only I hadn't promised my brother that I would look after you.'

'Perhaps I have an answer.'

Toni had almost forgotten the strange, ugly woman, who up until now had not spoken. Now she stared at her, as did her aunt and uncle.

'You, Madam Lashenka?'

'Certainly. I think I see what is required.' The woman spoke with an Eastern European accent that further strengthened Toni's impression of being in the presence of a Soviet athlete. Her voice was shrill, and there was a coldness in her tone that Toni instantly feared and disliked.

'Madam Lashenka was at the concert,' explained Aunt Gwendolyn. 'She was telling us about her finishing school in Estavia. We were hoping it might be suitable for you, but now she's seen the type of girl you are, I'm sure she wouldn't countenance taking you on.'

'On the contrary,' said the woman. 'We pride ourselves in accepting a challenge. I'm sure we have methods of knocking the sluttishness out of this one.'

'That seems precisely what she needs,' said Uncle Carl. 'My instinct is to throw her out, but unfortunately my duty doesn't allow it.'

'Why not place her in my hands then?'

'Do you think you could do anything with her?'

'As long as you allowed me free rein with my normal methods.'

'Naturally we would bow to your experience.'

'She will need punishing for tonight's misdemeanours.'

'Well I certainly agree with that,' said Aunt Gwendolyn.

'Good.' She turned to Toni. 'You, girl! Listen to me.'

She turned to face the woman.

'On the back seat of my car is a bag. Go and get it.'

'But I'm...'

'Go!'

Toni stared at her guardians, but they were stony-faced. Clearly they were happy for this woman to take charge of her. She began to back toward the door.

'Move!' shouted the woman. 'You have one minute!'

Toni hesitated for a second more, then turned and ran from the room, making for the front door. As she opened it she paused, reluctant to step outdoors in her unclothed state. She peered out, but the driveway seemed deserted apart from a single vehicle parked there. She took a deep breath and dashed out to where it stood.

The rear door was unlocked, and Toni flung it open. There, on the back seat, was a bag. It was a long one, the size and

76

shape of a golf bag, though with closed ends. She snatched it from the seat, slammed the door and ran back to the house, praying that nobody had been in the lane and witnessed her naked dash.

Once the front door was closed behind her, Toni slowed, suddenly apprehensive as to Madame Lashenka's intentions. The woman had spoken of a punishment. What could she have meant? And what was the function of the bag she was carrying? Toni glanced down at it. It was not very heavy, and seemed fairly empty. What could it contain that their strange guest required so urgently?

She pushed open the drawing room door slowly, once again aware of her nudity. It seemed extraordinary that she was naked in the presence of her guardians. Normally they would complain if she wore a dress with a hem even slightly above the knees. Yet neither said anything, simply regarding her with glances of contempt as she entered the room.

'Couldn't I go and get some clothes?' she asked, timidly.

'No. Come here.' The order came from Madame Lashenka, and it brooked no disobedience.

Toni approached the woman nervously and held out the bag.

'Place it on the couch, then go and stand by the table.'

Toni put the bag down as instructed, then crossed to the table. For the first time she noticed that the chairs that normally surrounded it had been moved back, so that they stood in a line against the wall.

'Turn to face the corner of the table, then wait.'

Toni made her way round so that she was in position at the corner of the table.

'Move closer.'

Toni shuffled forward until the edge of the wood was touching her crotch. She glanced down and saw, to her embarrassment, that her sex was making a damp smear on the polished surface. Not daring to catch the eyes of her guardians she remained where she was, staring ahead.

77

All at once she felt her wrist grabbed and something cold and hard closed about it. It was a steel manacle with a chain attached, joining it to an identical shackle.

'Lean forward over the table.'

Toni stared at the woman. What on earth was she doing? Smack!

Madame Lashenka brought the flat of her hand down hard on Toni's buttocks.

'Do as you're told!'

Toni gazed down at the shiny surface of the table. Then she leaned forward, slowly prostrating herself across its surface, the hard corner biting into her crotch. She shivered as her nipples and belly came into contact with the cool, unyielding wood.

No sooner was Toni prone than she felt her wrists grasped once more and pulled across to the opposite corner of the table. There, the chain was wrapped about the table leg and the second manacle was closed over her other wrist, stretching her arms out in front of her in the most uncomfortable way.

But Madame Lashenka hadn't finished yet. She reached into her bag and pulled out a stout pole, about three feet long, with a leather strap attached to each end. She crouched down, and Toni felt the strap being wrapped about her leg just above the knee and the buckle tightened, so that the stiff leather bit into her young flesh. The pole was passed round the inside of the table leg under her crotch and her legs were pulled apart. She struggled to spread them as wide as she was able, then felt the second strap being fastened to her other leg.

Toni was in an extraordinary position, quite unable to move. The pole held her legs wide apart, whilst her knees were bent under the table, forcing her to present her backside in the most blatant manner, so that her anus and vagina were exposed to all. She raised her head and glanced round. Her guardians were standing on the far side of the room, their faces impassive as they regarded their ward's naked body

78

strapped into this awkward and revealing position. Madame Lashenka, meanwhile, was reaching into her bag once again.

Toni's stomach tightened into a knot as she saw her pull out a thin bamboo cane. It was a cruel looking instrument, not much thicker than a pencil. Madame Lashenka took the ends in both hands and flexed it, and Toni saw that it was very supple indeed. The woman took a couple of practice swings, the instrument swishing through the air as she did so. Then she turned back to her young captive.

'A dozen strokes should teach her the lesson she deserves,' she said.

Her uncle nodded. 'I'm sure you know best, Madame Lashenka.'

'A dozen?' said Toni plaintively. 'But I...'

'Silence!' barked the woman. 'It's time you learned some manners, young lady.'

She moved round to stand behind and to the side of Toni, and the girl felt the hard wood of the cane tap against her bare, unprotected behind. She closed her eyes.

Swish! Whack!

The cane whistled down through the air and landed on Toni's buttocks with a crack that echoed about the room. For a split second the hapless girl felt nothing. Then the pain hit her and she gritted her teeth as the dreadful stinging almost overwhelmed her.

Swish! Whack!

Down it came again, laying a second stripe across the pale flesh of Toni's backside and doubling her pain as it bit into her. Tears filled Toni's eyes as she lay helpless before the onslaught, her body totally at the mercy of this cruel woman.

Swish! Whack!
Swish! Whack!

Madame Lashenka showed her captive no mercy. Toni had hoped that the beatings she had received from Alex would have prepared her for this punishment, but there was no comparison between the firm whip-strokes she had received from

79

her friend and the vicious lashes that she was receiving now.

Swish! Whack!

Swish! Whack!

Toni's impression of the woman being built like an athlete was strengthened by the force with which she wielded the cane. The muscles in her arms and wrist fairly bulged as she brought down the instrument with devastating force, leaving cruel weals criss-crossing Toni's soft flesh. The tears were flowing freely now, as the poor girl was overwhelmed by the pain of her punishment.

Swish! Whack!

Swish! Whack!

Each stroke seemed to find a fresh area of Toni's behind, forcing her hips down against the surface of the table and causing her clitoris to chafe against the wood. Toni had been unaware of this effect when the first blows fell, but now, suddenly, a new sensation was beginning to transmit itself to her, one which she fought to subdue under the gazes of her aunt and uncle. She could scarcely believe it was happening but, as with the beatings Alex had administered to her, she was beginning to experience a perverse sexual gratification from her punishment.

Toni was getting turned on.

Swish! Whack!

Swish! Whack!

Still the pain of the beating was excruciating, Toni's behind felt as if it was on fire as blow after blow rained down upon it with merciless regularity so that she writhed about on the table in a hopeless attempt to avoid the dreadful force of the cane. But even as she did so, she found herself pressing her hips down against the sharp corner of the table's surface, grinding her hard little clitoris against the wood and sending thrills of pleasure through her exquisite young body.

Swish! Whack!

Only one more stroke to come now, and Toni fought to control herself as her hips slammed down against the table, her backside pumping back and forth in the most lewd manner imaginable as she pleasured herself against the hard corner of the wood.

Madame Lashenka drew back the cane for the final time. Swish! Whack!

Toni screamed as it sliced into her already stinging behind. But the scream wasn't one of pain, it was one of release as a shattering orgasm shook her naked frame. She drove her protruding love bud hard against the table, prolonging her climax as long as she was able, the juices forced from her sex by the convulsions of the muscles inside.

Madame Lashenka watched as Toni's belly slapped down against the table's surface, her small body racked by convulsions that almost threatened to break her bonds that held her so fast.

'What on earth is happening?' asked Uncle Carl as he watched the young girl writhing on the table.

'It is simply the pain,' said Madame Lashenka.

'Extraordinary,' remarked the man. 'It's almost as if she's...'

'Perhaps you will allow me a few minutes alone with your ward now,' interrupted Toni's punisher.

'You want us to leave you?'

'It would be easier if we spoke alone.'

Uncle Carl inclined his head. 'I suppose you know what you're doing. After all, you are the expert. We'll retire to the lounge. Please join us there once you have finished with Antonia, and we can discuss the details of allowing the slut to join your institution. Come on, my dear.'

He took his wife's arm, and the pair of them left the room, closing the door behind them. Madame Lashenka turned back to her tethered captive.

'So, a good thrashing makes you come, does it?' she said. 'That's very interesting. Let's get a better look at you.'

She undid the manacles at Toni's wrists, releasing them. Toni rubbed at the angry red rings that marked where the cuffs had been, flexing her arms to try to restore the circulation. Meanwhile the woman was undoing the straps on her legs.

Toni rose to her feet in a gingerly fashion, wincing at the pain in her behind as she straightened up.

'Stand where you are!' ordered Madame Lashenka.

She stepped forward and examined the table. On the corner where Toni's crotch had been in contact with the wood was a wet stain, part semen, part Toni's own juices. Toni felt her face glowing as she glanced down at this betrayal of her own lust.

'Spread your legs,' ordered the woman.

Toni obeyed. The woman reached out a hand toward her crotch, and she instinctively shied away.

'Stay still!'

Madame Lashenka ran her fingers down over Toni's pubic mound, and the youngster gave a little gasp as she felt the woman's finger slide into her vagina. Despite herself, Toni felt her vaginal muscles contract about the intruding digit as they would about a lover's cock. The reaction was not lost on the woman, who glanced at her sharply.

'Such sensitivity,' she murmured. She pulled out her finger and held it up. It was shiny with semen and love juice. 'You are quite a find, little slut. Now lick my finger clean, then the table.'

She held out the finger in front of Toni's face. The girl stared at it for a moment, then leant forward and took it into her mouth. It tasted strongly of Frank's spunk and of her own feminine juices, and she licked it clean, swallowing them down.

'The table.'

Toni dropped to her knees. The stain was a large one, about three inches across. More had dribbled down the edge of the table. Protruding her tongue, the naked girl licked up the trail, then set about the pool on the table, lapping at it until all the fluid was gone. She glanced up at the woman.

'On your feet. Put your legs apart and place your hands

on the back of your head,' ordered Madame Lashenka.

Toni obeyed.

'That is the submissive position,' said the woman. 'It shows all your charms to those who wish to see them. From now on you will always stand like that in my presence. Is that understood?'

'Yes.'

Slap! Madame Lashenka's hand came down hard on Toni's already smarting behind, eliciting a yell of surprise from the youngster.

'Address me as Madam!'

'Yes Madam.'

'Good. Now, young lady, you have a lot to learn, and at the Lashenka Academy you will have to learn fast, or you will feel the cane on your behind on a regular basis. Is that clear?'

'Yes Madam.'

'Now get yourself upstairs and shower. Then you'd better start packing. I'm going to recommend to your aunt and uncle that you leave for the academy as soon as possible.

Madame Lashenka took a final glance at the naked, unhappy girl, then turned on her heels and was gone, leaving Toni staring after her.

Chapter 9

Toni's heart was thumping hard as she made her way down the stairs toward the kitchen, treading with the utmost care to avoid making the slightest sound. She knew she was taking a terrible risk. If her aunt or uncle found her there, after expressly forbidding her to even leave her bedroom, who knew what they might do to her?

But Toni was desperate. This evening they were taking her to the airport to catch the flight to Estavia. She had no idea when she would be back, if ever. What she wanted more than anything else was to talk to Alex one last time before her exile began, and this was absolutely her last chance.

She made her way down the corridor, scarcely daring to look at the secret door. Then her heart leapt. There, small but unobtrusive, was the whip and chain emblem. Alex was there.

With trembling fingers she pulled at the catch, and the door clicked open. She pushed it wider, and stepped into the room.

'Alex...'

'Oh, thank god, Toni, it's you.'

The girl ran across the room and took her petite friend in her arms, and the pair hugged one another hard.

'What happened? Where have you been? What did they do to you?'

Toni shook her head, smiling for the first time since her uncle had caught them.

'One question at a time, Alex,' she said. 'Oh gosh I'm glad to see you.'

'But tell me what's been going on?'

'All right, let's sit down. This room looks a bit different.'

'I cleared everything out as soon as your uncle had taken you away. It's all stashed in the barn. But what about you?'

Toni began to talk. It was nearly a week since the party. A week in which she had been confined to her room, even eating her meals there. In that time she had seen almost nothing of her aunt and uncle, something she was rather glad about. She told Alex about Madame Lashenka, and the beating she had received, and of how she was being sent to the academy. Alex clung to her hand as she spoke, the tears welling up in her eyes.

'But why didn't you tell them it was my idea to hold the party?' she said. 'You shouldn't have taken all the blame on yourself.'

'What was the point of telling them?' reasoned Toni. 'It wouldn't have made any difference to the way they treated me. I was naked with five men, and one of them was coming all over my face. They wouldn't have acted any differently.'

'But at least I'd have been there for you.'

'No you wouldn't. Not for long, anyhow. You'd have been thrown out, and possibly your father as well. And that's the last thing I'd have wanted.'

'And now you're going away.'

'Yes. Well, maybe that's not such a bad thing. I was just wasting away here. The only good thing to happen to me in the last couple of years was meeting you. At least I'll have your friendship.'

'You must write.'

'You too.'

'Don't forget to put our trademark on the letters. The whip and chain.'

'They seem quite appropriate, considering where I'm going.'

'Did this woman's beating really make you come?'

'Yes.' Toni felt her face redden. 'I guess I'm a bit of a pervert really.'

Alex laughed. 'I wouldn't have it any other way.'

Toni looked about her. 'Look Alex, I'd really better get back. If they find me here who knows what might happen.'

'Before you go, I've got a present for you.'

'For me?'

Alex reached into her bag and pulled out a long, narrow box.

'I was hoping I'd get a chance to give it to you,' she said.

Toni took the box from her and opened it, and her eyes widened.

'Oh wow, Alex. I suppose I might have guessed.'

Inside the box was a long, black phallus, shaped to precisely resemble a male penis. Toni took it out and ran her fingers down its length. It had a soft, rubbery texture and she traced the veins up to the bulbous end.

'I thought it might keep you company on the long, lonely nights,' said Alex. 'It's a vibrator too. Just twist the end.'

At the base of the phallus was a circular knob and, as Toni

turned it, the object began to vibrate silently.

'It's beautiful,' she said quietly.

'Why not try it for size?'

She looked at her friend. 'Alex!'

'Go on. Let me do it for you. Please?'

Toni looked at her watch. Already she had been gone from her room for nearly fifteen minutes. She couldn't afford to be much longer. But the vibrator felt wonderful in her hands, and the thought of having Alex use it on her was an exciting one.

'All right,' she said.

'Great. Bend forward over the bench and lift your skirt up.'

'Everybody seems to give me orders all the time,' protested Toni.

'That's because you like it,' smiled Alex. 'You're the submissive type, Toni. That's why we get on so well.'

Toni rose to her feet and crossed to the bench. What Alex had said was true, she mused. She was much happier when being given orders. It allowed her to abrogate responsibility for her actions, freeing her to follow her physical desires. She raised the hem of her skirt to her waist, then bent forward as instructed.

Alex moved up behind her, taking hold of her pants and sliding them down her legs. Toni stepped out of them. The air felt cool against her bare backside, and she shivered slightly as Alex ran her fingers over it.

'That must have been quite a beating,' she said. 'The marks are still there.'

Toni glanced round. In the mirror behind her she could see the firm, pale globes of her behind, the dark bruises still criss-crossing it.

'It doesn't hurt any more,' she said.

'Spread your legs.'

Toni leaned forward once more and widened her stance, at the same time pressing her backside backwards, presenting

86

her open sex to her friend.

A faint buzz told her that Alex had turned the instrument on. Then she felt the cool roughness of it against her inner thigh and she shivered with anticipation as Alex began to rub it up and down the smooth, creamy flesh.

A finger slid along the crack of her behind and stopped at the pink star of her anus. Then, to Toni's surprise, it pressed and twisted against that tight little hole, making her draw in her breath sharply, her hips squirming. It penetrated, so that the tip of the finger was just inside her, then it began to twist again, bringing fresh gasps from the lovely youngster.

Now the vibrator was moving again, sliding up her soft flesh to the very centre of her desires.

'Oh!'

The exclamation came involuntarily from Toni's lips as the buzzing object found her clitoris and pressed against it, moving back and forth over the little bud and causing a new wetness to swell inside her. She turned round to look at Alex, whose eyes were fixed on her crotch as she moved the phallus back and forth, whilst continuing to finger Toni's rectum.

Toni was gasping with desire now, her hips pressing back against her friend's hands. She badly wanted to be penetrated, and she moaned with quiet frustration as Alex continued to tease her.

'Oh please do it to me Alex,' she groaned at last. 'I need it.'

Alex smiled and moved the vibrator along Toni's glistening sex lips to the very entrance to her sex. Then she began to push, twisting back and forth as she did so.

Toni gave a cry as the long, thick object penetrated her, its ebony surface contrasting sharply with the pink of her sex lips as it drove into her. It felt wonderful, the vibrations sending sparks of excitement through her belly. Alex pressed it home as far as it would go, holding it there as the walls of her friend's sex contracted around it. Then she began to move it back and forth with a steady rhythm.

She worked the imitation penis in and out of Toni's vagina with smooth, sensuous movements, watching the way the girl thrust back against her hands, urging her on as she moaned with pleasure. At the same time she continued to twist her finger in Toni's nether hole, feeling her friend's sphincter tighten with every stroke.

Toni was lost in the joy of her arousal now, all her troubles forgotten as the exquisite pleasure of the vibrator overwhelmed her. She wanted the sensation to go on and on, but she knew she couldn't hold back her orgasm for long. Alex seemed to sense that she was reaching her peak, pumping the dildo back and forth with a new vigour, working her young friend expertly.

The orgasm, when it hit Toni, was a glorious one, her whole body shaking with passion as the exquisite release overwhelmed her. She lay flat on the bench, small grunts of satisfaction escaping her lips, her backside continuing to pump up and down. Alex kept on thrusting the dildo into Toni with vigour, feeling the way her sex muscles closed about the thick shaft of the vibrator as her passion slowly ebbed.

She continued to pump until the prostrate girl was still. Only then did she slip her finger from Toni's anus and withdraw the vibrator. Toni turned to her then, and gave her a weary smile.

'What am I going to do without you Alex?' she murmured.

Chapter 10

Toni awoke to the insistent ringing of the bell above her head. She reached out a hand for her alarm clock on the bedside table, but found only empty air. She fumbled about for a moment, then her mind cleared, and she remembered where she was. She opened her eyes and blinked at the stark, white-washed walls that surrounded her, and at the bare strip lights that shone down from above. Already the girl in the next bed to hers was responding to the rising bell, pulling herself into a sitting position and reaching for her slippers.

Toni knew she must do the same. At any moment one of the staff would enter the dormitory, and anyone found still beneath the covers would receive three strokes with a leather belt across her bare behind.

She sat up, wincing as her feet touched the freezing linoleum that covered the floor. She glanced at her watch. It was six o'clock in the morning. Still, she mused, the girls on kitchen duties had already been up for an hour and a half. She should be thankful for small mercies. She opened her drawer and pulled out her toothbrush and toothpaste. Then, pulling her towel from the rail, she joined the queue for the bathroom.

Toni had been at the Lashenka Academy for two weeks now, though it seemed longer. The whole time had been a litany of drudgery for the youngster. The academy was a finishing school in name only. Toni couldn't imagine a prison that could have a more severe regime.

The girls rose every morning at six, and by six-fifteen had to be in the dining room to consume the porridge and bread and margarine that served as their breakfast. After that came washing-up and cleaning their dormitory for inspection by Madame Lashenka at nine. Everything had to be spotless and in its place or the unfortunate girls concerned were strapped. Toni had already experienced the belt across her behind twice since joining, and she had soon learnt that nothing but perfection would satisfy Madame Lashenka.

After breakfast, the girls would be put to work about the house and gardens, or sent down to the town where they would act as maids and washerwomen for the local gentry. Lunch was a meagre affair, sometimes nothing at all for those working in the town, then all would assemble at five for an evening meal which generally consisted of a watery stew. The rest of the evening was spent doing the laundry for themselves and the staff, and waiting on table in the staff dining room. Thus

89

day followed dreary day at the academy with nothing to punctuate the dreadful boredom of the place.

Toni had tried to befriend some of the other girls, but with scant success. Most spoke no English at all and, since contact between girls was strictly forbidden at all times, life at the academy proved as lonely as with her guardians before she had met Alex. In the brief periods she had to herself, Toni had managed to write two letters to her friend, but since these had to be delivered unsealed to the staff before posting, she had had no opportunity to communicate the bleakness of her conditions, so the letters had been bland and uninformative. She had, as yet, received no reply, so she couldn't even be certain that her letters were being sent out.

She made her way out of the bathroom and back to her bed, where she peeled off her nightgown and pulled on the grey, shapeless dress that was the uniform of the academy. Then it was a rush to get into her place in the dining room before the gong sounded, indicating that the doors were to be closed, and those still outside punished.

As she ate the tasteless mush, she gazed about her at her fellow inmates. All sat with their heads down, avoiding eye contact with one another. She glanced down to the far end of the room, where half a dozen other tables stood empty. These had linen, condiments and knives and forks laid out on them, though she knew it would be a good few hours before anyone would arrive to sit at them.

The tables were reserved for the members of the Midnight Club. Toni had heard one of the staff using the name, but she had no idea what it was. All she knew was that club members enjoyed rare privileges. They were allowed to sleep late in the mornings, and had their breakfast served to them after ten, the meal consisting of cold meat, rolls, coffee and fruit. They were clearly a privileged group, and Toni wondered what they did to gain membership.

A bell rang, the sign that the meal was at an end. Toni dropped her spoon into her bowl and joined the queue to deposit the dirty crockery in the kitchen and then set about the mornings chores.

Madame Lashenka's inspection passed without incident for Toni. Normally, once this was complete, she would find herself on one of the rosters of girls who worked around the house and its gardens. Today, however, she was singled out with a number of others and taken to the main gate of the academy. A tall, stern looking woman awaited them, forming them into a line and marching them down the street.

It was the first time Toni had seen the town, and she glanced about herself curiously as they walked along. The houses were drab and characterless, relics of the communist past of Estavia. The townsfolk too were a colourless lot, gazing bleakly at the girls as they marched down the narrow, dusty street.

They rounded a bend, and all at once the scene changed. The small houses were replaced by larger ones with fine gardens an driveways in which stood shiny western European cars. As they passed each one, a girl would be taken from the group and sent up to the door. When Toni's turn came, it was outside an imposing red brick edifice and she eyed it with some consternation. But her escort was watching her, and she knew she had no choice but to knock on the door.

It was opened by a woman, about forty years old, with deep-set eyes and an expressionless face. She gestured for Toni to go in, then closed the door behind her. She led Toni down a long corridor, expensively carpeted, with large oil paintings on the wall. At the end was a kitchen. It was extremely untidy, the surfaces strewn with unwashed crockery and cutlery. The floor was dirty, as was the sink and table, and a bottle lay shattered on the floor, its contents making an ever-spreading puddle across the room.

'You clean,' said the woman. 'All dishes clean, then floor. You make clean, understand?'

Toni nodded. 'Yes Madam.'

'Good. Work now.'

91

The woman turned and left, closing the door behind her. Toni looked round at the state of the room. There was no doubt about it, she had her work cut out for her today.

She set to at once, absorbing herself in her tasks, the academy thrust to the back of her mind as she gathered the dishes by the sink. She worked speedily and efficiently, stacking the crockery on the draining board as she completed it.

Leaving the dishes to drain, she started on the floor. In the cupboard she found a mop and bucket and, having cleared the broken glass, set about cleaning it.

So intent was she on her work, that she didn't notice the figure enter the room. When she suddenly turned and confronted him she nearly dropped her mop in surprise.

He was a young man, about twenty-one, she estimated, well over six feet tall and rather overweight, his face spotty. His deep-set eyes told her that he was related to the woman, probably her son. They were small, beady eyes, and they stared at her with an intensity that immediately made her nervous.

She went on with her work, trying to ignore the new arrival as he stood and watched her every movement, his eyes never leaving her body as she went about her chores.

She finished the floor and put the mop and bucket back. Then she picked up a tea towel and was about to start drying the dishes when a hand closed about her wrist.

She looked up into the young man's face. 'What is it?' she asked. 'I have to get on with my work.'

'What is your name?' His voice had a high, almost girlish pitch.

'Toni.'

'Toni is boy's name.'

'It's short for Antonia.'

He nodded. 'I called Mika. You take off dress for me.'

Toni pulled her arm away, shocked. 'Don't be silly,' she said. 'I've got to get on with this work.'

'Take off dress,' he insisted. 'Or you get trouble. Other girl come here, she refuse to take off dress for Mika. I get her plenty trouble. Get whipped by Madame Lashenka and locked away in cellar with rats.'

Toni stared at him. She had heard about the cellar at the academy, where recalcitrant girls were locked, often for days at a time, without light or food. It was indeed rumoured to be infested with rats, and the idea sent a shiver down her spine.

'Take off dress,' he said again.

'No. Please leave me alone.'

He reached past her and picked up a pile of plates from the draining board, holding them high above his head.

'Take off dress,' he repeated. 'Or plates get smashed and my mother get plenty mad. Then you go in cellar.'

Toni eyed him. He was clearly serious, and she could only guess at the trouble that would ensue if the plates were broken. It would be simply his word against hers, and she had little doubt which of them would be believed.

'Put the plates down, Mika,' she said.

'First you take off dress.'

Toni knew he had her. She had no choice but to obey his command. She glanced about herself. She had seen no sign of the woman since she had been left in the kitchen a good hour earlier. In fact, she was fairly sure she had heard the car start up, so she guessed that her mistress had gone out. She gave a little sigh.

'You'll put the plates down if I remove my dress?'

'I drop them if you don't.'

'All right then. But stay where you are.'

Toni reached for the hem of her dress, once more looking about her to ensure they were alone. She began slowly to lift it. She was wearing a set of underwear that Alex had given her, consisting of matching black lace bra and pants, and she felt her face redden as it came into the young man's view. She pulled the dress over her head and let her hands fall to her side, allowing his gaze to rove over her creamy white flesh, acutely aware of how the black underwear contrasted with her pale skin. She dropped her eyes, embarrassed by the way

93

her bra enhanced her cleavage, pushing her breasts up and apart so that they swelled deliciously.

'All right?' she asked quietly. 'Would you put the plates down now, please?'

He shook his head. 'The bra now.'

'Look, I took off my dress,' said Toni, an air of desperation creeping into her voice. 'That was the deal wasn't it? Now please let me get on with my work.'

'You take off the bra, or I drop the plates.'

'You wouldn't.'

'I have already done it before. The girl was nearly sent mad by the rats.'

Toni stood, indecisive. She had little doubt that the young man would carry out his threat. There was something in his eyes that told her he was mad enough. But what he was asking went well beyond the pale. Stripping for her friends had been one thing, but baring her breasts to this unpleasant young stranger was quite another. Yet, as she reflected on the party, she was reminded how easy it had been, and how much she had enjoyed showing off her body to the men. Besides, the alternative was unthinkable. Taking off her bra was an awful prospect, but a small thing compared to incurring the wrath of Madame Lashenka.

She dropped her dress onto the kitchen floor. Then, reluctantly, she reached up behind her for the catch on her bra, noting the smile that came across the man's face as she did so. She undid it in a single movement and let it slide down her arms, leaving her firm young breasts bare. She glanced down at them, noting that, despite her reluctance, her brown teats had stiffened as soon as the man's eyes had fallen on them. She looked into his face.

'Satisfied?'

'You have beautiful tits.'

'Can I get dressed now, please?'

'One more thing to take off.'

In her heart, Toni had known he wouldn't stop at just the

94

bra, but still his demand outraged her.

'I can't,' she said. 'Not here. Someone might come along.'

He raised the plates above his head. 'Take off the pants,' he ordered.

Toni's shoulders slumped. She knew she was beaten. The thought of the wrath of the young man's mother, followed by that of Madame Lashenka made the embarrassment of stripping naked pale to insignificance. Yet she knew too that he was unlikely to stop at just looking at her, and for the first time she was forced to contemplate the possibility that he would fuck her, here in this strange house.

To her amazement, she found herself contemplating the idea quite calmly. She felt no physical attraction towards this overweight youth, yet she knew that, if it should prove necessary for her own well being, she would submit to him. At that moment she realised how much she owed to Alex for showing her the power of her own sexuality.

Slowly she reached down and hooked her thumbs into her panties. In her mind she was imagining that she was standing in front of the men in the secret room, and she felt a rush of wetness inside her as she began pulling down the scanty garment.

She dragged the pants off in a single movement and dropped them on the floor. All at once she was feeling very sexy indeed as she sensed the man's eyes on her crotch. It was as if she had been born to show off her body, but that it had taken Alex's coaching for her to recognise the exhibitionist within her. In an act of impulsive bravado she spread her legs and placed her hands on her hips, staring into his eyes.

'Is this what you wanted?' she asked.

For a moment he said nothing. The sight of her private parts seemed to have transfixed him, and he simply ogled her naked body, taking in her swelling breasts, the curve of her waist and the dark thatch that covered her pubis. Once again Toni found herself strangely excited by his attention, and she felt an unexpected tremor of excitement as she contemplated her situation. There was something about being naked before this stranger that was awakening the most basic of instincts within her.

The man put down the plates, then stepped forward so that he was standing only inches from the naked young beauty. Toni stood where she was, her heart thumping in her chest. When he reached out a hand, she shied back slightly, but kept her hands on her hips.

'You've seen me now,' she said. 'Let me get dressed.'

'You do as I tell you,' he replied. 'I can still break the plates.'

Toni said nothing, the inevitability of what was happening making any resistance to the man pointless.

'Go and wash dishes,' he said.

'But they're clean.'

'Wash again. Go now!'

Toni eyed him momentarily, slightly taken aback by this strange new demand. Then she walked slowly across to the sink, picking up the pile of plates he had been brandishing and placing them on the side of the sink. She filled it with water once more.

It felt strange to be standing there, her bare breasts hanging over the bowl, the cold edge of the porcelain pressing against her naked torso as she began to scrub the plates and dishes for a second time. She glanced down at the floor where she had discarded her clothes. They were no longer there. She gave a small sigh. He had complete control over her now, she knew, and a shiver ran through her as she imagined him standing behind her, contemplating the sight of her bare backside.

He left her to wash up for a full ten minutes. Toni guessed that the sight of her going about so mundane a chore whilst totally nude was something of a fantasy for him. The thought of him becoming aroused by the sight of her body was beginning to have an even greater effect on her, now, and she suddenly began to find her situation strangely erotic. She knew already of the latent exhibitionism inside her, a trait that had spurred her on during her striptease act with Alex. It surprised her, though, that being trapped in a kitchen with this odd young man could excite her, but the more she stood there, naked and unprotected, the more she felt the heat in her body increase so that, almost unconsciously, she found herself pressing her bare pubis against the side of the deep porcelain sink.

When he touched her, a tremor ran through her body that made her cease what she was doing, her muscles tensing. It had been a single, light touch on the smooth skin of her back, yet it was like an electric shock to the young beauty.

'Wash! Wash!' The words were whispered, but there was no mistaking the urgency in them.

Slowly she began to rub the dishcloth against the plate she was holding, though she was finding it increasingly difficult to concentrate on her task as his fingers traced the path of her spine all the way down to the swell of her behind before running up again to her shoulders.

Toni's hand shook as she reached for another plate and began to run the cloth over its surface. Her mind was now totally concentrated on the hands that were moving down her flanks, the palms pressed against her as they followed the contours of her curves down to her hips. He was standing close behind her now, towering over her petite figure. She could feel his clothes brushing against her bare skin as his hands began to move upwards again in a slow, gentle caress that was starting to make her heart beat harder as she tried to control her own emotions.

The hands slid higher, and with a shock she realised they were moving round her body to her rib cage. She glanced down at her breasts, noting how stiff her large brown teats had become as she anticipated his next move.

She gave a sharp intake of breath as his palms moved onto the soft firmness of her young breasts, the fingers closing about them. His large hands contained them completely. He started to knead them, his rough palms chafing deliciously against the sensitive flesh of her teats, sending ripples of pleasure through her.

'Wash!' he hissed.

She picked up another plate and began absent-mindedly wiping it with the cloth. She was trembling now, but not with fear. Despite the strangeness of her situation, or perhaps even because of it, her body was responding with a quite unexpected passion to the touch of this unpleasant, demanding stranger. He was pressing closer against her now, and she could feel his breath on her hair as he mauled her lovely mammaries.

All at once his right hand left her breast and began moving downwards once more. Toni bit her lip as she realised where he was groping for. She gave a murmur of protest, dropping the cloth into the water and reaching for his hand, but he was much too strong for her.

'Wash!' he said again.

Toni stood, all her muscles tense, simply staring ahead of her as she felt his hand creep lower. She tried to press her body against the sink, but in vain, as he forced his fingers in between, moving them down over her belly, toying briefly with her pubic thatch before seeking out the centre of her desires.

'Oh!'

Toni gasped aloud as his strong, rough fingers found her clitoris and began to rub it. The sensation for the wanton youngster was delicious, and all at once she found herself moving back from the sink and opening her legs in an unambiguous admission of her own arousal.

'You see? You like now,' he said.

Toni was silent, still unable to understand her own desires. Less than half an hour before she had been contemplating how repulsive she found this large, overweight bully of a man, and now here she was, standing naked before him, her body responding with total desire to his rough caresses.

His hands left her now writhing body for a moment, and she felt them drop to his trousers. She glanced behind to see him easing his large, stiff cock from his fly.

'Turn round!' he ordered. 'Lean forward, then wash again.'

Toni turned back to the sink, though her mind was completely occupied by the image of his thick member and the knowledge that it would soon be inside her. She was reacting almost like an automaton now, the cloth describing circles on the surface of the plate as she leaned forward over the sink. He took hold of her thighs in both hands, pulling her backwards. Then she felt the hardness of his erection as it pressed against the entrance to her vagina.

He eased himself into her with a series of short jabs, each one bringing a gasp of desire from her as she abandoned herself to him, suddenly no longer caring where she was or who it was that was violating her so intimately. He pushed all the way in, until she could feel his stomach pressed hard against the softness of her backside. Then he paused, his arms wrapping themselves about her body and reaching for her breasts once more.

He began to fuck her with strong, jerky movements that betrayed his own arousal and inexperience. His thrusts were hard, ramming her body against the sink as he grunted with passion. Toni responded by pressing back against him, her own arousal increasing with every stroke. She braced herself against the sink, the dish and cloth discarded as she accepted his onslaught, her breasts shaking back and forth, abandoning herself to the pleasure of being screwed hard.

The force of his thrusts was becoming stronger with every minute, and Toni guessed that he wouldn't be able to keep going for long. She herself could feel her own passion rising, the sheer eroticism of her situation suddenly blotting out all other thoughts. She was gasping now, her sex hotter and wetter than she would have believed possible as his penis slid in and out of it and she knew that her orgasm was not far off.

He came suddenly, his cock jumping as his balls pumped their contents deep into her. She cried aloud at the sheer pleasure of the sensation, her own climax engulfing her almost simultaneously. Together they rocked back and forth, their bodies locked together, their mutual passion filling them to the exclusion of all else. Toni felt her cunt muscles close rhythmically about his rod as he continued to spurt his seed deep inside her, each twitch of his cock bringing a fresh spasm of lust to shake her tingling body.

At last his thrusts began to slow, and she let herself relax, slumping against the sink, gasping as she fought to regain her breath. He withdrew from her slowly, his glistening penis sliding from her easily. She heard him zip his trousers as she turned to face him, her face crimson with exertion.

It was at that very moment that his mother entered the room.

Chapter 11

Toni stood outside Madame Lashenka's office, her heart beating hard as she waited to be summoned. She stared at the closed door, wondering what was being said behind it. She wasn't looking forward to the impending interview a bit.

Opposite her was a full-length mirror, and she studied her body as she stood, quite naked, her hands behind her head, legs spread apart.

Her backside still throbbed from the beating she had received at the house. The young man's mother had showed her no mercy, bending her over the kitchen table and setting about her with a riding switch. She had lost count of the number of strokes that had been administered on her bare behind whilst the boy had simply stood and watched, sniggering as he listened to Toni's cries of pain.

Then had come the humiliation of being taken back to the academy through the streets of the village, still quite naked. The people had come out and stared with a mixture of amusement and fascination at the beautiful youngster being driven past their doors by the angry woman, the whip cracking across her bare backside as she hurried along, trying desperately to cover herself with her hands.

She had been met at the entrance to the academy by a staff member, who had listened to the woman's complaints whilst the other girls stood and stared, many of them laughing at Toni's predicament. And now here she was, waiting to see Madame Lashenka, her thighs still streaked with the young man's semen as it continued to seep from her.

All at once the door to the office opened and Madame Lashenka's secretary came out. She was a tall dark-haired woman of about twenty-five. She wore a business suit, but her lovely figure was still obvious, her breasts pressing her white blouse forward whilst the skirt clung tight to her curvaceous hips. She wore her hair up in a severe bun, and had dark-rimmed glasses on her nose. She eyed the naked youngster grimly.

'Come inside,' she ordered.

Toni followed her into the office. It was a large room, quite out of context with the grim austerity of the academy. The carpet felt deep and plush under her bare feet, the walls were hung with expensive wallpaper and decorated with abstract art. At the far end, behind a large mahogany desk, sat Madame Lashenka. She had a pen in her hand and was writing. She didn't look up when Toni entered.

The secretary led Toni across the room until she was standing right in front of the desk, then indicated that she was to remain there. Toni at once took up her submissive stance, legs apart, hands behind her head, her bare breasts thrust forward in a manner that made her face glow red. The secretary stood beside the desk, saying nothing.

Madame Lashenka went on writing for some time. Toni, meanwhile, remained perfectly still, though her body trembled slightly as she waited to hear what the woman would say.

At last she put down the pen and gazed up at the naked youngster. Toni stared straight ahead, unwilling to meet the woman's eyes.

'What is that on your thighs?' said Madame Lashenka suddenly, the harsh tones of her voice making Toni start.

'I...'

'Well? Speak up girl!'

'It's semen, Madame.'

'Who's semen?'

'The young man in the house.'

'What young man?'

'I don't know his name.'

'You don't know his name, and yet his semen is leaking from your cunt?'

'He didn't tell me. He made me strip. I didn't know he was going to...'

'Going to what?'

'To fuck me,' said Toni, her face scarlet.

'Yet you acquiesced.'

'I couldn't stop him.'

'So he raped you?'

Toni hung her head. 'No. Not exactly.'

'Did you come?'

'Yes,' she said quietly.

'I see. You'd better tell me the whole story.'

Toni related exactly what had happened. Madame Lashenka listened carefully, interjecting with questions. When Toni had finished, she sat back in her chair and eyed the girl coldly.

'This is the second example of lascivious behaviour since you and I have met, young lady,' she sniffed. 'What do you think we should do with her, Miss White?'

'There's always the cellar, Madame. That's a good place to take the sluttishness out of a girl'

Toni felt a cold pang of fear at the words. The cellar was precisely what she had been trying to avoid by giving herself to the man. Now it seemed that she would get the worst of both worlds.

Madame Lashenka sat back in her chair. 'You're right,'

she mused. 'The little slut certainly deserves it. Perhaps a week naked with the rats will teach her a lesson.'

'No!' The word had leapt from Toni's lips before she was aware she had said it, and now she clamped her lips shut, cursing herself for her indiscretion.

'So, you don't like the idea, young lady?'

Toni didn't reply, aware that the outburst might already have sealed her fate.

'There is an alternative, Madame,' said Miss White.

'Yes, but do you think she's cut out for it?'

'She certainly seems to have an appetite for entertaining men. And she has the body for it.'

'Perhaps you're right. Turn round girl.'

'Madame?'

'You heard me. Turn round. I want to see your backside.'

Toni obeyed. She wished that they would allow her some clothes. Showing off her naked body in this way was painfully embarrassing to the youngster. She stood still whilst the two women examined the pert swellings of her behind, now criss-crossed with the thin red marks of the whip.

'Right, face me again. Tell me, young lady, have you ever waited on table?'

'No Madame.'

'No matter. You can be taught. Miss White, take her down and get her an outfit. She can start tonight.' She turned back to Toni. 'I'm giving you a chance to redeem yourself, and to use your talents for a useful purpose,' she said. 'But the cellar will still be there if you disappoint me. You understand?'

'Yes Madame.'

Toni didn't understand, though. She had no idea what was happening to her. But if it meant that she didn't have to visit that awful cellar, then she would acquiesce with anything they suggested.

Madame Lashenka returned to her writing, indicating that the interview was at an end. Toni turned to Miss White, who nodded towards the door. Toni made her way towards it, her hands still clutched to the back of her head.

Miss White led her downstairs and out across the courtyard in the centre of the academy. The girls who were going
about their daily chores stopped to watch as the red-faced,
naked girl passed them, giggling and pointing. Toni knew
that they could see the streak of white fluid that ran down her
thigh and the evidence of the thrashing on her behind, and her
face glowed red as she tried not to catch their eyes.

Miss White took her down a flight of stairs into a part of
the building she had not previously visited. She led her along
a corridor and opened a door at the end. It was a large changing room, with a stone floor and lockers all about the walls.
On one side was a row of shower cubicles.

'Go in there and get yourself cleaned up,' ordered Miss
White. 'Hurry up, now.'

There were no doors on the cubicles, and Toni was obliged
to shower in full view of the secretary. She washed herself
carefully, removing all traces of the ravishment she had received earlier. When she emerged, Miss White threw her a
towel and she dried herself.

'Come over here.'

Still clutching the towel to her breasts, Toni walked across
to where the woman was standing.

'Try this on.'

She held something out to Toni, who took it from her. It
was a single piece garment, a sort of leotard, but decorated
with sparkling sequins. Toni stepped into it, pulling it up her
body, grateful for a chance to cover herself at last. There
were cords dangling from the top and she fastened these behind her neck in a bow, then stood, waiting for Miss White's
next order.

'Go across to the mirror,' ordered the secretary.

Toni did as she was told, stopping short when she saw her
reflection.

The garment was red in colour, with silver edging about
the straps and legs. It had a built-in bra that lifted her breasts,

104

accentuating their perfect shape and the depth of her cleavage. The front was cut inwards on both sides, so that it was no more than three inches wide at her midriff. The crotch, too, was narrow, barely covering her sex, leaving tufts of pubic hair visible on both sides. She turned round and glanced back over her shoulder. The costume cut up the crack of her behind, leaving the cheeks exposed so that the stripes of her punishment were clear to see, a narrow belt running across just above her cheeks. In all, it hid very little indeed.

'Hmm, you'll have to trim your pubic hair back,' mused Miss Smith. 'But otherwise it seems to fit fine. Find yourself a razor and see to it, then report at the reception area in half an hour. Get on with you now.'

And with that she walked away, leaving Toni staring after her in confusion.

Chapter 12

When Toni arrived at the reception area there were half a dozen girls already there, all dressed in the same way as herself. She glanced round at them in surprise. She didn't recognise any of their faces. For their part, they paid the little English girl scant attention and continued conversing together in a language Toni didn't understand.

She paused by a mirror, checking her appearance. She had carefully shaved her sex, so that there remained only a thin, dark line of hair over her pubis and none at all about the lips of her vagina. It felt odd to have the material of the outfit pressing against her bare skin, but then it felt odd to be so scantily clad anyway, and she found herself blushing as she considered how much of her body was revealed.

A few more of the girls arrived and joined the others. Toni felt rather excluded from them, so she simply stood quietly on her own, waiting to see what would happen.

All at once a man appeared. Toni was quite startled, since

she had never encountered a man on the premises of the academy before. He was tall and heavily built, dressed in a dark evening suit with black bow tie. He was about forty years old, Toni estimated, with a thin, dark moustache decorating his upper lip. His eyes were green and penetrating, and Toni fond herself shivering under his icy gaze. The girls fell silent the moment he appeared, and lined up against the wall. Toni joined them at once.

He made his way down the line, inspecting the girls in turn. He stopped when he reached Toni and said something to her.

'I don't understand, Sir,' she said.

'Ah, English girl eh?' he said. His voice was deep and rich, his accent almost imperceptible.

'Yes Sir.'

'Your name?'

'Antonia Sir.'

'You are the one who has been fucking with your employer's son in the kitchen.'

Toni dropped her eyes. 'Yes Sir.'

At this a titter went up from the other girls, and Toni felt the blood rush to her face.

'You know why you are here?' he asked.

'No Sir.'

'No matter. You will find out soon enough. Just follow the other girls and do as you're told.'

He barked an order, and the girls turned and set off down the corridor, with Toni at the back of the line. They went through a door that Toni had never seen opened before. Beyond was a spiral staircase, and they made their way down to the bottom. There, the decor was quite different from anything Toni had encountered before in the academy. The floor was carpeted in rich burgundy, the wall coverings of a similar hue. Everywhere was soft lighting, with thick velvet drapes across doors and windows. In the distance she could hear music playing.

They continued through two more curtained doorways before they found themselves in a large room. It was furnished as a nightclub, with tables set about the floor and a low stage at one end on which a number of spotlights played. Above the stage was the legend 'The Midnight Club'. To her left was a bar, and four of the girls immediately made their way behind it and began setting up bottles and glasses.

The man spoke a few words to one of the girls, who turned to Toni.

'You waitress tonight,' she said shortly. 'Get tray and money from bar. Do like I do.'

Toni nodded nervously. She felt very odd indeed, standing in this bar so scantily dressed. She couldn't imagine what the customers would make of the stripes across her behind.

At that moment the door opened and a group of men came in. There were about six of them, all casually dressed and in their early twenties. They were laughing and joking as they entered, and the sight of the girls brought wolf whistles from them as they found themselves a table.

One of Toni's companions made her way across to where they were sitting with her tray and began to take orders. As she wrote down their drinks they groped at her, running their hands up her legs and squeezing the soft globes of her behind. Toni watched in trepidation as she twisted away, clearly unworried by the treatment she was receiving. It was obvious that to be groped by the customers in this club was the norm.

She wondered that such a place could exist so close to the academy. In fact it was part within the very building. The more she thought about it, the more it became clear that the club was actually part of the academy, and was run using the resources of it. In particular the supply of beautiful young girls. It looked as if the institution was even more corrupt than she had at first suspected.

Another group arrived, then another. All at once Toni felt a hand on her shoulder. It was the man in the bow tie. She had learned that his name was Mr Vilenski, and he was clearly the manager of the club. Now he leaned forward and spoke close to her ear.

'Take that table over there. And mind you make no mistakes.'

Toni looked across at the group of men that had just arrived. There were four of them, sitting at a table close to the bar, and they were shouting and waving to her.

Nervously she made her way across to the table. As she approached they called out again and, although she couldn't understand what they were saying, it clearly was about her, and she could hear the laughter of the occupants of the other tables around her.

One of the men crooked his finger, beckoning her close. She stood beside him, but still he urged her closer. As she bent down by his face she felt a hand close on the bare flesh of her buttocks and squeeze her there.

The man said something, and she shook her head.

'English,' she said, trying hard to ignore the fingers that were running over the smooth flesh of her behind.

The man's face brightened. 'Ah! Little English rose. You like to fuck with Estavian guy Rosie?'

Toni blushed. 'What would you like to drink, Sir?' she asked.

He slid his hand up her inner thigh so that she could feel it pressing against her crotch.

'Get four beers,' he said.

Toni headed back to the bar, grateful to be free of his groping for the time being. It wasn't so much his attention as the way her body was responding that concerned her. The sensation of his fingers touching her bare flesh had sent tremors of excitement through her small frame, and when his hand had touched her between the legs she had had to bite her lip to prevent herself gasping aloud. Now, as she stood at the bar, she was only too aware of the eyes on her punished bottom and of the comments that were being passed by the men all around her.

She collected the beers and made her way back to the table. The men watched her as she approached, their gazes drifting over her cleavage and her long, shapely legs. She avoided their eyes as she unloaded the tray, trying not to think about the sight her backside must make as she leaned forward across the tables. Once again hands stroked her pale flesh, and once again she fought down the sensation of pleasure that their touch brought.

Toni worked on, busily carrying her tray from table to table, delivering drinks to the customers, all the time trying to dodge their groping hands. Each trip to and from the bar meant running a gauntlet of stroking, pinching fingers, the men's laughter ringing in her ears as she struggled to prevent the drinks on her tray from spilling. And all the time she felt her arousal increasing, the attention from the men simply reminding her of how sexy she looked, and of how enjoyable had been the fucking she had received that day.

How she got through that introduction to the Midnight Club Toni never knew. She simply focused on what was demanded of her, and accepted the way the men treated her as a commodity that they were buying in the same way as they were paying for the drinks she was delivering to them. Her already sore behind was a mass of pinch marks by the middle of the evening, yet her crotch was so wet that she wondered that it wasn't showing through the material of her outfit

It came as a surprise to her when, at about half-past ten, one of the girls placed a hand on her shoulder as she stood at the bar awaiting her next order.

'You break,' the girl shouted above the noise of the band. 'Fifteen minutes, then back here.'

Toni looked at her in surprise. 'Where can I go?' she asked.

'Back room,' the girl replied. 'Through there.'

She indicated a door at the back of the stage, behind the four-piece band that had been playing for some time. Toni made her way across to the stage, still dodging the outstretched hands, and slipped through the opening.

Behind the door she found a narrow corridor that opened up at one end into a small open area. It was furnished with a couch, behind which was a hot-plate on which a pot of coffee was gently simmering. One of the other girls was seated on the couch, but at the sight of Toni she stood up and pushed past her, heading back toward the club. Toni poured herself a cup of coffee and settled down on the couch, glad to be out of the hurly-burly of the club for a while. She sipped at the coffee and tried to relax.

All at once she heard a sound. It sounded like a cry. She listened hard, but all she could hear was the music coming from the next room. Then she heard it again, like a muffled shout of pain. She put her cup down and rose to her feet, looking about her.

The sound had come from the opposite direction to the club. There was a door on the far wall, and Toni approached it cautiously. Turning the handle she pushed it open and glanced through. It led onto another passageway, at the end of which was a door. The door was slightly ajar, and a light showed through the crack. As she stood there, another cry reached her ears. Slowly, her heart beating hard, she began to make her way along the corridor.

She reached the door and paused outside, almost too afraid of what she might find. Slowly she pushed it open and peered round it.

The room itself was quite dimly-lit. What light there was came from a spotlight that was trained on the far end of the room. When Toni saw what it illuminated, she gave a gasp of surprise. Against the wall was a heavy wooden bench, and a figure was bent across it. It was a girl, one of her fellow waitresses, and she was totally nude, her costume discarded beside her. She was bent forward at the waist, so that the pale moons of her backside and the pink gash of her sex were perfectly displayed. Her legs were wide apart, and Toni's jaw dropped as she realised that the girl was tethered in position,

110

strong cords about her wrists and ankles holding her where she was. Beside her stood another of the girls, still dressed in her brief outfit. In her hand she was holding a long, thick dildo, and as Toni watched she rubbed the bulbous end along the girl's slit, bringing another cry from her as it slid over the trapped girl's clitoris.

Suddenly Toni became aware that the two girls were not alone. Between her and the bench was a row of chairs, and on these sat a group of men, sipping drinks and watching as the girl with the dildo began to force it into her helpless companion's vagina, bringing fresh cries from her as she pressed it between her glistening sex lips.

One of the men shouted something, and the others laughed. The girl laughed too and immediately renewed her efforts, pressing and twisting the thick object, sliding it ever deeper into the trapped girl's gaping sex as her cries rang about the room.

Toni watched with rapt attention as the dildo all but disappeared into the girl's love hole. Then the moaning started anew as her tormentor began moving it back and forth inside her, fucking her hard with it whilst the men shouted their approval. The girl with the dildo glanced back and smiled at her audience as she worked the object back and forth. It was shiny with her companion's juices now, and she was beginning to writhe about, clearly in a high state of arousal.

She came with a cry, her backside thrusting back as the wetness leaked from her onto her pale thigh, betraying the genuineness of her passion. The men cheered as her cries rent the air, the lips of her sex closing about the thick shaft as spasms racked her lovely young body. Toni found her own fingers slipping down to her crotch as she watched the extraordinarily erotic sight before her.

Then a hand dropped onto her shoulder and pulled her round.

'What are you doing here?'

It was Vilenski.

111

Toni stood against the cold wall of the cell, blinking into the bright light that spotlighted her, wondering what was now to befall her. She tugged at the cuffs that held her wrists together, her hands pulled high above her head by the chains that were attached to them. Her arms ached from being held in such a position for so long. She tried to shift her stance, but the shackles about her ankles allowed her to do no more than shuffle.

She glanced across at the mirror opposite her on the wall. Like those in the secret room, it had clearly been placed there to allow anyone imprisoned as she was to see their reflection, and to contemplate their fate. She wore a tattered dress, not much more than sackcloth really, the holes in the fabric showing her bare white skin beneath. It came down to just below her crotch, leaving her long, slim legs bare. The overall impression given by her outfit, along with the shiny chains that held her, was that of a slave girl in some mediaeval dungeon.

They had brought her straight from Vilenski's office, where he had dragged her immediately after discovering her at the door of the room. She had been shocked and unnerved by what she had witnessed, but more so at the man's anger on finding her there.

'What were you doing at that doorway?' he stormed.

'I'm sorry, Sir,' stammered the frightened youngster. 'I was just looking.'

'Spying more likely,' he replied. 'Do you get your kicks from watching girls frig each other?'

'I heard noises, Sir. I wanted to know what was happening.'

'Don't you know better than to pry into other peoples' affairs?'

'I didn't know what was happening.'

'What you saw was a private viewing. Those men paid a lot of money for that. They are all important people. It would harm their reputations to be seen in a place like this. They were very angry that you had seen them.'

'But I wouldn't give them away. I don't even know who they were.'

'That isn't the point. You were spying, and you'll be punished for it.'

'P-punished?'

He said nothing, simply pressing a bell-push on the side of his desk. Immediately the door opened and two of the girls entered. It was the same pair she had witnessed in the room, both now wearing their costumes.

'This little spy is to be taught a lesson,' he said. 'To placate the men you were entertaining I have promised a midnight show.'

The two girls grinned as he said this. Toni was surprised that he addressed the pair in English, but assumed it was for her benefit. She wondered what a midnight show could possibly be. The other two clearly understood, and they nudged one another, giggling. Then Toni realised that Vilenski was speaking again.

'Make sure the appropriate club members are informed,' he said. 'The longer standing members wouldn't want to miss the show, especially with it being a new girl.'

'Yes Sir,' chorused the smirking pair.

'Now get her out of here and prepare her.'

They had taken her down to the cell, where they had made her strip, laughing at her embarrassment at having to denude herself before them. Then they had given her the tattered dress, before chaining her to the wall, clearly enjoying her discomfort as they pulled the chains tight.

That had been more than an hour ago. An hour of acute discomfort and agonising anticipation as she contemplated what was in store for her. There was no doubt that she was due for another chastisement, but what form could it take? Just what was a midnight show, and who were the privileged club members who were to attend? She shivered slightly as she contemplated the prospect.

And yet there was another emotion stirring itself deep within her. An odd desire that she couldn't ignore. There was something unmistakably exciting about her bondage and near-nudity. Something that gave her a warm feeling in her belly.

Despite her fears, Toni was becoming aroused.

She was quite unable to understand the feeling. After all, she was being kept against her will, her body tormented and aching. What was it that Alex had kindled inside her in those delicious sessions in the secret room? Why was it that she felt these desires when any normal girl would be simply terri-fied? Toni didn't know the answer. All she knew was that, whatever happened to her tonight, she was more likely to be aroused than hurt by their treatment of her.

All at once she heard the sound of footsteps approaching. Toni froze, her heart suddenly thumping hard as the sound of the bolts on her cell door being drawn across echoed through the small room.

The door swung open, and there stood her two warders. They had changed their costumes, and now wore black leather outfits of the same style as those they wore for waiting on table, but with black fishnet stockings, knee-length boots and small black caps on their heads. Toni was reminded of the outfit Alex had worn when she had beaten her for the first time, and the memory sent another shiver of anticipation through her small frame. The pair swaggered into the small cell, their faces wreathed in grins at the sight of their beauti-ful young captive.

They released Toni's arms, and the grateful girl rolled her shoulders and flexed her muscles, the feeling gradually re-turning to her aching limbs whilst the pair set about undoing the shackles on her ankles. Her relief was short-lived, how-ever, as they immediately dragged her arms behind her back and placed cuffs on her wrists. Then they joined her ankles with shackles linked by a chain no more than fifteen inches long. Once these were secure, they fitted a leather collar about her neck to which was attached a chain. One of the girls took hold of this and, tugging at it, dragged her out of the cell and down the corridor.

Toni felt very nervous indeed as she stumbled along behind her two escorts. When she heard the sound of voices ahead she became even more apprehensive. She tried to hang back, but the two women simply tugged at her lead, forcing her to keep up with them. The chain between her ankles made walking difficult, but the pair seemed heedless of her plight, simply pulling all the harder when she stumbled.

As they progressed, the sound of the voices grew louder, and Toni guessed that they were approaching the club. Her stomach churned as she realised that the crowd was awaiting her arrival, and she tried not to think about what lay in store.

All at once a door was flung open in front of her, and she found herself stepping directly out onto the stage, the strong lights blinding her temporarily as she staggered out. There was a general hubbub of voices as she appeared, and she blinked into the blinding beams, trying to make out the people who sat at the tables.

The room was about half full, mainly older men, unlike the clientele that had been there earlier. Despite the lights, Toni was able to make out some of the other waitresses, as well as the unmistakable shape of Madame Lashenka sitting in the front just beyond the stage. As Toni was led to the middle, the talking died down. Then she realised that Vilenski was standing at her side.

He took her lead from the girl who was holding it and the two escorts backed away to the rear of the stage. Then he began to address the crowd. Toni was unable to understand anything that was said, but his words clearly amused his audience, and his speech was punctuated by bursts of laughter and the occasional cheer. For her part, Toni simply stood quietly, staring straight ahead of her, wishing that the ordeal would end and that they would let her down from the stage and away from the bright lights that so drew attention to her.

All at once Vilenski turned to her and began addressing her in English.

'You understand why you are here?'

'I-I'm not sure, Sir.'

'It is for punishment. You see the box up there at the back?'

Toni squinted through the lights once more. There, at the back of the room was a recess set into the wall, not unlike the boxes one saw in the grand opera houses of Europe, although this one was relatively plainly decorated. The box was in darkness but, as she watched, Toni caught a movement inside it. Someone was sitting in there, probably more than one person.

'Those are the people you so insulted by your intrusion this evening,' said Vilenski. 'They will wish to see you afterwards. Meanwhile they have ordered that you receive fifteen strokes with the cane.'

'Fifteen?'

'Certainly. The rest of the audience are trusty club members who have been with us a number of years. You see the real Midnight Club only gathers at the stroke of midnight, after those stupid boys have gone home. These are sophisticated men. Men who have a penchant for watching a beautiful young girl being punished.'

Toni glanced out into the audience once more. It seemed that the academy had more secrets that she had dreamed. She wondered how many other innocent youngsters had been brought up onto this stage in the past. Then she saw the long, thin cane that lay on the table beside her, and a knot formed in her stomach.

Vilenski beckoned the two girls forward and they came up and stood either side of the hapless youngster. Toni gazed down at herself. Despite its tatty state, the dress she wore clung to her body, accentuating the swell of her breasts and the curve of her hips. Through the holes she knew the men could see her pale, bare flesh, one tear in the bodice revealing the underside of her right breast, the brown half-moon of her

116

areola just visible.

One of her two escorts removed the collar from her neck. Then there was a clanking sound, and Toni looked up to see that a chain was being lowered from above her. The other girl had gone to the wall and was turning a handle that wound the shiny links down. Her companion moved behind Toni and undid the cuffs that held her wrists together.

The leather-clad pair took hold of an arm each and pulled them above Toni's head. Attached to the end of the chain was a stout wooden crossbar about three feet long, at the ends of which were metal manacles. These were closed about Toni's wrists, holding her hands wide apart. Then the handle was turned again, this time cranking the chain upwards, pulling Toni's arms above her head until her body was stretched and she was standing almost on tiptoe.

They turned her to face the audience. Vilenski was speaking again, and his words brought a murmur of approval from the audience. He turned and issued an order to Toni's warders.

The pair stepped forward and took hold of Toni's dress at the neck. Then, without warning, both tugged hard. The flimsy material came away like tissue paper, the dress ripping completely in two. A shout went up from those watching as the girls discarded the now useless rags, leaving Toni completely nude.

It had all happened so fast that Toni had scarcely realised what they were doing. The dreadful realisation that her petite young body was now on open display to this roomful of strangers brought the blood suddenly rushing to her cheeks. She wondered at the sight she must make, her firm, plump breasts jutting forward, her trimmed pubic bush drawing the men's eyes down to her bare sex lips below.

She barely had time to consider her plight, though, as her two attendants dropped to their knees and undid the shackles at her ankles, then turned her round to face away from the audience. The new position gave Toni some scant comfort as

117

her breasts and belly were turned from the men's hungry eyes, but she knew that they would be scanning her backside with equal interest, and she thought of the stripes so recently laid across it by the woman that morning. She wasn't sure if she could take another beating so soon after that one, but it was clear she would have little choice.

Suddenly she realised that the two young women were at work again, each taking hold of one of her ankles and pulling them wide apart before clamping yet another shackle about each. She glanced down to see that these irons were attached to the floor at about the same distance apart as those on her wrists. She was trapped now, her arms and legs pulled wide, her body describing a large X shape as she hung in her chains, her feet barely touching the ground.

She watched as one of the girls picked up the cane. It was made of bamboo, about a quarter of an inch thick. As the girl described an arc through the air with it, it made a swishing sound, and, once again, Toni was reminded of the secret room, and of the beating that Alex had administered. She was grateful, now, for that experience. At least she knew what to expect. Then a cold feeling gripped her as she recalled the other effect the beating had had on her. What if she were to be turned on again, in front of all these people? It didn't bear thinking about.

'Five strokes each, then five for me I think,' said Vilenski.

The girls both nodded, then the first of them took up her position behind Toni and tapped the cane against her behind. She braced herself.

Swish! Whack!

The cane struck her hard across the cheeks of her bare backside, making her gasp with the pain as it cut into the soft flesh, rekindling the fire of the beating she had had earlier that day.

Swish! Whack!

The second blow came down almost immediately, the sound of cane against flesh cracking about the room as she

118

was rocked forward, her beautiful young body shaken from top to toe.

Swish! Whack!

Down it came again, striking her behind with unerring accuracy and laying another angry stripe across it. Toni clenched her teeth in a determined effort not to cry aloud as the pain seared through her like a hot knife. The girl drew back the cane once more.

Swish! Whack!

Swish! Whack!

There followed a brief but blessed respite as the girl, now breathing heavily with her exertions, handed the cane across to her companion. Toni glanced over her shoulder at the audience, suddenly acutely aware of the sea of eyes upon her naked body. The thought brought a strange tingle of excitement to the wanton beauty and, to her consternation, she felt her nipples begin to harden as the first stirrings of arousal began within her.

She looked at the second girl. This one was left-handed, so that she stood on the opposite side to her companion. Toni shivered slightly as she braced herself for a fresh onslaught.

Swish! Whack!

Once again the cane descended onto her backside with stinging ferocity, this time catching her right buttock first before wrapping itself about her and laying down yet another stripe.

Swish! Whack!

Swish! Whack!

The blows fell relentlessly, the girl showing no mercy to her helpless young captive, bringing the weapon down with all the force she could muster, each blow making the fleshy globes of Toni's pert behind quiver deliciously.

Swish! Whack!

Swish! Whack!

Toni had lost count of the strokes that had been meted out to her, but when the girl stopped and lowered the cane she knew she had received ten. Her body was bathed in sweat now, her smooth skin gleaming with moisture, the fluid running from her face and forming a rivulet between her breasts.

But there was another wetness that troubled her more. A wetness deep in her vagina that was increasing by the second. Once again, inexplicably, Toni found herself extraordinarily aroused by her situation and, despite the unbearable pain in her behind, the burning sensation in her sex was beginning to dominate her thoughts as Vilenski took the cane from the girl.

Swish! Whack!

This time Toni cried aloud as the cane came down with unbelievable force, biting into her flesh so deep that she feared it might draw blood.

Swish! Whack!

Vilenski was putting every ounce of his strength into the beating, his blows making those of the two girls pale to insignificance. Toni screamed with the pain, the tears streaming down her face as her behind glowed with pain.

Swish! Whack!

The beautiful youngster's body was thrown forward by the force of the cane, her arms feeling as if they would be torn from their sockets as they took the weight. Only two strokes left, she knew, but she seriously wondered how she would stand them.

Swish! Whack!

The penultimate blow landed with undiminished force, then Vilenski drew back his arm for the final time.

Swish! Whack!

Once again Toni's screams filled the room as the man lowered the cane. The girl barely noticed that the punishment was at an end, though, such was the agony in her behind. For a few more seconds she writhed about in her chains as the pain seared her, then slowly she began to relax, exhaustion overcoming her until she hung, gasping and sobbing in her chains.

Vilenski stretched out the cane and touched her between

120

her legs.

The effect on Toni was electric, her whole body convulsing as an indescribable shock wave of excitement shook her. All at once the pain was forgotten as the realisation of her arousal overwhelmed her and her sex pulsated with excitement, her teats standing out like thick knobs from her swelling breasts.

Vilenski smiled when he saw her reaction.

'So, what I have been told about you is true,' he said. 'That beating has really got you turned on.'

Toni said nothing, but the bright red glow in her cheeks told him all he needed to know, and she hung her head, unable to meet his eye.

All at once the tension in her body was decreasing and she looked across to see one of the girls turning the handle on the wall, slackening the chain above her. The pair came forward and undid her cuffs, then the manacles on her legs.

'Turn around.'

Slowly Toni turned to face her audience. Her instincts told her to cover her breasts and sex with her hands, but one look from Vilenski told her she dare not. Instead she placed her hands behind her head and spread her legs, blushing brightly as she revealed the wet sheen that covered the lips of her throbbing sex.

Vilenski said a few more words to the crowd, who nodded their satisfaction with what they had witnessed. Then he called the girls forward and Toni felt her arms pulled behind her and the cold embrace of the handcuffs about her wrists once more. The collar was replaced about her neck and she felt a tug at her lead. To a round of applause she was led from the stage and out of the bright lights.

For Toni, the relief of being out of the gaze of the men was a wonderful one, and she gave a sigh as the door closed behind her. But instead of leading her back the way they had come, she found herself being taken up a new corridor. Then she remembered Vilenski's promise that she was to meet the strangers in the darkened box, and her heart sank once more.

They climbed a flight of stairs and came to a small, unobtrusive door. One of her escorts knocked on it, then opened it
and pushed Toni inside, closing it behind her.

At first she could discern nothing in the box, the bright-
ness of the club room beyond making it difficult for her eyes
to adjust. Slowly, though, the scene began to become clear.
In the centre of the room was a large leather chair of the type
that an executive might have behind the desk in an office. A
figure was sitting in it, facing away from her. On either side
were two smaller chairs. Their occupants, both men in their
forties, were gazing back at the naked youngster with obvious interest. Toni stood where she was, uncertain what to do
as the seconds ticked past.

The person who was facing away from her raised a hand.
Instantly the man on the right rose to his feet and came forward. He took hold of her lead, allowing his hand to brush
against her nipples, which still stood out proud from her
breasts.

'The Count wishes to see you,' he said curtly.

Her heart beating hard, Toni allowed herself to be led round
in front of the dark figure. The man tugged on her lead and
she dropped to her knees at his feet. Once again she had an
overwhelming urge to cover herself, but the cuffs made that
impossible. Instead she stared down at the ground, acutely
aware of the creamy swell of her breasts.

The man was slim, about fifty she estimated with grey,
wavy hair and a small goatee beard. He was dressed in an
expensive dinner suit with a black bow tie at his neck. As
Toni looked up at him a shiver ran through her. He had the
most penetrating eyes she had ever seen. They seemed to
bore into her very soul. She knew that, even had she been
clothed, his gaze would have made her feel quite naked.

'What is your name?' His voice was deep and laden with
authority.

'Antonia Sir.'

'Is it true that this mistreatment arouses you?'

'I...' Toni dropped her eyes once more.

'Your nipples are hard. Only two things make a woman's nipples hard, cold weather and sexual arousal. It is not cold here, is it?'

'No Sir.'

'Check her cunt. I want to know if she's wet.'

'Spread your legs,' hissed the man holding her lead.

Toni stared at him for a second, then back at the Count. What right did they have to treat her thus? To drag her naked into this dark room and make her kneel before this man? And why was it that she felt so turned on by her whole situation? She felt deeply ashamed by the humiliating way they were treating her. Yet the heat in her sex was undeniable, and the more they mistreated her, the greater that heat became. Slowly she moved her knees apart, then looked at the man beside her.

He reached for her, running his hand down her belly, his touch sending a tremor of excitement through her. He slid his hand over her pubic mound and his index finger slipped into her vagina, bringing an involuntary gasp from her as he probed her most private place. He moved his fingers back and forth, watching as she fought to control her emotions, her hips pressing forward against his hand whilst the muscles of her sex closed about his finger. He withdrew the digit, leaving her panting quietly.

'She's wet as hell down there,' he announced, holding his shiny finger up for the man in the chair to see..

'Interesting,' mused the man. 'I think I shall be taking a close interest in this young lady. Meanwhile, you'd better fuck her.'

Toni stared at him in shocked surprise. Once again her acquiescence was being taken for granted by this stranger. It was as if she had no will of her own. And yet the words had sent a shiver of arousal through her young body that she knew must be obvious to the men.

There was a tug on her lead and she climbed to her feet.

She looked at the man, wondering where he would take her. Then, to her surprise, he spun her round and pressed her against the edge of the balcony that overlooked the club. The rail was at about the height of her crotch, her body projecting over the edge into the bright lights of the room, her breasts dangling below her.

She heard a rustle of clothing behind her and, with a sudden shock, she realised that he was going to fuck her then and there, in full view of all the people in the club. She could scarcely believe it was possible that she was to be taken so publicly. Then she glanced back and saw his stiff cock projecting from his fly, and she knew she would make no protest. She wanted him more than she could imagine.

'Open your legs.'

Toni obeyed at once, spreading her legs wide and bending further forward, offering him the access to her sex that she knew he wanted. Below, faces were turned up to her, all clearly aware of what was happening, but by now Toni didn't care. All she cared about now was the burning need inside her.

He wasted no time, pressing his thick cock up against the entrance to her vagina and pushing hard, slipping easily into the well-lubricated well of her sex. She moaned aloud, almost coming there and then as he forced himself deeper and deeper until she felt his belly press against her backside, bringing a brief reminder of the punishment she had received such a short time before.

He started to thrust against her soft young body, the violence of his fucking forcing her hips against the balcony, bringing hoarse cries of lust from her as the delicious sensation of his cock within her drove her to new highs of ecstasy. She gazed down at the crowd below. They were silent now, the intensity on their faces telling her that they too were aroused. She thought of their cocks hardening in their pants as they witnessed her ravishment, and a new surge of excitement swept through her small frame.

The soft grunts from her anonymous lover told her that he

124

too was approaching his peak, and she glanced back at him. He was holding her by the hips, his pelvis thrusting rhythmically forward as he took her. Behind him the Count sat, apparently impassive, though his eyes never left the tableau in front of him.

The man's onslaught was harder than ever now, and it was all Toni could do to hold her position, her breasts bouncing back and forth with every stroke to the obvious delight of those watching.

He came suddenly, his thick penis twitching violently inside her as jets of hot spunk filled her vagina. His orgasm triggered her own almost at once, her shouts of passion echoing about the club as her whole being was engulfed in lustful pleasure. He went on thrusting into her, spurt after spurt of his semen flooding her love hole, keeping her at the peak of her own climax. Then, with one final heave, he collapsed against her, momentarily winding her as the last drops of his seed pumped into her.

He withdrew quickly, releasing a stream of sperm that ran down her thigh as she slowly straightened. She turned to face the Count, her hands still cuffed behind her, her hair a mess, her lovely young breasts rising and falling as she fought to regain her breath.

The Count nodded. 'Very good,' he murmured. 'I find you more interesting by the minute, young lady.'

Chapter 14

After that first night in the club, life began to settle into a kind of routine for Toni. Along with the other privileged girls she was allowed to sleep later and to partake of much better meals than the rest of the inmates at the academy. All pretence of educating the girls was abandoned for those who were part of the Midnight Club. Their job was to wait on the tables and to endure the hands that were forever groping their bodies as they wound their way between the tables.

Toni soon became something of a favourite amongst the club's patrons. They would love to squeeze her succulent breasts and stroke her inner thighs, laughing as she fought to control the emotions these caresses aroused in her. The other girls too would tease and laugh at her, and she never felt comfortable in their company, preferring to take her breaks on her own.

There were further visits by dignitaries, too. Toni would notice girls in ones and twos disappearing down the corridor behind the rest room, but she never followed them again, only too aware of the painful and humiliating consequences of her first venture into the rooms beyond. She worked hard and diligently at her job, being careful to stay out of trouble, and the stripes on her backside soon faded away.

There were other midnight shows, she knew, though she was never invited to attend, being sent back up to her bed at midnight every night. She always knew when something was happening because half-a-dozen of the girls would be kept back, and she would occasionally see Madame Lashenka making her way towards the club as she was on her way upstairs.

Then, one day, the Count returned.

It had begun as an ordinary evening. Toni had been waiting at table in the usual way, receiving her customary slaps, pinches and caresses as she moved from table to table. Then, as she made her way back to the bar for another order, she became aware of Vilenski standing by the counter.

The man had scarcely spoken to her since her public beating and fucking that first night. Toni hadn't minded that at all, preferring to keep as low a profile as possible. Now, however, he was there, and as she approached he beckoned to her.

'Sir?'

'Deliver those drinks, then come with me.'

'Yes Sir.'

Toni's stomach was a mass of butterflies as she placed the

drinks on the table, and she scarcely noticed the way the men were groping between her thighs as she did so. When she turned around, Vilenski was waiting by the door, and she hurried across to him.

'Follow me.'

He led her down, through the rest room and out the door at the back. Once again she could see the light in the room at the end of the corridor, but instead of taking her there, he led her to another room halfway down the corridor.

'Stand there.' He pointed at the centre of the room.

Toni obeyed at once, immediately grasping her hands behind her head and taking up an open-legged stance. Vilenski walked round her slowly, his eyes scanning her closely. He seemed content with what he saw, because he nodded his head slowly.

'You have been sent for,' he said.

'Sir?'

'The Count. He has asked for you. That is an honour. The Count is one of our most important customers.'

'Yes Sir.'

'Have you ever stripped?'

'I beg your pardon Sir?'

'Have you ever stripped? Performed a striptease to music?'

Toni looked at him with wide eyes. 'No Sir.' It wasn't strictly true, she knew. After all, she had put on that act with Alex. But then she had been guided by her friend. She couldn't imagine doing it on her own.

'Think you could do it?' he asked.

'Take my clothes off to music?'

'Yes.'

'All of them?'

'Of course all of them, you stupid girl. Have you ever danced?'

'Yes Sir. I took dancing classes at school. I was quite good at it.'

'Good. You'll just have to improvise. I'll play the tape whilst we find you a costume.'

'But I don't know what to do.'

'Just take your clothes off slowly and sensuously. And play with yourself.'

'Play with myself?'

'Yes. You've frigged that pretty little cunt of yours before, haven't you?'

Toni didn't answer. Vilenski turned away from her and pressed a button on a tape machine built into the wall. All at once the room was filled with loud, throbbing music. Then, as she looked on, he opened the door of a wardrobe and began rummaging inside.

Half an hour later, Toni was standing on her own beside a doorway, her heart pounding as she waited to be summoned. There was a mirror on the wall opposite where she stood, and she studied her reflection with some trepidation. She was wearing a tight silken top, against which her firm breasts pressed delightfully. The open neck showed the pale flesh of her cleavage, its shape enhanced by the low-cut bra she wore, which pushed her soft globes together and up. Her skirt was short and almost transparent, so that her black panties showed through underneath. She wore black hold-up stockings, the tops of which were only just covered by the skirt. On her feet she had tall black stilettos. All in all the outfit made her look very tarty indeed, and she wondered what her aunt and uncle would think if they could see her now.

Toni considered what was being asked of her. To be made to strip her clothes off in front of strangers was an outrageous proposition. At least on the previous occasion that she had stripped she had had Alex beside her to assist her and to give her support. Here she was alone, and not facing a group of friends, but of total strangers, possibly hostile ones. She thought of the way the Count's eyes had bored into her on that first occasion they had met. There was something about his stare that had unnerved her then, and she wasn't looking forward to baring her all to him again.

And yet Toni's thoughts weren't simply fearful ones. As she glanced at the beautiful young girl in the mirror, she couldn't help the shiver of excitement that ran down her spine as she considered what was about to happen. She, Toni, was about to bare all to a group of men. To display her private parts to them in the most suggestive and lascivious way. And afterward, who knew what would happen? If they decided they wanted to fuck her, there was little she could do to prevent them. As this thought occurred to her she felt a wetness creeping into her sex, and an odd warmth in her belly.

The door opened suddenly, giving her a start. Vilenski was standing there, his eyes taking in her outfit with obvious approval.

'Come on,' he said. 'They're ready for you.'

Toni stepped reluctantly through the door. She found herself standing on what appeared to be a stage, behind a curtain in the wings. The curtains on the stage were open, and a spotlight picked out a single chair in the centre. Vilenski took her arm and indicated the chair.

'Out there,' he said.

At that moment, the music started, its loud, booming notes bringing a knot to Toni's stomach. She hesitated for a second, suddenly overawed by what was being asked of her. Then she caught Vilenski's eye, and she knew it was time.

She stepped tentatively out into the spotlight. As on her previous encounter with the Count, the lights were extremely bright, making it almost impossible for her to discern how many people were watching her. The applause that greeted her entrance, however, told her that it was at least a dozen, possibly more.

She made her way to the centre, and paused, her mind suddenly blank. Then she heard the beat of the music change, and her body responded automatically, dropping into the rhythm at once as she began a swirling dance that brought another round of applause from below her.

Toni danced as if she were born for it, her lithe young body gyrating sensuously as the music took command of her. She swayed her hips from side to side, occasionally thrusting her pelvis forward, moving about the stage with the grace of a cat.

The music changed again, and Toni recognised her cue to undo her top. Slowly, one by one, she began to unfasten the buttons, scarcely thinking of what she was doing as she concentrated on getting it right. When the last one was undone she let the blouse fall open, revealing her skimpy bra from which her breasts were bulging.

As the dance continued, Toni released the buttons that ran up the side of her skirt, beginning at the bottom and working up. As each one came undone she revealed more and more of her thigh, the creamy flesh making a striking contrast with the top of her stockings. She reached the final button, popping it undone, then shimmied across the stage holding her skirt shut with her fingers. The men below began to whistle, and for the first time she found herself beginning to enjoy herself, a slight smile coming to her face as she responded to them.

She pulled the skirt off in a single movement, holding it up and waving it about her head before tossing it in the direction of the spotlight. She wore only her underwear, stockings and shoes now, and she knew that her slim, lithe body looked good as she gyrated at the front of the stage, moving her belly in small circles in a movement that resembled something out of a Turkish nightclub.

Once again a change in the music told her that a new phase of her dance was beginning, and her stomach tightened as she realised that she was about to bare her breasts to those watching. Nevertheless the idea was thrilling to her and already she could feel her nipples puckering to hard points under the brief bra.

She reached behind her for the strap and undid it . Then, moving her hands round to the front, she cupped her breasts, rubbing the material round in circles so that it chafed against her nipples, sending thrilling sensations down to her crotch, which was becoming wetter by the minute.

She continued to hold the bra against her chest for a few moments longer, whilst the men whistled and shouted at her. Then, slowly but surely, she began to push the garment downwards, revealing the brown flesh of her areolae to the cheering crowd.

She pulled the bra away in a single movement, tossing it into the audience and standing still momentarily, her firm mounds on open display, the nipples standing out like brown knobs. Then she was dancing again, her breasts bouncing delightfully as she shook her shoulders back and forth, much to the obvious enjoyment of the men.

All at once, Toni was in her element, revelling in the attention she was receiving as she showed off her body to the men. At that moment, Toni knew that it was her destiny to share her body, and that her previous prudish behaviour was behind her. Now she wanted to bare all. To show them exactly what she had, as the heat in her belly increased with every moment.

It was all she could do not to rip off her panties then and there, but she knew she must give the men the full show, so she sidled across to the chair and sat down daintily, raising her right leg and crossing it over her left.

She began to remove her stocking, sliding the nylon down her soft, smooth thighs, over her legs, then pulling it off, raising her leg in the air as she did so. She did the same with the other one, tossing it aside before rising to her feet once again.

The music had slowed now, and Toni slunk about the stage with extraordinary agility, her slim form describing gracious movements as she drifted back and forth. Then she moved to the centre of the stage and stopped, hooking her thumbs into the waistband of her pants.

The room was quiet now, and she knew all eyes were on her. She turned to face away from those watching and began slowly to work the brief garment downwards. First she revealed the crack of her behind, then she pulled the pants lower so that her pert buttocks were on display. Then, in a single movement, she pulled the pants all the way down and kicked them away, leaving her totally nude. She waited a moment longer, savouring the anticipation, then she spun round and ran to the front of the stage, standing with her legs apart, staring into the spotlight as the men enjoyed a perfect view of her open sex.

A cheer went up, and Toni stayed where she was, enjoying the adulation, aware that the wetness inside her must be visible, but suddenly not caring, wanting the men to ogle her charms. Then the music reached a crescendo, and the curtains closed.

Toni staggered to the side of the stage, where Vilenski was still standing. He nodded to her.

'A good show. You have many talents young lady.'

As he said the words his gaze dropped pointedly to her crotch, with its thin, dark line of pubic hair and shaved lips, and she blushed.

'Could I go and get my clothes please? she asked quietly.

'Eventually. But the show is not over. There is a second act, a duet, in fact, especially requested for the Count.'

As he spoke the music started again and the curtain opened. Vilenski took hold of Toni's arm and began to lead her back onstage. Toni held back, suddenly dreadfully embarrassed. Somehow stripping naked during the dance had seemed all right, fun almost. But to go out on stage now, with no clothes on, seemed very different, as if she was offering herself to those watching.

But her reluctance was ignored by Vilenski, who simply tightened his grip on her arm and dragged her out in front of the audience once more. A cheer went up as the men saw her again, and Toni's face reddened still further as they began to whistle and call to her.

Vilenski addressed the audience in their own tongue, one

132

of which Toni could understand not a word. As he spoke there was much hilarity and catcalls, and Toni knew that something was being planned for her. She wondered how she had come to be in such a position. A few weeks before she was a modest youngster who wouldn't have said boo to a goose, and was totally unaware of her own sexuality. Now here she was, standing naked on a stage in front of a group of strangers, whilst they hatched up some plan for her, and all the time she was growing more aware of the excitement that was increasing within her.

Vilenski stopped speaking and turned to her.

'You have one more act to perform for the Count and his friends,' he said. 'For this they have chosen a partner. He will join you on stage in a moment. Do not disappoint your audience.'

With that he stepped aside, leaving Toni alone centre stage. For a few seconds she remained there, uncomfortable and embarrassed. She wanted to cover her breasts and sex with her hands, but knew that such an act would invoke Vilenski's disapproval. Instead she stood, hands by her sides, her face cast down.

There was a movement to her right and she turned to see someone entering the stage door and walking toward her. It was a man, a large, broad-shouldered figure, and as he came closer she noted how tall he was, at least six foot six inches. As he stepped into the light she saw him properly for the first time. He was a great Adonis of a man, with long fair hair and a deeply tanned complexion. He wore a white kimono and, even through its loose folds, Toni could discern his powerful muscles in his heavy arms and broad chest.

He stopped just in front of her, towering over her petite frame. Toni's face was scarlet as his eyes roved over her naked body, taking in her charms.

A shout came up from the audience, and the man responded with a smile.

'They want you to undo my belt, pretty one,' he said, his

voice deep and smooth.

Toni dropped her eyes to his waist. The kimono had no buttons, the belt was all that was holding it closed. Beneath it she knew he was naked, and a sudden tremor of desire ran through her as she felt his closeness and masculinity begin to overcome her. Slowly she reached out a hand and took hold of the white sash. It came undone in a moment and the garment fell apart, revealing his body to her.

He was indeed muscular, his hairy chest bulging, his hips slim, his legs powerful. But it was none of these that caught Toni's attention. Her eyes were fixed on his cock.

It was a beautiful cock, long and uncircumcised, hanging straight down in front of a massive scrotum and surrounded by a mat of pubic hair. She licked her lips as she stared at it, fascinated. He dropped the robe behind him.

'Suck me,' he said quietly.

It was not a request, it was an order. One given with the quiet confidence of someone who knew he would obeyed. A man who could sense the lascivious nature of the young English beauty who stood before him, and was confident that she would already be so horny as to want him.

Without a word Toni dropped to her knees. He moved closer to her, so that the scent of his maleness was strong in her nostrils. Toni was becoming more aroused by the second, the closeness of this beautiful, naked man sending a surge of wetness to her sex. She glanced out to her right, to where she knew other men sat, waiting to see her seduction. She knew instinctively that what she was doing was wrong, and that no normal girl would submit to a complete stranger before an audience, but she new too that she was no ordinary girl, and that the desires she felt were not those of a normal young woman. After all, what other woman would have stripped off as she had that evening and displayed herself so blatantly? She glanced up at the man, who was standing impassively before her, then reached out for his cock.

It felt soft and flexible in her hands. She was unused to

encountering a flaccid penis, and she squeezed it between her fingers, wondering how this soft protrusion could ever be used to give her pleasure. But even as she handled it she could feel the blood begin to pulse within it, and a faint stirring as he responded to her touch.

She pulled back his foreskin to reveal the smooth head of his glans. Then she leaned forward and, opening her mouth, took him inside. She began to suck him, gently at first, her tongue worming under his foreskin as she caressed his heavy balls with her hands. At once she felt him begin to swell, his ball sac tightening as a regular pulse flowed through his organ. Toni sucked harder, her excitement growing as his cock began to stiffen. It seemed to have grown to twice its size already, yet still it was by no means erect. She wrapped two fingers about the base of his shaft and started to wank him, pulling his foreskin back and forth whilst her lips and tongue continued to work on him.

By the time he was fully erect, her mouth was stretched wide open, unable to contain more than half of the length of his great throbbing organ. He was responding to her now, giving short grunts of pleasure as she moved her head back and forth, still sucking hard. The audience had gone quiet again and she knew they were watching her with rapt attention as she fellated her partner, her breasts shaking delightfully with every movement she made. She wondered if she was simply to bring this man to a climax with her mouth, to swallow his seed for them. But she suspected they would expect more of her, and when the man suddenly withdrew his cock from her mouth, her suspicions were confirmed.

'Get on your hands and knees.'

Once again the quiet authority in his voice brooked no disobedience from the lustful youngster and she dropped forward onto all fours, deliberately pressing her body down so that her stiff nipples brushed the floor whilst her backside was raised high, her legs spread to ensure that her anus and sex were perfectly displayed.

The man moved round behind her. Then, to her surprise, he took hold of her thighs and lifted them. As he pulled her up, she straightened her arms, so that she was in the same position as when she and her friends had played wheelbarrow races when they were children. But now she was a mature young women, with succulent breasts that dangled down and a wet slit that ached to be penetrated. He lifted her higher, his strong frame supporting her effortlessly. Then she felt the tip of his penis rub up against the entrance to her vagina, and she gave a gasp of desire as he began to press.

He forced himself into her with short jabs, his saliva-coated cock working its way into her tight love-hole. Toni gritted her teeth, doubting for a moment that she would be able to contain his massive organ, but still he kept pressing, sliding deeper and deeper into her until she felt she could take no more. Then, at last, she felt the wiry hairs of his pubic bush against her outer lips and she knew he was fully inside her. For a moment he paused, and Toni was able to savour the sensation of being so totally filled by a man. Every fibre of her was concentrated on the exquisite sensation in her crotch as his heavy weapon twitched within her.

'Walk forward.'

She glanced round at him.

'What?'

'Walk forward. On your hands.'

So it was to be like the game of her youth, but this time with an eroticism she could never have imagined then. This time it was to be a show, a display for those watching. She began to step with her hands, moving forward, then going around in a circle as he guided her. The men were laughing now, and she blushed at the spectacle she knew she was making, her breasts swaying with every step. The motion of Toni's body with his caused a delicious friction within her, his engorged penis jabbing into her sex with every step he took. For Toni the sensation was extraordinary and she moaned softly as he led her about the stage, impaled on his thick organ.

136

They walked back and forth half a dozen times in this odd formation before he eased himself out of her once more and dropped her legs to the floor. She remained crouching there, her panting audible to those watching as she struggled to bring herself under control.

'Get up.'

Toni's legs were shaky as she pulled herself to her feet. He took her hand and led her across to the chair, which was still in the centre of the stage. He sat down facing the audience, his long cock still stiff as a ramrod.

'Turn round.'

Toni obeyed, turning her back to him. Then she felt his hands on her waist, pulling her back. She opened her legs, so that she straddled his, moving backwards until she was poised above his rampant organ.

'Sit.'

Slowly she lowered herself, biting her lip as she felt his cock enter her once more. She continued to crouch, small mewing sounds emanating from her lips as she felt his organ stretch her, driving ever deeper until it was, once again, all the way in. She squinted into the spotlight, able just to discern the silhouettes of those watching, only too aware of the erotic vision she made, the man's cock visibly embedded in her throbbing vagina.

'Fuck me.'

Toni didn't need asking twice. She began to move, flexing her knees and easing her body up and down his shaft. It felt delicious to be so totally penetrated and she moaned aloud at the sheer pleasure of what she was doing.

All at once she was seized by a desire to climax. The prolonged ordeals of the striptease, followed by the man's appearance, the taste of his cock and the extraordinary wheelbarrow exercise had all combined to turn her on more than she could imagine, and now she could feel an orgasm building inside her.

She increased her pace, her head thrown back, her mouth

open in a silent scream of lust as she worked herself off on the man. As she fucked him harder, her breasts bounced up and down in a way that brought cheers from the crowd. Toni heard this, and her face turned crimson at the thought of her behaviour, but she was too far gone to care now.

Her orgasm was long, loud and public, her body moving frenziedly as she milked her pleasure from his massive organ. Her shouts rang about the room as she came, ramming herself down on his erection with a force that threatened to break the chair on which he sat.

At last, though, her movements slowed as she descended from her peak, her hips describing a gyratory movement, her body sinking lower and lower until she was slumped on his lap, her head bowed, her hair covering her face.

He let her sit there for a few moments as the crowd shouted their appreciation, then he pulled her face round to his.

'My turn now,' he said.

He lifted her bodily from his cock and stood her in front of him on the stage. Then he rose and led her down to the very front.

'I'm going to spunk all over your pretty face and tits,' he said. 'Kneel down. And be ready to swallow some.'

He pressed her down to her knees, so that his cock was, once more, just in front of her face. Then he guided her hand to his shaft.

She began to masturbate him, one hand working his foreskin back and forth whilst the other squeezed and caressed his balls. He stood, his hands on his hips, his pelvis thrust forward, letting her do the work. Her hand flew back and forth, sensing his arousal increase with every stroke. Then he gave a grunt and she felt him stiffen.

The first gob of spunk launched itself from the end of his organ and splattered onto her cheek. She opened her mouth, in time to catch the second and third. Then she closed her lips to swallow and another hot, sticky load struck her chin, dribbling down her neck. Another gush of come hit her, then

138

another. She seemed drenched in his semen as spurt after spurt exploded from him into her mouth and onto her face, neck and breasts. He went on coming for a full thirty seconds or more before, at last, the flow decreased. In the end there was just a dribble hanging from the end of his organ.

'Clean me.'

Toni leant forward and protruded her tongue, catching the trickle before it dropped and swallowing it down, Then she took him in her mouth once more, licking and sucking every trace of semen from him. Only when he was completely clean did she release her hold on him.

Without a word he turned, scooping up his kimono. Then he was gone, leaving the naked, spunk-spattered youngster kneeling in the spotlight on her own whilst the applause of her audience rang in her ears.

Chapter 15

In the weeks that followed, Toni found herself entertaining the Count on a number of occasions. Every time he visited he would ask for her, and Lisa would find her heart sinking as she wondered what new degradation he had in mind for her. Once he had her take on two men at once, sucking off one whilst simultaneously being screwed by another. On another visit he made her dance a striptease then draw from a hat the name of the man who was to publicly fuck her. On yet another he had her simply tied naked to a post whilst a party went on around her, leaving the guests free to feel her up as they wanted.

Toni's feelings about these ordeals were ambivalent. On the one hand she was ashamed and humiliated at the way she was forced to offer her body to the men, and to allow intimacy with whoever the Count decreed. On the other, her lascivious nature led her to achieve orgasm after orgasm at his hands, and she never failed to find an exquisite if bittersweet pleasure in the way she was treated.

The Count had another effect on her, though, one that she couldn't understand. There was something about him that she found extraordinarily attractive and, though he never touched her himself, she found herself longing for him to do so. Despite his age, Toni found him fascinating, and, as time passed, she became more and more willing to obey his whims.

The feeling frightened her. How could she possibly be attracted to one such as him, a man who had never shown any vestige of affection? She knew too that her feelings toward the Count were becoming obvious to those around her. She was acutely aware of the interest her fellow waitresses took in her sessions with the Count, and she always knew when he was visiting from the general air of amusement amongst the girls when she arrived for work. She sometimes wished that he would take an interest in another of the girls for a change, though she was sure that if he did so she would be jealous. She had even considered asking Vilenski if she could be excused from her duties with the Count, in the hope that this might free of her of her obsession, but she had been unable to pluck up the courage.

Arriving at the club one evening, Toni knew at once that the Count was in the building. There was no mistaking the way the other girls nudged one another and pointed in her direction. She waited to receive the call to him with rising excitement, but the evening wore on and none came. Disappointed, she set about her business as usual, dodging the groping hands as she doled out the drinks.

It was nearly eleven o'clock before things began to happen. Things that would eventually change the whole path of her life, though she wasn't to know it at the time.

She had been taking a break, and was about to return to the club when a man entered the room. She recognised him vaguely as having been in one of the Count's entourage, and her stomach tightened as it occurred to her that he might be here at the club even now, but had declined to send for her.

She tried to avoid the man's eye as he came in, but he walked right up to her.

'We have met, I think.' His accent was similar to the Count's, his English somewhat broken.

'Have we Sir?' She eyed him. He was quite good-looking, aged about thirty with short, dark hair and the craggy face of one who has spent a lot of time in the sun.

'You are the beautiful English girl who entertains the Count.'

Toni said nothing, but the colour that suddenly flooded her cheeks gave him his answer.

'I am looking for the Count. Have you seen him?'

'No Sir. Not tonight.'

'I believe there is a room out the back here that he sometimes uses.'

Lisa remembered the room where she had witnessed the two girls entertaining the Count the first time she had encountered him.

'It's through there, Sir,' she said, indicating the door.

'Perhaps you could show me?'

Once again Toni eyed him. His face betrayed no emotion. Perhaps his enquiry was genuine. In any case, she knew she must do as he asked or risk incurring the wrath of both Vilenski and the Count.

'Come with me, Sir,' she said.

She led him through the door at the back of the rest area and up the passage toward the room at the end. When she reached it she pushed the door open and stepped in. It was empty, though the lights were on.

'I'm sorry Sir, he doesn't appear to be here.'

'It doesn't matter.'

The man closed the door behind him, and Toni was suddenly aware of his eyes on her. She took a step backwards, but he moved quickly, taking hold of her arm and pulling her close.

'Please, you're hurting,' she complained.

'I do not wish to hurt you, little English beauty,' he said.

'What do you want?'

'This.' He planted his lips over hers and she felt his tongue probe into her mouth.

Toni struggled for a moment, but he was a powerful man, and she was no match for him. As he pulled her close, his hand slid inside the top of her costume and closed over her breast, caressing it. At once she felt her nipple harden and a tingling sensation ran down her spine as she smelt his masculinity.

The kiss went on, and Toni found her body responding to it. His hand kneaded her soft breast, sending renewed shocks of pleasure through her. It was nearly two weeks since she had last been screwed and, despite her reluctance to accede to his demands, she found her breath begin to shorten as he caressed her.

He broke away, staring down into her eyes. As he did so he pulled down the front of her costume, exposing her firm young breasts to his gaze.

'You mustn't,' she murmured as he caressed them once more.

'Why not, you like it don't you?'

'I have to get back to work. If Mr Vilenski finds I'm gone I'll be punished.'

'He won't.' The man bent forward and took her left nipple into his mouth, sucking at it as he ran his tongue over the hard flesh. Toni let out a gasp at the intimacy of the manoeuvre, a sudden wetness invading her crotch as his hand explored her other breast.

He slipped a hand behind her, and she felt him take hold of the zipper that ran up the back of her costume.

'No,' she said.

But he took hold of it and pulled it all the way down.

The costume fell away, leaving her quite naked. Toni instinctively glanced about her, suddenly afraid that someone might be watching. Then she felt his fingers probe between

142

her legs and she gave a sigh of arousal as his digit penetrated her vagina.

'No,' she repeated, but offered no resistance as is fingers slid deeper inside her.

'You want me, don't you little English one,' he murmured.

'Someone might come in,' she protested lamely.

'So what if they do?' He forced her back against the wall of the room, leaving her costume behind where she had stood.

'But I...' her words were lost as he pressed her back against the cold surface of the wall, his hands roaming over her soft flesh. He placed his lips over hers once more.

She made a final effort to push him away, but already her own desires were building inside her at an alarming rate, her sex flooding with lubrication at his caresses.

He slid a hand down over her belly. She reached down to stop him, but h was too strong for her, brushing her arm aside as he slid his finger down between her legs.

'Oh'

Toni couldn't suppress an exclamation as he found her hard, wet love bud and ran his coarse fingers over it, sending extraordinary thrills through her young body as he fingered her in the most intimate way imaginable.

He began to frig her, his lips closed over hers, his tongue deep inside her mouth whilst his other hand continued to squeeze and caress her firm breasts. Toni was on fire with lust now, leaning back against the wall her legs spread wide, her hips thrusting against his fingers. She couldn't believe how quickly he had managed to kindle the base emotions that lurked within her, but now she was lost, her entire being consumed with a desire to be fucked and fucked hard. She reached down for his trousers, her hand closing over his crotch. He felt hard down there and a new shiver ran through her as she imagined his cock straining against his pants. She took hold of his zipper and began to slide it down.

At that moment there was a crash from outside, followed by the sound of men shouting and women screaming. The man froze for a second, then pushed her away.

'Police raid!' he shouted.

'What?'

'It's a police raid you idiot. You didn't think this place was legal did you? I've got to get out of here.'

'I don't understand...'

'It's okay for you. Just a fine and you'll be free. It happens all the time. But I've got my reputation to consider.'

He grabbed her hand and dragged her toward the door.

'But I'm naked,' she protested.

He ignored her, taking her down the corridor and back toward the main club and the only exit. Toni tried to pull back, desperate that the people in the club not see her nude, but she was no match for the man.

When they reached the club there was uproar. There were about twenty policemen, and they were wielding truncheons as they rounded up the people in the club. The clients were being driven back against the wall on one side, whilst all the waitresses were being lined up on the other. Toni's partner made immediately for the door which was, at that moment, unguarded, but one of the policemen spotted him and ran across to cut him off. As the officer came close, however, the man swung Toni round and thrust her forward so that she crashed into him, sending them both sprawling across the floor. Then he dashed for the door and was gone.

Toni tried to follow, but the policeman was too quick for her, taking hold of her shoulders and thrusting her against the wall alongside her fellow waitresses.

Toni clutched her hands to her breasts and sex, mortified at being naked amongst all these people. Despite their own dilemma she could see the other girls nudging one another and giggling at her obvious discomfort. The policemen too were eyeing her with some amusement, and made no effort to cover her.

Slowly a resemblance of calm and order settled over the room. A police officer set up a table and began taking the

144

customers' names, whilst the girls were taken across to another, behind which sat a fat police sergeant.

He began speaking to them, and the others all nodded. Toni looked at him in confusion.

'Please, I don't understand.'

'Ah, you are English, little shameless one.'

Toni nodded, blushing. 'What's happening?'

'I am imposing an on-the-spot fine for serving liquor without a licence. Fifty Zluvas each.'

Toni looked at him. It wasn't a large amount, about as much as she could earn in tips in a week. The other girls were reaching into the money pouches on their costumes and counting out the notes.

I don't have any money with me,' said Toni. 'It's in my costume. I'll have to go and get it.'

'Nobody is going anywhere,' said the policeman. 'Either pay up or you'll be arrested. Now, where is the money?'

'I told you I haven't got it,' insisted Toni. I can get it though.'

The sergeant beckoned one of his men over, then turned to Toni once more.

'Pay or be arrested,' he said.

'But I can't.'

He spoke a couple of words to the policeman and turned away. All at once Toni felt her hands pulled behind her, forcing her to uncover herself, and the cold metal of handcuffs closing about her wrists.

'No!' she exclaimed, but already she was being dragged off to the door, her naked charms on display to all as she struggled and pleaded.

The policeman took her out of the club, where a small crowd had formed from the village. There was much shouting and hilarity at the sight of the naked, shackled girl as she was manhandled across the courtyard.

On the far side was a van. The policeman pulled open the rear doors and thrust the hapless youngster inside. Then the doors were closed, plunging her into darkness.

A few seconds later she heard the engine start, and the van lurched off with its naked and reluctant passenger.

Chapter 16

Toni stood, gazing out through the bars of her small police cell, still barely able to comprehend what was happening to her. The cell was a single room, surrounded on three corners by bars and with a blank wall at the back. It was furnished with a mattress and nothing else. There were no windows in the room, just a single heavy door beyond the bars of the cell that was kept locked.

She wondered how long she had been her. Two hours? maybe three? They had brought her in here from the van, through a small back entrance and down a flight of stairs. Nobody had spoken a word to her, they had simply pushed her inside and slammed the door, leaving her by herself.

Toni glanced down at herself. She was still quite naked, with her hands cuffed behind her. She had begged them for some clothes as they were leaving, but her pleas had fallen on deaf ears. She cursed her plight. If only she hadn't allowed that man to seduce her. If only she'd had something on when they raided. To be alone and naked like this was awful.

All at once she heard the sound of a key turning in the outer door. Having no better way to cover herself she retreated to the back of the cell and pressed herself against the wall, doing her best to cover her backside with her hands. The door opened and someone came in.

'This is the one, is it?'

'Yes Sir.'

They were both men's voices and, surprisingly, they were talking English. Toni glanced over her shoulder and saw that both were in uniform, one a young man, the other in his late forties, his tunic bearing a number of badges of rank that showed him to be the senior of the two.

'Come over here, young lady,' he ordered.

'I can't, I'm naked.'

'I can see that. Now come here at once, or it'll be the worse for you.'

Reluctantly Toni turned to face the pair, her face glowing as she saw their eyes drop to her breasts, then her crotch. She walked hesitantly across to where they stood on the outside of her cell.

'Please give me some clothes,' she begged.

'Silence. Speak when you are spoken to,' barked the young officer.

'What is your name girl?'

'Antonia.'

'You are now in the custody of the State Police. You will be taken out and properly registered, then we will discuss what will happen next. Defaulting on a fine is a serious offence here.'

'Bu I...'

'Silence!' shouted the young policeman again. 'One more word and you'll be beaten for your insolence.'

Toni fell silent.

'See to her registration, then bring her to me,' ordered the older man. He turned on his heels and walked out.

The policeman unlocked Toni's cell and ordered her out. He pushed her into the corridor and indicated a room at the end. On reaching it, Toni saw that it was a kind of bathroom, with a sink at one end and tiled walls. In the centre was an old zinc tub about two feet across, filled with water. He pulled a key from his pocket and unlocked Toni's cuffs.

'Bathe yourself. Wash all over,' said the man. 'And face me whilst you're doing it.'

He settled himself on a bench by the wall.

Toni eyed the bath. There was a single cake of soap beside it and a towel attached to the wall by a cord. She stepped into the water. It was lukewarm. She glanced back at the policemen. He was sitting, his eyes fixed on her. Clearly there was no question of privacy. Reluctantly she turned to face him, then bent down and picked up the soap.

Toni washed herself thoroughly under the man's watchful eyes. She glowed with embarrassment as she ran her hands over her bare breasts and between her legs, her discomfort clearly enjoyed by her warder. When she had finished she dried herself carefully, then stood whilst he inspected her.

'Next door,' he ordered.

In the next room sat a small bespectacled man whose eyebrows shot up at the sight of the naked beauty. There was a scale on one side of the room and he took her to it, his hand lingering on her bottom as she was made to stand on it. He had a clipboard in his hand and he made a note of her weight. Then she had to stand against the wall whilst a marker was moved down onto her head and her height was noted.

What happened next took Toni by surprise. The man produced a tape measure from his pocket and, ordering Toni to stand in the centre of the room with her legs apart, he began to measure parts of her body.

He measured her breasts at least three times, his fingers lingering on the soft flesh, stroking her nipples and grunting in appreciation as they puckered to hardness under his touch. He measured both inside legs, his fingers brushing against the soft outer lips of her sex, rubbing against her love bud and making her bite her lip to avoid gasping with the sensation. He measured her low on her hips, running his hand through her pubic hair and stealing another touch of her swollen clitoris, sending shock waves of pleasure through her young body.

By the time he had finished, his touches had left Toni's body tingling with arousal, her nipples hard, her sex lips twitching as she fought to control her emotions.

The policeman led her out and into another room. This was set up as a photographic studio. The man behind the camera was about forty, and he licked his lips at the sight of Toni.

148

He gave her a strip, bearing a number, and made her hold it in front of her whilst he posed her facing the camera. He told her to hold the strip just below her breasts, so she knew that the picture would show that they were bare. He took two more shots sideways on, then told Toni to put down the board.

Thinking he had finished, Toni walked across to the policeman, but the man called her back.

'Over there,' he said.

At the back of the studio was a small stage draped with a white cloth. As Toni approached it, the man turned on a number of switches, flooding the area with light.

'Stand there and spread your legs apart,' he ordered. 'Put your hands on your hips.'

'But you can't photograph me like this,' protested Toni.

'Do as you're told,' barked the policeman.

Reluctantly Toni adopted the pose, and the man snapped a full-length shot of her naked body.

'Right, turn your back and look over your shoulder. Sick out your arse, that's it. Round a bit further, let me see your tit, Good. Now get down on all fours and spread your legs, I want a clear view of your pussy. That's right. Now play with yourself. Come on, just finger your cunt a bit. That's right. Okay, onto your back.'

The orders came thick and fast as he photographed every inch of her lovely young body. In spite of her embarrassment, Toni found herself becoming strangely turned on by the whole idea. She thought of the magazines in the secret room, and how they excited her. The idea of men seeing photos of her flaunting her body like this appealed to her baser desires, and she imagined men wanking over the sight she made, their hands rubbing up and down their shafts as they studied her image. Her arousal increased as the session went on, the poses becoming more and more outrageous until she was lying on her back, her pelvis thrust upwards, her fingers wet with her own juices as she masturbated herself.

By the time he had finished, she was close to orgasm, and

it was all she could do to cease masturbating as he ordered her to her feet and back into the charge of her escort. It was a somewhat shaky Toni that was marched into the senior officer's room five minutes later and made to take up her submissive pose before him, her sex lips still glistening with wetness.

'So,' said the man as she was brought in. 'I trust she has been fully registered.'

'Yes Sir,' replied the policeman.

'Good. Now, young lady, we must discuss what happens to you. Failure to pay a fine is a very serious offence, punishable by an automatic two month prison sentence.'

'Two months?' Toni's jaw dropped as she heard the words. 'But I can't possibly. It was only fifty Zluvas.'

'The amount is immaterial,' he said. 'You failed to pay, that is all.'

'Of course,' put in the younger man. 'You have two days in which to pay.'

'Then let me go back to the club and I'll get the money,' begged Toni.

The policeman shook his head. 'Out of the question. You cannot leave police custody.'

'Then how can I possibly raise the money?'

'Some prisoners find a way to work in the cells to raise it,' said the senior man. 'With the men it's generally breaking stones, but I don't think that would be suitable for you.'

'Then what else is there?' pleaded Toni. 'I'll do anything.'

'Anything?' The man's eyes drifted over her young charms.

'Wh-what do you mean?'

'Well, there's one obvious way in which you could raise some money. The local men are always interested in some new talent, especially a lovely young Englishwoman such as yourself.'

'You're not suggesting that I...'

'That you sell your body. It's as simple as that.'

'No.' She shook her head. 'It's out of the question.'

The man shrugged. 'Of course that is your decision. I'll

call for the prison van at once.'

'No, wait. Isn't there some other way?'

'Not as far as I can see.'

Toni stared at the floor. 'What would I have to do?' she asked quietly.

'Well, the standard rate for a prostitute in this town is twenty Zluvas. However they have their own accommodation, and it is considerably more comfortable than your cell. Then, of course, I shall have to charge you for use of the facilities. I imagine you could earn five Zluvas per customer.'

'Five Zluvas? But that's ten men!'

'You have two days. That should be time enough, surely?'

'But...'

'The alternative is two months in prison. The decision is yours.'

Toni stared from one to the other. What they were asking would have been unthinkable under any normal circumstances. But the idea of two months in prison was even more unthinkable and, knowing the lawless state of this country, might prove to be no less of an ordeal. She had no doubt that the prison warders would desire her as much as any man, and that she would have little power to fight off their advances.

She sighed. 'Where would I find such men?' she asked.

'I can procure them for you easily.'

'Then I suppose I'd better earn the fine.'

The man smiled. 'A wise decision,' he said. He turned to the younger policeman. 'Take our new whore back to her cell and send for her first customer.'

Toni stood in her cell, her back to the wall, staring at the door. It had been more than twenty minutes since her interview with the police chief and she knew the time was near when the first of her customers would materialise.

Customers! She couldn't believe she was using the word so casually. She was about to give herself for money, sell her body like a common whore to a man she had never met. Here she was, waiting to entertain him stark naked, her breasts and sex totally available to him. So why did she find the whole idea so incredibly exciting?

In any normal circumstances she knew that the idea of giving herself freely for money should be totally abhorrent to her. After all, she was an Englishwoman, brought up to be modest in her behaviour and to bestow her favours with care. Never had she imagined being in a situation where she would be awaiting the arrival of a man who she knew would fuck her, whatever her own feelings were, and who she would almost certainly never see again.

So why, then, was her cunt so wet? And why were her nipples stiff with anticipation?. She couldn't explain her emotions. All she knew was that she was totally turned on, and, but for the fact that the policeman had cuffed her wrists and attached them to a ring set in the wall above her head, she would even now be masturbating.

She heard the sound of footsteps and voices outside, and her stomach filled with butterflies as she realised that the moment had come. Whoever it was that was to enjoy her pleasures was just outside the door, and was about to see her naked body.

There was a rattling of keys, then the door swung open and the policeman came in, followed by another man. Toni stared at him, unconsciously thrusting her firm young breasts forward and widening her stance as his eyes fell on her. He was in his mid-forties, balding on top and with a bit of a paunch, hardly the man she would have chosen for a partner. She wondered if he was married. Almost certainly he was, so what was he doing here? Perhaps his wife didn't satisfy him, or maybe she too sought her kicks away from the marital bed. All Toni knew was that it was she who would be providing him with what he desired today and, since he was paying for the privilege, she was expected to perform as if he was an intimate lover.

The policeman opened her cell and the man walked in. He stopped just in front of Toni. his eyes roving over her body.

'Is she satisfactory?' asked her jailer. Toni noticed that he was using English, and guessed that the chief had insisted that she understood every detail of her degradation.

'Very nice,' the man replied. 'She will do as I ask?'

'Tell him,' said the policeman.

Toni took a deep breath. 'I am yours to use as you will,' she said, repeating the words she had been ordered to use. 'For five Zluva I will do whatever you ask, Sir.'

The man moved up close to Toni, his eyes roving over her naked flesh. She gave a little shiver as he examined her breasts, the sense of his eyes on them making the nipples harden even as he watched. He stretched out a hand and ran it over their soft surface, his fingers closing about her nipples and pinching them, nodding with approval as he felt how hard they were.

Toni stayed as still as she could, not allowing her eyes to meet his, trying as best she could to control the emotions his caresses were kindling in her. His hand fell away from her breast and ran lightly over her belly, making the tiny downy hairs there stand up on end as he did so. It dropped further, stroking the short black hairs that covered her pubis, his fingers tracing the line along which she had shaved them. Then he probed between her legs, seeking out her love bud, which was shiny and wet with her juices.

He teased the hard knob of flesh out from the folds of her sex lips. He did it slowly and carefully, his eyes never leaving her face as he probed the young English beauty in the most intimate way imaginable. Toni knew that her expression and the whole posture of her body would convey to him the effect he was having on her. She felt the muscles of her sex tighten, and she was certain he must have felt it.

'I see you enjoy having your body caressed,' he murmured. 'You are very sensual, little English whore. I think it is not just the money that makes you give your body to men.'

Lisa said nothing, but a low moan escaped her lips as he began to probe her vagina with his finger, feeling the wetness inside her so that she knew he was aware of how turned on she was.

The man turned to the policeman. 'Release her hands, then leave us,' he said.

The policeman undid the cuffs, and Toni rubbed her wrists as he went out, locking both the cell door and the outer door.

'So, my dear,' said the man. 'It seems we are both prisoners for the time being. You will suck my cock now.'

Toni looked at him. The words had been spoken with the casual air of someone telling a minion to perform some minor task, though what he was asking was something totally intimate. Yet the way he was taking charge was serving only to increase her own arousal. To have all responsibility taken from her and to simply be obliged to obey, somehow made her submission that much easier, allowing her to detach herself from the sluttish way she was being asked to behave and simply become an automaton, obeying orders to the letter. Yet nobody seeing this warm, sensuous beauty would ever have considered her a automaton, and the barely suppressed eagerness with which she dropped to her knees and began unfastening his trousers betrayed the fact that she was very aroused and anxious to taste his manhood.

She pulled down his zip and reached inside. His cock was short and thick, standing stiffly from his fly, the foreskin pulled slightly back so that she could see the small hole from which she knew would soon come spurts of spunk inside her vagina.

154

She took him into her mouth at once, sucking hard at him whilst her fingers reached into his pants and cupped his balls. This time it was his turn to moan as she began to fellate him, tasting his maleness, her head moving back and forth, coating his swollen knob with her saliva.. He stood, his hands on her head, his eyes glued to her as she sucked him.

'That's good,' he murmured. 'You seem to be something of an expert at satisfying men.'

Toni lowered her eyes, concentrating on the job in hand, her breasts shaking with every thrust forward of her head.

'Enough,' said the man suddenly. 'I have paid to fuck you, and fuck you I will. Now stand up, then bend over and take hold of the cell bars.'

Toni' had a tight feeling in the pit of her stomach as she rose to her feet. She turned away from him and grasped the cell bars at about waist height., bending forward, then widening her stance. She felt his fingers probe between her legs once again, moaning aloud as he ran his index finger along the length of her slit. All restraint abandoned now, she pressed her backside back at him, grinding her hips down on his fingers, urging him to probe ever deeper inside her.

'Good,' he said. 'I see you are ready for me.

His fingers left her, then she felt his cock brush against her leg. She reached behind her, grasping his shaft and guiding it toward her vagina until it nuzzled against the soft, pink flesh there.

He penetrated her with a single push, his thick cock sliding deep into her. Then, taking hold of her hips, he began to fuck her hard. Toni gave a cry of arousal as she felt the force of his onslaught. She braced herself against the cell bars as her body was shaken by his thrusts, his stomach slapping against her behind with every stroke. She pressed back at him, matching his rhythm with her own, her lovely breasts swaying back and forth deliciously, her breath coming in hoarse gasps. The cell door clanged with each thrust, and she knew that the policeman outside would hear the sound and would know she was being taken, but she was past caring now, her entire being consumed by the pleasure she was receiving from her ravisher.

They came simultaneously, he grunting with pleasure whilst she screamed aloud at the exquisite pleasure of feeling her cunt filled with spunk. Toni was in a state of ecstasy, the tension that had been building in her ever since her registration finally finding its relief in an explosive orgasm. For his part, the man continued his thrusts with unabated vigour, pumping the contents of his balls deep inside the wanton youngster.

At last, though, he was spent, pulling his knob from her, leaving her still pressed against the bars, her chest heaving.

'Clean me,' he ordered.

Slowly Toni straightened. Then, turning to face him, she dropped to her knees once again and took him into her mouth, the taste of her own feminine juices mixed with his spunk bringing a new spasm of pleasure to her as she licked every last vestige from him.

He pushed her away and tucked his cock back into his trousers. Then he shouted something and Toni heard the sound of the key turning in the outer door once more.

When the cell was opened he left without a word. The policeman eyed Toni's dishevelled state with some amusement and she blushed as she felt the spunk dribble from her sex and trickle down her thigh.

He took a five Zluva note from his pocket and attached it to a clip that hung by the door.

'Another forty-five and you'll be free to go,' he said. 'Now come with me. We'll have to get you cleaned up for your next customer.'

Toni lay on her back in her cell, gazing up at the ceiling. She knew she must have been asleep, but she wasn't sure for how long. For the last two days her life had been something of a blur, as she had entertained man after man, allowing them to enjoy her body in any way they had demanded.

She could scarcely believe that she had gone through with it, but now, at last, her fine was paid and her stint as a whore was at an end. It had been a gruelling ordeal, yet one that her body had responded to with an extraordinary enthusiasm, giving her more orgasms than she could remember.

The men's demands had been many and varied. Some had simply taken her on her back on the mattress. Others had had her on her hands and knees, or in various other positions. One man had had her cuffed to the bars in a spreadeagled posture and had fucked her twice, clearly turned on by her helplessness, as had been Toni. One had watched her wash the spunk from her by her previous customer before bending her over the tub and filling her vagina once more. Two of her partners had succeeded in coming in both her mouth and her cunt in quick succession. All the time Toni had been in a state of total arousal, sometimes enjoying two or three orgasms during a single fuck. When the last man had paid his money she had been exhausted and had simply flopped down in her cell, falling at once into a deep sleep. Now, as she gazed about her, she wondered how long she had slept, and when they would return her to the academy. Rubbing her eyes, she rose slowly to her feet, stretching her aching limbs.

She was alone. She wondered where her warder was. Surely they should have set her free by now? After all she had paid her fine hadn't she? She shivered as she remembered what that had involved, still scarcely able to believe she had gone through with it.

She went across to the door of her cell and leant against it, meaning to call out to her captor. To her surprise the door opened. It had been left unlocked! Cautiously she made her way to the outer door and tried that. It too was not locked. Toni paused. Dare she go out? Perhaps they would punish her if she did. Then there was her state. She was still totally naked, hardly a condition in which to try to make an escape. But the alternative was to stay here in this dingy cell, a prospect that did not appeal to the youngster. Perhaps she would take a look in the corridor. With any luck she might find something to wear.

She crept out. She knew that to her right lay the bathroom and the other rooms where she had experienced her registration. She went left, toward a door at the end that had always been closed and locked. Once again, though, it opened when she turned the handle. She peered through and saw beyond a dingy corridor lit by a single naked bulb. At the far end was a staircase that led up to the left. Taking a deep breath, Toni stepped out onto the cold linoleum floor.

She climbed the stairs on tiptoe, wincing every time she made the old wooden treads creak under her weight. At the top was yet another door and she pushed it open cautiously.

What met her eyes made her jaw drop in surprise. Far from finding the grim austerity of a police station, the door opened onto a hallway carpeted with a rich navy blue pile, the walls lined with oak panelling and decorated with very old looking oil paintings. She stepped out, her bare feet sinking into the soft carpet. Once again there was nobody about. Toni resolved to find something to wear. Perhaps there would be a bathroom offering the comfort of a towel to wrap about herself, or even a bedroom where she might find some real clothes.

She made her way up the hallway. At the far end was hung a long mirror in a gilded frame and she found herself blushing as she caught sight of her bare breasts and the dark covering of pubic hair over her mound. She hoped desperately there was nobody about.

When she reached the mirror she stopped. She appeared

to have reached a dead end, apart from a single door to her left. She glanced behind her. There seemed little point in retracing her steps without investigating further. Slowly, her hand shaking a little, she reached for the handle and pushed the door open.

'Ah, there you are young lady. I was beginning to think you weren't coming. Step inside and close the door.'

Toni froze. At the far end of the room was a desk with someone seated behind it. In the dim light of the room, with the only illumination a low lamp on the desk, she couldn't at first discern the identity of the figure beyond.

'Come on, come on,' the man said impatiently.

Then she recognised the voice, and Toni gasped.

It was the Count.

'You...'

'Come over here, closer to the desk.'

Toni moved closer. As she did so the Count clicked on a light, so that she could see him more clearly. His eyes bored into her an she felt, once again, the curious sexual magnetism that, despite her better judgement, drew her to him.

'How are you enjoying your stay in my castle?' he asked.

'Your castle? But I thought...'

'You thought you were being held by the police? A neat little subterfuge, and one that rather amused me.'

'You mean those weren't policemen at all?'

'The raid was real enough. It's actually quite routine for them to raid the club. The fines and bribes come in useful. Naturally I was informed of the impending raid.'

'So you set me up?' Toni was incredulous.

'Something like that.'

'And that man who was seducing me...'

'Was working for me. That's very perceptive of you. I knew that a hot little thing like you wouldn't be able to resist him coming on at you. Getting you naked was part of the plan. It not only ensured that you'd have no money to pay, but it also amused me to have you as a naked captive.'

'And all those men...'

'You mean these.' The Count flicked a switch on his desk and suddenly half a dozen television screens lit up on the wall beside him. On each one was a video of Toni being screwed by a different man. The girl's jaw dropped as she watched herself impaled on the rampant cocks of six different men.

'You had no right,' she cried, her face turning crimson at the scenes before her.

'When you are in my position, you can do what you like,' said the Count. 'You see I wanted you to come here, and the raid seemed an obvious way. The business of earning your fine was simply a harmless diversion, that's all. It amused me to watch you give yourself so freely.'

'But I thought I had to. The fine.'

'You didn't have to pay in the way you did. But with such a lovely body, it was the obvious way.'

Toni was suddenly reminded of her nudity, and she tried as best she could to cover herself with her hands. The Count smiled.

'Your sudden modesty becomes you,' he said. 'But don't you think it's a little late?'

She dropped her eyes. 'How long do you intend keeping me here?' she asked.

'That rather depends on you.'

'But I'm being held a virtual prisoner.'

The Count glanced about him. 'I see no bars or shackles here,' he observed.

'You know what I mean.'

As far as I'm concerned you are free to go,' he said.

'What, like this?'

'That is how you arrived. However I concede that you will require some clothes. For that reason I have had a wardrobe prepared for you upstairs.'

'And how am I to get back to Madame Lashenka's?'

'A car will be organised. That is if you want it.'

'Of course I do. Why wouldn't I?'

'I have an alternative proposition. You could stay here.'

She stared at him. 'Why would I want to do that?'

'Because I want you to. It would be on my terms of course.'

'I don't understand. what are you suggesting?'

'I'm offering you your own suite of rooms in my castle. The best food in the district. A salary. The run of my castle and its grounds. Complete freedom within its walls.'

'Within its walls?'

'That's one of the conditions, that you do not stray from the castle unless escorted.'

'One of the conditions? What are the others?'

'That you are completely obedient to me whilst you are here. And that you perform certain hostess functions for my special guests.'

'What kind of functions?'

'Once again, total obedience, whatever they ask of you.'

'More whoring?'

'That's something that you have already shown yourself to be extremely adept at.'

'It's an outrageous suggestion. No decent girl would even consider it. It's quite out of the question. Now please find me some clothes and call that car.'

'I hadn't mentioned the salary. If you agreed to stay for three months I would pay you two thousand pounds Sterling per week.'

'Two thousand...' Toni's jaw dropped.

'I see the whore in you surfacing again.'

Toni reddened. 'That's a lot of money,' she said.

'Certainly.'

She shook her head suddenly. 'No,' she said. 'I couldn't consider it. What on earth made you think I'd accept?'

'The alternative is to return to Madame Lashenka's.'

'I have to return. My aunt and uncle are paying my fees.'

The Count laughed. 'There are no fees paid at Madame Lashenka's. She makes her money by treating her girls as drudges and whores, then pocketing the takings.'

'You mean...'

'Eventually the girls cotton on. But getting out of there isn't easy. For one thing, how would you buy a ticket home? No, young lady, girls sent to Madame Lashenka's are girls abandoned by their families. Why would you want to go back there? Just to be a waitress in that dreary nightclub and to satisfy the odd man? It's not much of a life, surely?'

'She doesn't lock me up in prison cells.'

'What would you call that ghastly institution, if not a prison cell? And as for the food, any self-respecting prison governor would have sacked the chef years ago.'

'Even so, I couldn't possibly stay here.'

'Why on earth not? What I'm offering you is three months spent amusing me, after which I'd give you an air ticket and enough money to set yourself up in a flat and find a job. After all, it's only three months.'

'But what would people think?'

'Nobody you know will ever be aware you were here. No matter what demands are made of you, you'll leave here with a clean character.'

'Why are you making this offer to me? There must be plenty of local girls who would jump at the chance. Even some of the ones at the Midnight Club.'

'Such girls are two a penny. I'm sick to death of watching women fake their orgasms to try to please their men. You, on the other hand are totally different. You actually enjoy the treatment, and your orgasms are genuine. I have never come across that in a woman before. You act so prim and proper, the typical blushing English rose, yet you fuck like a bitch on heat with total strangers and you come every time. That is why you fascinate me. And that lovely young body you flaunt so openly.'

Toni hugged herself even closer. 'I see.'

'So, You are interested?'

'I... I'm not sure.'

'But you are considering the idea?'

'How many of your guests would I have to entertain?'

'Only the special ones. I estimate that you would have at least a third of your time to yourself. But you would have to stay the full three months. Once you agree, you consent to hand over full power to me. If you refuse to co-operate or manage to escape before the three months are up the deal is cancelled.'

'And these guests, they would expect me to do anything for them as well?'

'That's right. Some may just want a companion, others a partner at tennis or bridge. Some would want to fuck you, to chain you, to use you as a slave, even to whip you.'

Toni shook her head. She couldn't believe he was even suggesting such a deal. What she should do was slap him across the face and walk out. But to where? He was right, the idea of returning to Madame Lashenka's held no appeal to her at all. The thought of living here, on the other hand, in all this luxury, was very appealing indeed. Then there was the money.

Toni had never had any money of her own. All her life she had relied on others to pay her way. But two thousand a week! That would mean that in a few months she could afford to return to England and set up on her own. Begin her life anew with enough capital to find a place to live and a job. Maybe even take a holiday.

Then there was the fact that, if she stayed, she would be close to the man who fascinated her so much. The idea of pleasing him was one that she found almost irresistible, though she was at a total loss to understand the power he held over her.

There was something else occupying Toni's mind though. Something she could barely bring herself to acknowledge. The idea of being a sex slave to the Count's guests, whilst it frightened her, also thrilled her more than she cared to admit. She knew that what he had said about her was true, that her sexual appetite was far in excess of other girls'. Even the thought of

163

the bondage and whipping sent a delicious shiver of excitement through her.

'Could... Could I see the room?' she asked hesitantly.

'Certainly. I was sure that you would accept.'

'I haven't accepted yet.'

'But you will. You are too turned on by the idea to say no.'

'You're very sure of yourself.'

'One other thing. Whilst you are in my employ you will speak only when spoken to and you will call me Master. Do you understand?'

Toni stared at him for a moment. She opened her mouth to make a remark, then closed it again. Instead she allowed her arms to drop to her sides, revealing her body to him fully once more.

'Yes Master,' she said.

Chapter 19

The next few weeks were amongst the strangest of Toni's life. True to his promise, the Count gave her a luxurious suite of rooms for her personal use and the run of the castle. The grounds were extensive and beautifully cultivated and she spent many happy hours walking, swimming in the large pool or simply relaxing in the warm sunlight. Her meals were served in her room by the Count's servants and she was free to go where she wished.

Entertaining the Count's guests was the only task she was called on to do, and it proved something she could do well, though she often felt shamed by her behaviour. Most of the men were businessmen in their forties or fifties. A few simply wanted her companionship, but most made more rigorous demands on her. They would make her dress in sexy clothes and wait on them at dinner. Often she would not be permitted underwear, allowing them to grope her at will. Many took her to bed with them, sending her upstairs to wait naked for them between the sheets. One man had a servant tie her to his bed, spreadeagled so that he was able to take her at will during the night. Another made her sleep on the floor at the foot of his bed, waking her three times in the night to suck him off. For Toni the visits were occasions of mixed emotions. Her natural shyness made her uneasy with her various masters, yet their treatment aroused her hugely, so that she would enjoy orgasm after orgasm in their hands.

She saw surprisingly little of the Count during those weeks, much to her disappointment. He seldom seemed to bother with her, though she felt certain that hidden cameras often filmed her antics with his guests, and it comforted her to know that he would have found enjoyment in watching her give herself to other men. Occasionally he would dine with his visitors so that she would be obliged to wait on both men, something that gave her great pleasure. On these occasions he seldom addressed a word to her, yet still she sensed that he had an affection for her, and sometimes she would turn to find him watching her with an expression of genuine tenderness on his face.

Then, one day, about two weeks before her three months were up, he summoned her to his office.

It was the first time she had entered the room since her first meeting with him after her ordeal in the cell, and her heart was beating fast as she knocked on the door.

'Come,' he called.

She stepped inside. He was seated at his desk, and she felt a flutter of excitement as he looked up into her eyes.

'You asked to see me Master?'

'Ah yes.. Stand there,' he said indicating the spot in front of the desk.

Toni obeyed, placing her hands behind her head and placing her feet apart as she always did when in his presence.

'I hear good reports about you from my visitors,' he said.

'Thank you Master. I do my best.'

165

'Evidently. They tell me you have a tight cunt.'

She blushed and said nothing.

'The time is drawing close when I must meet my side of the bargain.'

'Yes Master.'

'I shall be sorry to see you go.'

'I... I shall too Master.'

He gave a little smile. 'I'm almost prepared to believe that,' he said.

Toni herself wasn't certain quite how she felt about her impending departure. If truth be told she loved the castle and its grounds. It was the first place she had ever lived where she had felt at home. Oddly, although she was a virtual prisoner here, she had never felt so free. As for the sex, it provided an excitement she had never dreamed of in her life. Most of all, though, it meant that she was close to the Count.

'Anyhow,' he went on, returning to his usual businesslike manner. 'You still have two weeks here, and I have a new task for you. I have another visitor arriving tomorrow.'

'I'll do my best to please him, Master,' she said.

'I'm sure you will. He is a very important man, and you are to be especially obedient to him. Do you understand?'

'Yes Master.'

'I will be holding a reception for him tomorrow night. There will be many rich and influential guests there. I want you to behave exactly as he orders.'

'Yes Master.'

'Good. Just make sure you do. That will be all.'

'Yes Master.'

She turned to leave.

'Wait.'

'Master?'

'This man is... He is very powerful.'

'Master?'

'Just be careful, that's all.'

'What do you mean Master?'

He looked into her face, and she sensed the concern in his eyes.

'Nothing. Go now.'

She gave a little curtsey and left the room. As she made her way upstairs she puzzled over the interview. Why had it taken place? He never normally warned her of the arrival of new guests. This man must be very important indeed. She shivered slightly as she thought of what he might demand of her, and her fingers crept down between her legs where a warm wetness was already seeping into her crotch.

When her guest arrived Toni was, as always, at the door to meet him. He was about fifty years old, with an arrogant air about him and he glanced disdainfully at her when she bade him hello. His name was Bastik and he had olive brown skin and dark hair flecked with grey.

'Take this briefcase and look after it,' he said brusquely, thrusting the bag into the youngster's hand. His voice was harsh, with an accent that sounded eastern to Toni.

She showed him up to his room with two servants following carrying his luggage. The suite was huge, much larger than those allocated to any of the men Toni had entertained previously, indicating the man's status.

The servants put down the cases and he waved them out.

'You stay,' he said to Toni.

'Give me the briefcase,' he ordered once they were alone. 'Then unpack my bags.'

Toni set about dutifully doing as she was told. He seemed to have an enormous number of suits, shirts and ties, but the wardrobes were more than sufficient to contain them. As she worked he sat watching her, making her feel more nervous by the second as he fixed his eyes on her.

At last the final shirt was stowed and all the drawers were shut. Toni turned to him.

'Will there be anything else, Sir?'

'Get me a drink. A whisky and soda. Then strip naked.'

'Sir.'

Toni tried to keep the tremor from her voice as she turned to the drinks cabinet. The order to strip had been given in precisely the same tones as the order for the drink. Clearly he had no illusions about Toni's status, and neither should she have.

Her fingers trembled as she poured the drink, her stomach like a tight knot. Despite the many times she had given herself to men during her stay in this country, it still gave her an extraordinary thrill when she contemplated baring her body to another man, and the ice cubes rattled in his glass as she passed it to him.

'Stand in front of me,' he ordered. 'And take everything off.'

She began to undo her blouse, her fingers barely able to work the buttons so nervous was she. She reached the bottom eventually, though, and pulled it open, revealing the small black bra beneath. It lifted her breasts and enhanced her cleavage wonderfully, though Toni's young breasts were in little need of support. She dropped the blouse to the floor and reached for the zipper on her skirt. She pulled it down and pushed the tight garment over her hips and off, stepping out of it and kicking it to one side. Her panties were very brief indeed, not much more than a G-string, and she felt a hot flush invade her cheeks as she stood, facing him in such scanty attire.

Her bra fastened at the front, and she reached up for the catch, snapping it undone. For a second she held the cups to her breasts, then she saw an impatient look cross Bastik's face and she knew she could delay no longer. She let the bra fall open and slide down her arms and off. The colour in her cheeks deepened as he studied her succulent young breasts, the nipples hardening to stiff points even as he watched. She let her hands drop to her waist. Once again her natural modesty made her pause for a second. Then she pulled the pants down her thighs and kicked them aside. Now she wore only her high-heeled shoes, but she sensed he would want her to

168

leave them on, enhancing as they did the slim tapering of her shapely legs, so she simply placed her feet wide apart and grasped the back of her head in her classic submissive stance. Bastik sat back in his chair and eyed her body, his gaze roving slowly over her soft flesh in a way that made her shiver. She could already feel the wetness seeping into her sex as it always did when she flaunted her body before a man.

'Turn around.'

Obediently Toni turned her back on him, revealing the firm pertness of her backside to him.

'When were you last thrashed?'

'About two weeks ago Sir.'

'Hmm. That behind of yours could do with some fresh stripes. Bend forward and pull your arse cheeks apart.'

Toni bent at the waist, her supple young body allowing her to bend almost double. No man had ever asked her to do this before, and she wondered at the sight she was presenting to the man as she moved her hands up onto her bottom cheeks. She pulled them apart, aware of the fact that the tight star of her rear hole was being perfectly presented to him. She held the pose for a full minute, almost physically feeling his gaze on her backside as she did so.

'Stand up and face me.'

Once again Toni's response was instant as she exposed her breasts and sex to him.

'Pass me that phone.'

Toni scuttled across the room to where the telephone stood on a side table. It was cordless, so she was able to take it across to him. He punched in three numbers, then began to speak in a tongue she didn't understand. Toni, meanwhile, resumed her spread stance in front of him.

He switched off the phone, then handed it back to her.

'What time is the party?'

'Six-thirty Sir,' said Toni.

'Be here at six.'

'Yes Sir.'

She paused for a moment longer, but he had picked up a magazine and begun to flick through it, so she knew the interview was at an end. Picking up her clothes from the floor she headed for the door.

She arrived back at six on the dot and rang the bell. A voice sounded from a small intercom.

'Yes?'

'It's me, Sir. Antonia.'

'What are you wearing?'

'My dress for the party, Sir.' Toni had chosen a particularly elegant gown that complemented her curves beautifully.

'Take it off. Leave it outside and come in naked. And be quick!'

The intercom went dead.

Toni glanced about her. Two servants were working across the corridor on a broken door lock. They were no more than ten feet away. She wondered if they had heard the conversation and, if so, whether they had understood it. Until now only the most senior of the Count's servants had seen her naked whilst they had prepared her for her guests. She waited a few moments in the hope that they might go away, but there was no sign of that. She knew she could delay no longer, so reached behind her and undid the catch of her dress, then pulled the zip down. She slid the dress down her body, aware that this was the second time in only a few hours that she had been made to strip like this. She glanced across at the men, who had stopped work and were eyeing her intently. Then, her face crimson, she turned her back on the pair and removed first her bra, then her panties, discarding them on the floor.

She pressed the bell again.

'Are you naked?'

'Yes Sir.'

'Those two workmen, tell them to go away and come back later. The noise is disturbing me. Hurry now girl, I'll be pressing the button to admit you in thirty seconds.'

Toni mentally cursed him for the way he had read her embarrassment so well. She had no time to think though. She daren't delay any longer. She turned and rushed across to the two men, whose eyes were still fixed on her. She addressed the older of the two.

'Mr Bastik says come back later.'

The man replied in a language Toni didn't understand.

'Go away now,' she said gesticulating with her hands.

He said something to his colleague, who laughed aloud.

'Please go,' pleaded Toni. 'Now.'

The man shrugged and the pair began picking up their tools. At that moment Toni heard the buzz of the door lock and she flew across to it, gasping with relief as it opened under her hands. She almost staggered into the room, pulling up short in front of Bastik and adopting her submissive pose at once.

'Are they going?'

'I think so, Sir.'

'You think so?'

'I don't speak their language, Sir, but they were packing up.'

'Let's hope you're right. Now, what about the clothes you were wearing?'

'I put on a lovely dress. I was trying to please you, Sir.'

'In future you are to put no article of clothing on your body without my approval. Understand?'

'Nothing? Not even underwear?'

'Nothing.'

Toni couldn't believe what she was hearing. All the other guests had expressed their preferences about what she wore, but none had taken it quite that far. She began to realise what the Count had meant about this man.

'I understand, Sir,' she said. 'It won't happen again.'

He nodded, then once again he picked up a magazine from the table beside him and started to read it.

Toni's mind was confused. She just didn't know what to

make of her new master. Making her expose her body to the two servants had been quite unnecessary, yet he had clearly done it as a test. This whole affair was as puzzling to her as it was arousing. The encounter with the servants had been humiliating, yet it had appealed to the perversity of her nature. Indeed her juices were flowing freely now, and she knew it was only a matter of time before they began to seep from her. Yet Bastik was acting as if she wasn't even there, despite the fact that her lovely body was on display to him.

About five minutes passed, then the doorbell rang.

'Answer that.'

Toni gazed down at herself in dismay. Whoever it was, they were going to see her naked, whether she liked it or not.

Her heart thumping she went to the door and opened it. There, standing before her, was one of the servants, a man she recognised as the Count's personal barber.

'Someone need a shave?' he said, his eyes fixed on Toni's crotch.

'I think Mr Bastik must have called for one,' she said.

'He call, but shave not for him.' The man grinned. 'For you. In bedroom please.'

'For me?' Toni stared at him.

'In bedroom.'

She turned to Bastik, but his face was buried in the magazine once again.

Toni took the man into the bedroom. In the centre was a huge four-poster bed, and in the corner a much smaller one. This was an arrangement that for Toni was useful, as the Count's guests often called for her in the night, but preferred not to share their beds with her. The man went across to the bed and, pulling the pillow out from the eiderdown, placed it in the centre of the bed. Then he withdrew a towel from his bag and spread it over the pillow. He turned to Toni.

'You lie down on bed, backside here,' he patted the pillow. 'Spread legs wide open.'

Toni was perplexed. Did he intend to fuck her? In which

case why him? Surely there were plenty of men Bastik could have called on apart from the Count's barber.

'You lie down,' he said again. 'I come back soon.'

He disappeared into the bathroom, leaving Toni on her own. She glanced at the door. Bastik was apparently still absorbed in his magazine. Clearly whatever the man was doing, he was doing it with her new master's blessing. With no alternative in mind, Toni crawled onto the bed and lay back, the pillow beneath her backside so that her pubis was thrust upward in the most lewd manner. Then, slowly, she spread her legs as he had ordered. As she did so she felt her vagina with her fingers, noting with embarrassment that she was, indeed, very wet down there.

The man bustled back in. He was carrying a mug and was stirring something around inside it. He grinned broadly when he saw her position, sitting down on the bed beside her. He ran his fingers through her pubic hair.

'A pretty bush,' he murmured.

He pulled a brush covered in soapy foam from the mug and held it up in front of her, the warm water dripping onto her belly. Then he began to coat her pubis with the foam.

All at once she understood. He was going to shave her cunt!

She gazed down between her breasts, her face a picture of consternation as he spread the foam over her mound and down between her legs, the warm softness of the brush sending involuntary shivers of pleasure through her as he worked it into her nether bush. Then, when he had coated every inch, he reached into his bag and pulled out the razor.

Toni shivered as he ran it up and down a leather strop, noting how it gleamed in the light. She froze as he leaned over her crotch and she felt the chill of cold metal on her bare flesh.

He worked in small, even strokes, gliding the sharp steel across her mound, gathering a small pile of soap and black hair with each stroke, then wiping it clean. When every wisp of hair had been removed from Toni's mons, he started between her legs, making her shiver as the blade slid along her sex lips. He shaved her expertly, removing each hair down to the follicle and leaving the soft flesh as smooth as a baby's, his fingers moving over the most private part of Toni's anatomy in a way that had her shaking with excitement.

At last he was done, and he wiped the last vestiges of foam away with a cloth. Then he spread an ointment over the shaved area, one that burned slightly.

'That kill hair roots,' he explained. Make you bare down there for long time. Maybe two years.'

He left the ointment on for about five minutes before washing it off. Then he pulled Toni to her feet and led her across to a mirror. She could scarcely believe what she saw. Her pubis was completely devoid of hair, as was her sex. Her thick nether lips had never been so exposed, and there was an odd coolness between her legs that she had never felt before. He stood behind her, running his hand down over her mound and along the length of her slit, pausing to rub her clitoris so that she gasped aloud.

'You like shaved cunt?' he asked. 'Only slut and whore have shaved cunt. Right for you I think?'

Toni said nothing, her eyes still fixed on her crotch. He was right. Being shaved down there was something a woman did only to advertise her availability. She shivered again as she thought of what men would think when they saw her like this.

'One more thing Mr Bastik orders. You lie on bed again like before.'

Toni went back to the bed and prostrated herself on it. The man pulled something else from his bag. It was a sort of pen, with a very fine fibre nib. He bent over her crotch and began drawing, each stroke leaving a fine black line on her pale skin. He worked for no more than a minute, then sat up.

'That okay I think.'

Toni raised herself on one elbow and gazed down at herself and her jaw dropped. He had drawn a small black arrow on her skin, less than an inch long, but thick and unmissable. It ran down at an angle on her pubis from right to left. And the point was directed precisely at her cunt. It was like a signal to anyone seeing her that this was where she wanted them to look.

Toni was still in a daze as the barber led her through to where Bastik was sitting. He put aside his magazine and beckoned her closer, inspecting her sex. Then he nodded.

'Better,' he said. 'The mark. It will remain?'

'The ink was indelible. It will be there for a week, maybe longer.'

'Hmm, a tattoo would be better. Maybe some other time. You may go, barber.'

The barber gave a bow and left. For a few seconds there was silence, then Toni plucked up the courage to speak.

'Excuse me Sir?'

'Yes?'

'What am I to wear to the party?'

'I have picked out some jewellery and other items for you. They are on the table.'

He indicated an expensive looking jewel box that lay on the table next to him. Toni picked it up and opened it. Inside was the most exquisite diamond necklace she had ever seen, the stones glittering in the light of the room. With it was a matching bracelet. Toni crossed to the mirror and put them on, her eyes positively dazzled by their beauty. She turned to face him and he nodded his approval.

'And my clothes, Sir?' she asked meekly.

'I told you, on the table.'

Toni looked down. Beside the jewellery box, all she could see was a pair of hold-up black stockings and black high-heeled shoes.

'But what dress should I wear?' she asked.

'How many times must I repeat myself? All you are to wear is on that table.'

'But...' Toni stared down at the stockings and shoes.

'Now get them on, girl,' he ordered. 'We are due at the party in five minutes.'

Chapter 20

Toni's stomach was churning as she stepped out into the hall-way. She couldn't believe what was happening. Here she was on her way to a grand party, which she knew would be full of beautifully dressed people from the upper echelons of local society, yet she wore only stockings, her breasts and sex on view to all. Worse, she was shaved, as if she intended to be seen like this, with that awful mark pointing to her most private place. She watched as Bastik, resplendent in full dinner suit, locked the door, then turned to her.

'There are special instructions for you,' he said suddenly.

'Sir?'

'Usually, when you entertain the Count's guests you do so with deference, am I right?'

'It is how I am told to behave Sir.'

'Whilst in my care you are not to show me the deference of a slave, you are to act as my partner.'

'Your partner, Sir?'

'You will drink and talk as a normal member of the guest list. You will call me Masad, which is my first name, and I will call you Antonia. It will be so much more amusing if people think that you are attending like that voluntarily, don't you think?'

'I... Yes Sir.'

'I beg your pardon, Antonia?'

'Yes Masad.'

His suggestion had confused her at first, but now she saw the ingenuity of his mental torture. Had she attended as his slave, she could at least have argued that she had no choice but to be nude. However, as his partner, they would assume she was naked by her own choice, and that she wanted to display her bare sex, even to the point of drawing attention to it with what was apparently a tattoo. The beautiful jewels were the final touch. Jewels were a sign of vanity in a woman, and their expensiveness proved her equality with Bastik. All who saw her at the party would assume she wanted to be seen like this, driven by some perverse exhibitionism or simply a desire to be fucked.

' Let me take a look at you,' said Bastik suddenly.

At once she placed her hands behind her heads and spread her legs.

'No,' he said. 'From now on you just stand with your arms by your side. Keep your legs apart at all times, though, understand?'

'Yes Sir - I mean Masad.'

'I can't see your clitoris. Make it more visible.'

'I beg your pardon?'

'You heard me. Let me see your clitoris.

Toni bit her lip. Then, her face glowing, she lowered her hands to her crotch, using the fingers of her left hand to pull her sex lips apart and teasing her hard little bud out with the other, until it was visible protruding between them. It was very wet.

'Lick your fingers clean.'

Toni did as she was told.

'That is better. Make sure you do that every time you stand.'

'Every time?'

'Yes. See to it that your clitoris is always visible.'

'Yes Masad.'

'Now, during the party you are to refuse your favours to nobody. Whatever they ask of you, you will do. And you will do it willingly and with enthusiasm, is that clear?'

'Yes Masad.' Toni could barely suppress a cry of consternation at his order. Tonight she would have to play the slut in every way, whether she liked it or not.

Yet, even as she contemplated the idea, a tremor of perverse excitement shook her. There would be men at the party who would have been anxious to fuck her had she attended clothed. Like this there was no doubt she would be propositioned. And she was forbidden to refuse.

'Good,' he said 'Two other instructions, first you are to concur with whatever I tell them about you, both in words and acts. Second, on no account are you to express a wish to clothe yourself, even when I suggest it.'

'Yes Masad.' There was no doubt about it now, he wanted the guests to believe that her state of undress was her choice and hers alone.

'Come along now,' he said. Walk beside me as we go down. Remember, you are my partner.'

He took her arm and led her toward the stairs. Below she could hear sounds of talking and laughter. The party was already under way, and she could see women in long designer gowns, their husbands in evening dress or military uniforms. She glanced down at her bare breasts and felt the heat in her face increase as people's eyes began to turn in her direction.

The walk down seemed to take forever. With every step she took, more and more people ceased their conversations and turned to stare at the naked beauty descending the stairs. Toni could hear the tut-tutting of the women and the sniggers of the men as she approached the foot of the staircase, and she stared straight ahead of herself, trying not to contemplate how she must look amongst these finely dressed people.

They reached the bottom of the stairs, where the Count stood wearing the uniform of an army general. He cast his eyes over the naked youngster without a flicker of emotion, then turned to Bastik and greeted him warmly. He led them across to where a group was standing and made introductions, introducing Toni simply as Antonia.

'You must excuse Antonia's extraordinary decision to attend the party naked,' said Bastik. 'She is a woman of perverse sensibilities, with no shame at all. Isn't that so my dear?'

178

'I just didn't want to wear any clothes,' she said quietly

'Extraordinary, isn't she? I requested that she at least wear some underwear, but she refused. Go on, my dear, won't you go upstairs and put something on? You're embarrassing me in front of these people.'

'I prefer to be nude,' said Toni.

'You see what I mean?' he said. 'I think it excites her to be without clothes. That is probably why she shaves her crotch and has that tattoo. Later, I have no doubt, she will give herself to as many men as desire her.'

. Toni watched the reactions as she shook hands, her face scarlet with embarrassment. Some of the older women were clearly disgusted, other younger ones giggled and covered their mouths. The men's eyes dropped immediately to her breasts, then to her crotch, their eyes wide. Toni mumbled her greetings, then took up her position beside Bastik, being sure to keep her legs apart. A waiter arrived with glasses of wine. As he offered Toni hers, Bastik looked into her eyes, then let his glance drop to her crotch as he raised an eyebrow.

Toni stared at him for a moment, then realised what he meant. She took a deep breath. All eyes were upon her, yet she dare not refuse. Placing her glass back on the tray she reached down to her crotch as she had before, gently easing her clitoris out between the folds of her slit. Then she placed her fingers in her mouth, sucking off the juices before taking the glass again.

For a moment there was silence as all eyes were on Toni's sex.

'The wine is rather good, Antonia, don't you think?' said Bastik suddenly.

'Yes,' she replied quietly.

'But then the Count always did keep a fine cellar.' He turned to the man beside him. 'Tell me, have you tried the seventy-three claret?'

All at once the conversations resumed. Toni stood silent, listening. Behind the man opposite her was a long mirror and she could see her reflection clearly, her small, naked body totally out of place amongst the beautifully dressed people all about her. She looked at her firm breasts, the nipples standing proud and hard from the pale orbs, then down at her bare mound, and at the arrow that pointed directly to where her protruding clitoris glistened in the lights of the room. The stockings, far from providing any concession to modesty, seemed to enhance her nudity, making her a sight that any man would find extraordinarily erotic. She could scarcely believe that she could be doing this, standing apparently calmly, sipping her drink, yet at the same time aware that she was outraging all about her by her lack of clothing.

'Excuse me my dear, there's a man I must talk some business with. I'm sure you'll be all right on your own.'

The words were spoken by Bastik, who nodded to the rest of the circle and strode away. Toni was taken completely by surprise by his words, and a sudden panic rose up inside her as she realised he was leaving her alone with these people. She stared at him as he walked away, wanting to run after him. He wasn't exactly the company she would have chosen for the evening, but at least, by his side, she had felt slightly protected. Now she was alone and naked in a roomful of clothed strangers, and she was expected to act naturally with them.

She glanced about her group. Two of the older women looked positively hostile toward her. There were two or three young men who she could see were keen to speak to her, but their wives were with them and, whilst some of them were amused at Toni's condition, there was no way they were going to allow their husbands near her.

The group disbanded within a few minutes, all the members making their excuses to one another and avoiding Toni's eye as they moved off. Soon she found herself standing alone, though there was no shortage of interest in her as she stood, sipping her drink.

Toni felt very uncomfortable indeed. She had always hated

parties where she knew nobody, and would, even had she been properly attired, have made her excuses and left by now. But she couldn't leave this party, and how could she possibly speak to these people when she knew what they must think about her?

She decided to seek out another drink. She made her way through the throng, excusing herself as she pushed past people, trying to avoid their gazes as she did so. She found a table at the side of the room and topped up her glass from a bottle standing there. Then she turned to face the party once more, shamefacedly slipping a finger into her crotch to make sure her love bud was properly displayed.

She felt nervous and embarrassed as she stood there, yet deep inside she couldn't control the arousal that her nakedness was eliciting within her. Every glance in her direction sent another shiver through her lovely young body as she thought of the sight she made, and all the time Bastik's orders ran through her head. She was to refuse her favours to nobody, and she was to be willing and enthusiastic.

All at once she became aware of three men making their way toward her. They were young men, all in their early twenties. Even from a distance she could detect the arrogance of rich youth, and she guessed they were the sons of the local gentry. All three stopped in front of her, grouping themselves about her.

'Hello,' said the one in front of her. 'My name is Mika. What is yours?'

'Antonia. People call me Toni.'

'But Tony is a man's name, surely? And it is obvious to all of us that you are not a man.'

At this his friends laughed.

Toni looked at the three of them. All had dark hair and were quite good looking. She wondered how many young women they had seduced between them, probably with promises of money and power. Mika spoke almost perfect English, the American twang in his accent indicating that he had almost certainly studied in the USA. The three had the air of experienced and powerful young men, and they were regarding her with some interest.

'Did you have no dress to wear this evening?' asked Mika.

'I had one. I chose not to wear it, that's all.'

'What a strange decision. Do you normally show off your breasts and sex to complete strangers?'

'Sometimes. When I'm in the mood to,' Toni spoke quietly, trying to keep her voice as calm as possible.

'What is that thing you keep doing with your crotch?' asked Mika. 'Are you playing with yourself?'

'No. I'm... I'm just getting comfortable.'

'When you do it your fingers are wet. You are horny I think, showing us your body? You want us to look at your clitoris?'

'You can look if you want to. I don't mind.'

'What is the arrow for?'

'It's just a mark.'

'But where is it pointing?'

'You can see.'

'Tell me.'

'It's pointing at my cunt.'

'Because you want men to look at your cunt?'

'I suppose so.'

'You suppose so?'

She hung her head. 'Yes,' she almost whispered. 'It is because I want men to look at my cunt.'

'And your clitoris?'

'And my clitoris.'

'Does it make you horny when you rub your clitoris?'

'Sometimes.'

'Rub it now.'

Toni looked about her. A number of people were still staring at her. This whole conversation was getting out of hand. Already she had replied to him in ways that she could barely bring herself to. She couldn't masturbate here, could she? Yet

182

all the time Bastik's words were ringing in her ears, and she knew she had to obey. She turned back to the man.

'Do you want to go outside with me?' she asked, almost in desperation.

He grinned. 'You really are horny, aren't you? Maybe I'll come out soon . Right now I want you to rub your clitoris.'

She sighed. 'All right.'

She gave a final glance about her in a vain hope that attention would have moved from her, but she wasn't surprised to find a number of people still watching her. She put her glass down on the table. Then, gritting her teeth, she placed her hand on her belly and began sliding it slowly down over her bare pubis.

As her index finger touched her love bud she drew in her breath sharply, a tremor running through her body. She paused for a second, afraid of how obvious her reaction would be when she moved it.

'Go on,' he said.

Toni began to move her finger in small circles over the hard little knob of flesh. At once the action began sending pulses of excitement through her young body, so that she could scarcely stop herself from moaning aloud. She looked up through lowered lashes at the three young men, who were staring at her with unblinking eyes. Beyond she could see others watching her. She tried to fight down the extraordinary arousal her fingers were bringing her, but already she could feel herself close to orgasm. As she rubbed on, her hips began to move, thrusting forward against her hand in the most lewd fashion. She whimpered slightly, trying to blot from her mind the sight she must make, naked and openly masturbating amongst all these grandly dressed people.

'Stop now.'

With a relief tinged with frustration, Toni withdrew her finger from her crotch.

'Show me your fingers.'

Toni raised her hand and held it out for him to see. From

all around her she heard murmurs of surprise as those watching saw the love juices glistening on it.

'Lick it clean like you did before.'

Toni placed the finger to her lips and sucked on it, tasting her juices.

'God, but you're something else,' the man murmured. 'Do you want us to fuck you?'

Toni dropped her eyes. 'If you like.'

'Where?'

'We could do it in my room.'

'Not public enough. What about outside on the lawns.'

'Some of the party guests might see us.'

'So what? That's where we want you.'

'All right.'

'Come on then.'

Two of them took an arm each, whilst the one called Mika walked alongside. Toni was aware of dozens of eyes following her as she was led from the room by these three virile young men, and she knew that they knew what were their intentions.

'Antonia, you're not leaving so soon are you?'

Toni drew up short at the sound of Bastik's voice. He was standing with a group of about ten others just beside the door.

'I... I was just going outside with these young men.'

Bastik turned to Mika. 'You're not going to deprive me of my guest for the evening are you?'

Mika seemed taken aback. 'I'm sorry, Sir,' he said. 'She came with us willingly. Naturally we'll leave her with you.'

Bastik turned to Toni. 'You want to go outside with these men?'

Toni recognised his desire to humiliate her once more, and recognised too how helpless she was to prevent it. She was playing his game tonight, and she had to stick to the rules.

Yes Masad, I do want to,' she said.

'Will you be long? What are they going to do?'

Toni looked round at the group standing with Bastik. As

184

always, they were all staring at her.

'They want my body, Masad,' she said quietly.

'Your body? You mean they want to have sex with you?'

'I expect so.'

'All three of them?'

'Yes.'

Some of those listening gasped, whilst others shook their heads.

'Well, if that's what you want.'

'It is what I want,' she whispered.

'Then, go and enjoy yourself. Bring her straight back to me when you've finished with her, young man. I want to hear how she enjoyed it.'

'Yes, Sir,' Mika replied.

They led her from the room and down the corridor. From all sides the other guests turned and stared as she passed, her eyes fixed on the ground in front of her. Outside the flood-lights were on and she could see a number of people standing by the swimming pool. Mika indicated a bank of grass barely hidden by two small bushes.

'Here I think,' he said.

'Couldn't we go somewhere more secluded?' asked Toni.

'No, I like it here. Come closer and let me feel your cunt.'

Toni approached him, flanked on both sides by his companions. When she got close to him she stopped, her legs apart as always. He placed a hand on her belly, his fingers sliding down to her pubis and tracing the mark. His touch was light, sending shivers through her as he felt the newly-shaved flesh. Toni was becoming more turned on by the second, and the sensation of his fingers so close to the centre of her desires was almost too much for her.

She moaned aloud as his probing fingers found her clito-ris, rubbing back and forth over the sensitive little nut of flesh that was so wet and swollen after her ordeal inside. He stroked her gently yet firmly, describing small circles about her love bud, watching her face as he did so.

Toni came suddenly, the pent up frustrations of the last hour finally releasing themselves in the most delicious way possible. She bit her lip to stem her cries of pleasure as he held her at her peak with his fingers, scarcely moving them as she drove her hips forward against his hand. The orgasm went on and on, her breasts shaking as her lovely young body writhed with pleasure. When she finally came down she was breathless. Over his shoulder she could see people watching from across the garden and her face flushed with shame as she stood there, leaning back against the two men, her legs spread wide, her hips pumping back and forth.

'Put her on the ground, boys,' said Mika. 'It's time she had a cock in her.'

They lay her on her back on the grass and she watched as Mika unbuttoned his trousers. His cock arched up from his fly, long and pink, and she found herself thrusting her hips up once more as she urged him to penetrate her.

He knelt between her legs and she reached out and took hold of his cock.

'Fuck me,' she gasped. 'I want it so bad.' This time she wasn't acting.

He needed no further urging, pressing forward as she guided him towards the entrance to her vagina. He penetrated her with a single smooth movement, eliciting a small scream from her as he did so. Then he was pumping into her with gusto, grinning at her as she cried aloud with lust.

It was a swift and unceremonious fucking. He came quickly, grunting as he filled her with semen. Toni came too, the second orgasm even more delectable than the first as she felt his seed spurt deep inside her.

No sooner had he finished than the second man was on her, mauling her soft breasts as he penetrated her. He fucked her with less finesse than Mika, but Toni scarcely noticed, and soon her third orgasm was coursing through her, her exposed position forgotten as her cries rent the air. Then yet another cock was invading her as she bent her knees and thrust her pubis up at him, revelling in the glorious sensations that were filling her body.

By the time the third man had ejaculated inside her she was exhausted, stretched out on her back, her legs spread wide, a white trickle of spunk oozing from the pink, swollen lips of her sex. She gazed up at the trio, all of whom were now decent once more.

'Just leave me,' she gasped. 'I'll be all right in a minute.'

'I cannot do that, little English slut,' said Mika. 'I promised Mr Bastik I would take you back to him.'

'Yes, but not like this!'

'Come on boys,' said Mika. 'Grab her arms. We're taking Antonia back to the party.'

Chapter 21

It was a very reluctant Toni that allowed herself to be led back toward the house. The semen inside her was escaping and leaking onto her thighs, tricking down to the tops of her stockings, clear evidence of what she had been doing with the three men, the black arrow on her pubis simply serving to draw attention to it. There was grass in her hair and a grass stain on her backside. All in all she knew she looked wanton and debauched as she walked down the hallway amongst the guests.

'Ah, Antonia, there you are,' said Bastik as he caught sight of her. 'This is my guest, Antonia,' he went on, turning to the group he was standing with.

Toni went through the ritual of shaking hands once again, feeling more embarrassed than ever as she felt the cold fluid continue to run down her inner thigh.

'You do look rather a mess, my dear,' said Bastik. 'What have you been doing?'

'I've been in the garden with those young men.'

'Rolling on the grass by the look of it. I hope it wasn't damp. After all, you've got no clothes on.'

187

'It wasn't damp.'

'What's that stuff on your leg?'

'It's nothing.'

'It must be something. What is it, Antonia?'

'It's sperm,' she said as quietly as she could.

'Antonia!' he said in mock surprise. 'So you've been misbehaving again. You really should control your appetites.'

'I'm sorry, Masad.'

'Go to the ladies' room and clean up, there's a good girl. And please put some clothes on. You really are making an exhibition of yourself.'

Toni found the ladies and went inside, relieved to be out of the public gaze, even though it was only a temporary respite. She slipped into a cubicle and cleaned herself up, removing as much of the spunk as she could from her thighs and from inside her vagina, though there were still stains on her stocking tops. When she emerged, there were two other women standing at the mirror, so she waited until they left, both giggling at the sight she made. She cleaned the grass from her behind and tidied her hair as best she could, then took a deep breath and went back outside.

'Come on, Antonia,' said Bastik when he spotted her. 'We're going to eat. Still not wearing any clothes, I see.'

'No, Masad, I'm not.'

He shook his head and turned to his companions. 'Such lack of modesty in one so young,' he sighed. 'It makes you wonder if any of them are being taught morals any more. Certainly no young girl would have flaunted herself like that in my day.'

The food was laid out on long tables and they filed along making their selections. Toni wasn't particularly hungry, but she put a few things onto a plate and joined Bastik and some other men and women at a table. She was embarrassed to discover that the woman opposite her, who was introduced as Jennifer, was English, as was the man sitting to her right. Somehow behaving as she was before people of her own na-

188

tionality seemed to make it twice as shameful, and she kept her face lowered, not joining the conversation, picking unenthusiastically at her food.

Then, quite unexpectedly, she felt a hand on her leg. She glanced sideways. The man beside her was the Englishman, a man in his fifties, grey-haired and distinguished looking. He was conversing with Bastik across the table, yet it was certainly his hand that was resting on Toni's stockinged leg.

As he continued to converse he began to move his fingers, stroking the fine nylon. The sensation was not at all unpleasant, and Toni made no move to stop him. Indeed, she daren't, not after what Bastik had said.

He began to slide his hand higher up her leg, moving it very slowly. When he touched the smooth flesh of her inner thighs just above her stocking tops Toni shivered but still did nothing. His fingers went higher, and she felt her sex lips convulse as she anticipated what was to come. When the edge of his hand grazed against her clitoris she gave a small gasp.

He manoeuvred his hand round and a finger slipped into her vagina, probing her deliciously so that she had to use all her willpower to keep still whilst he fingered her, his thumb stroking back and forth over her swollen love bud. Yet still he gave no intimation to the other diners of what he was doing, continuing his conversation as normal.

Toni was almost crying aloud with arousal as he continued his intimate caress, squirming in her seat and clenching her fists to try to contain her emotions.. At last there was a pause in the conversation and she turned to him.

'If you don't stop I'll come right here,' she said in a low voice.

He smiled. 'I'd like to see that,' he said.

'We could... Oh!' she gasped as he probed even deeper. 'We could go outside together. You can do what you want with me out there.'

'You are a wanton little thing, aren't you?'

'Do you want me?'

'Go and wait for me by the door to the gent's toilet,' he said.

'Where?'

'The gent's. It's just down the corridor. Go on, now. I'll follow you in a minute.'

Toni hesitated for a second, then she nodded.

'All right.' She rose to he feet.

'Where are you going, Antonia?' asked Bastik.

'I... I just need to go outside for a minute.'

'An assignation I've no doubt. When you're in this kind of mood you seldom go long without finding a man to service you. Or two or three. Is it a man you're meeting?'

'Yes, it is.'

'Naked?'

'Yes, Masad. I'll be naked, just as I am now.'

'And will you give yourself to him?'

'If he wants me.'

'With that arrow on your pubis, he's bound to, I'd have thought. That's why it's there isn't it, to show men they can have you?'

'It's just a mark, that's all. I'll be back in a moment.'

Toni crossed the room and went out the door, conscious of the eyes that followed her as she made her way to where the gents toilets were located. On arrival she stopped and waited, pretending to study a large oil painting on the wall. Two or three people passed her, but she kept her face firmly away from them and she wasn't approached.

It was about five minutes before the man appeared. She turned to greet him and he took her arm at once.

'In here,' he said, propelling her towards the door of the toilet.

'But I can't go in there,' she protested. He took no notice, though, opening the door and shoving her inside. Fortunately for Toni the room was deserted. He led her down a row of stalls and pushed her into one. locking the door behind them.

'Christ you're a gorgeous little slut,' he gasped, his hands reaching for her breasts and caressing them as he pressed her back against the wall of the cubicle. 'Never seen anything like it, a pretty young girl who wanders round naked with her cunt shaved, just asking for a cock inside her. You're dying for it, aren't you?'

'Yes,' she whispered as he penetrated her vagina with his fingers once more. 'Please fuck me.'

'Right,' he said. 'Turn round and put your hands on the cistern. Then spread your legs. '

Toni did as she was told, taking hold of the cold, smooth porcelain and bending forward, her breasts dangling before her as she thrust her behind back at him. As she did so she heard the sound of his zip being pulled down.

His cock was a large one, stiff as a ramrod as it probed at her sex. She spread her legs wider and he pressed it against her, then slid it deep into her sex.

Toni moaned as he began to thrust into her, heavy, violent thrusts that shook her small body with their power. He fucked her hard, his hips pumping back and forth, the sound of his breathing close to her ear. Once again Toni reflected on the crude simplicity of the sex. No foreplay, not even a bed or a mattress, simply the starkness of a toilet cubicle and a hard fucking from a stranger satisfying his basic needs. Yet she was not dismayed by this total lack of romance. On the contrary, the sheer wantonness of her behaviour seemed to excite her all the more, and she relished the casual way he was taking her. As his movements became stiffer, and his breath shortened she tightened her cunt muscles about his knob, preparing to accept his seed inside her.

He came with a grunt, spurting his semen into her and bringing another delicious orgasm to the lustful youngster, her cries echoing back from the walls of the room as she let herself go.

He withdrew quickly, tucking his still stiff member back into his trousers.

'Follow me back in a couple of minutes,' he said to her,

then unlocked the door and left.

Toni remained where she was for a few moments longer, still savouring the last vestiges of her orgasm. Then she slowly straightened, pulling some paper from the roll and wiping the semen from her thighs. She waited a minute longer, then cautiously pushed the door wide and emerged from the cubicle. At once she came to a halt. There were two men leaning on the sinks staring at her.

'I think you are in wrong place, little naked lady,' said the first. He was about thirty, with dark sleeked back hair and a Latin look about him. His companion was slightly older. Both wore evening dress.

'I... I'm sorry. I must have gone in the wrong door,' stammered Toni.

'Go in wrong cubicle too,' said the man. 'Someone else in with you. We hear you fuck.'

Toni blushed. She made for the door, but the man put out a hand, barring her way.

'No fuck for my friend and me?'

She stopped short.

'I beg your pardon?'

'You fuck with old guy. What about with us?'

'I...' Toni 's speech faltered. She wanted to get out of this place. A gent's washroom was not exactly somewhere she felt comfortable. But what the man had said was true. If she could give herself to an older man, why not to these two? Besides, she really had no choice. Bastik's orders had been clear. She could refuse these men, but what if it got back to him? She daren't think of the consequences. She eyed the pair

'You can fuck me if you like,' she said in a quiet voice. 'That's why I'm nude. I want men to fuck me all the time, so what's the point of wearing clothes?'

She could scarcely believe she was saying what she was, but she knew it made her hornier than ever, and if she was to survive this night she might as well enjoy the sex.

The man raised his eyebrows. 'You fuck here?'

'Wherever you like.'

He spoke a few words to his companion, then they moved forward. They took Toni by the arms and, turning her round, lifted her up onto the shelf where the sinks were installed, sitting her right on the edge. The marble felt smooth and cold under her backside as she leaned back against the mirror and spread her legs.

The man wasted no time, undoing his fly and plunging his stiff cock into her open sex at once. He fucked her with smooth, long thrusts, grasping her thighs and sliding his long tool in and out of her with some enthusiasm. To Toni the sensation was exquisite as she lay back in this bare, functional room and let him take her, every jab of his hips bringing her to new highs of excitement.

The door behind him opened and two men entered. They stopped short at the sight of the young English beauty perched naked on the shelf being ravaged by the man. Toni looked across at them, too aroused to care about the sight she made, openly screwing in a men's washroom.

The men said something to the second of the pair that had lifted her where she was, and the three laughed. Then they leaned against the wall, watching her, and she knew that they would fuck her too.

The man inside her came suddenly, catching her unawares, his cock twitching as it filled her with spunk. Then, in no time, he had withdrawn and his companion took his place between her open thighs, triggering another orgasm in the young beauty as he penetrated her.

In the end she was more than an hour spreadeagled on the washroom shelf whilst man after man took her. Some of those entering the washroom expressed disgust at what they saw, the naked English slut being gang-banged by whoever wanted her. Others came over and felt her breasts and body whilst she was being taken. Many simply joined the queue to screw her, laughing when she came and jostling for a view of her.

The ordeal went on and on, the faces becoming no more than a blur to Toni as she accommodated each and every one of them, her orgasms following one after another until she lost count of the number of times she had come. At last, though, the crowd thinned, and eventually she found herself with a single companion. who had her quickly, then left.

Toni dropped to her feet. Her cunt was running with spunk, a great pool of it dribbling down from the shelf where she had been sitting. It trickled down her legs now, feeling cold and sticky, and she knew she must find somewhere to clean up. She was unwilling to stay in the men's room though, for fear of more men wanting her.

She slipped out of the door and made her way as fast as she was able to the ladies room, acutely aware that the evidence of her debauchery was clear to all. She reached the room with a sigh of relief. It was empty, and she grabbed a paper towel and began to wipe the sperm from inside her.

Then the door slammed open, and she turned to find half-a-dozen women standing glaring at her.

Toni's first reaction was to run into one of the cubicles, but the women were too quick for her, blocking her way. She could see that their faces were angry, and she backed away as they came closer.

'What the hell you do with our men?' asked the leader. She was a tall redhead with fiery green eyes and she spat the question at Toni with an expression of pure hatred on her face.

'Wh-what men?' asked Toni nervously.

'You been in men's room fucking with many men. We think you fucked by our husbands. That true?'

'I don't know. I don't know who they were.'

'You don't even know who fuck you? How many?'

'I don't know. A dozen, maybe two.'

'Filthy whore.'

'Look, I'm sorry if it was your husbands. I didn't ask them to.'

'Of course you did, going about bare like that. All the

194

men see your breasts and cunt and they want to fuck you. Look at that arrow pointing at your cunt. Filthy whore.'

'Listen,' said Toni, as quietly as she could. 'I must go now. Let me out please.'

'What, out to flaunt your naked body to our men again?' said the woman.. 'No! You will stay here and discover what happens to sluts like you when they fuck another woman's man.'

Toni took a step backwards. The women were clearly in no mood to argue with her. Their leader in particular had an evil glint in her eye. The youngster backed away until she could back no further, her bottom pressed against the sink shelf.

The women closed in around her, and all at once she felt her arms grabbed.

'Turn her round,' shouted the leader, and Toni found herself being thrust up against the sink unit. Someone was wrapping tape about her wrist, and before she could pull away they had secured her hand to one of the taps. Moments later her other wrist was similarly secured, leaving her unable to move from the spot. Hands took hold of her ankles, pulling her legs apart before attaching them in a similar way to the uprights that supported the unit. Now she was helpless, the edge of the marble pressing against her pubis whilst her breasts were forced down on the cold, hard surface of the unit top. She glanced behind her fearfully as two of the women undid leather belts at their waists and passed them forward to the redhead and one of her companions.

'Now we show you how we deal with English sluts,' she said.

'No!' pleaded Toni, but the plea fell on deaf ears as the women took up position on either side of the helpless young beauty. They drew back their arms.

Thwack!

Thwack!

The belts came down in rapid succession, each one cracking into Toni's bare skin with terrible force, sending an awful stinging pain through her helpless body

Thwack!

Thwack!

Down they came again, the ends wrapping about Toni's naked behind, each one leaving a long angry stripe where it had fallen.

Thwack!

Thwack!

The women showed no mercy as they beat the youngster, the blows falling with a steady rhythm, each one stinging worse than the last.

Thwack!

Thwack!

Thwack!

Thwack!

Toni was screaming at every stroke now, her backside positively on fire as the blows rained down upon it. She tugged frantically at her bonds, but in vain. She was held fast by the tape and must endure the punishment for as long as it lasted.

Thwack!

Thwack!

Thwack!

Thwack!

Toni had lost count of the number of strokes she had received, yet still the women went on, cheered by their friends as they saw Toni's pale skin decorated by stripe after stripe until her backside was completely covered, barely an inch of the soft globes of her behind left without a red weal decorating it. Toni's screams rang about the room, echoing back at her as she fought vainly with her bonds, her pleas for mercy lost on the cruel women who wielded the belts.

At last, though they tired, the force and frequency of the strokes slowing until finally they stopped, the pair of them gasping for breath. Then the redhead stepped forward and grabbed Toni's hair pulling her round to face her. Toni could barely see her through the mist of tears, her body wracked by sobs.

'There, little whore,' said the woman. 'Maybe now you remember to keep your tits and cunt covered in company.'

Then, with a sniff of derision, she turned and left, the other women following her, leaving Toni slumped where she was.

For what seemed ages she remained there, whilst women came and went from the washroom, most of them either ignoring her or laughing at her plight. Toni, meanwhile, regained her composure. The beating had hurt, but had done no damage aside from leaving a network of stripes across her bare flesh. The pain soon subsided. Her stance was desperately uncomfortable, though, and she longed to be free and to stretch herself. Her position was not an elegant one, with her legs spread wide so that anyone entering the room was immediately confronted by her hairless crotch, the sperm still leaking from it.

It must have been half an hour later when the door opened and she heard a voice behind her.

'There you are. Masad's been asking where you were.'

Toni strained round to see a woman staring at her punished behind. It was Jennifer, the Englishwoman who had dined with her and Bastik. For the first time Toni looked closely at her. She was older than Toni, but still a young woman, probably in her mid twenties She had blonde hair and a lovely figure encased in a tight silk dress. Toni gazed enviously at her, wishing that she too could cover her body.

'Got your behind thrashed did you?' the girl went on.

'Yes. The women beat me with their belts.'

'Well, I'm not surprised, and nor should you be. You're asking for it really. You want me to release you?'

'Yes please.'

'I suppose someone's got to.'

The girl pulled a pair of nail scissors from her bag and began to hack through the tape. Soon Toni was standing upright and stretching her limbs again.

197

'Better get yourself cleaned up,' said the girl.

Toni filled a sink and, using a series of paper towels, washed the spunk from her for a second time. The girl lent her a comb and she untangled her hair.

'You're English aren't you?'

'Yes.'

'I heard you got gang-banged in the gents toilet, that true?'

'Yes.'

The girl shook her head. 'All of us enjoy a bit on the side, you know,' she said. 'But you don't have to go that far. What possessed you to come to the party with no clothes on?'

'I wanted to.'

'Aren't you embarrassed? My god I know I would be.'

'I just wanted to be in the nude.'

'Don't you mind the men all seeing you like that?'

'I don't care.'

'Look,' said the girl, rummaging in her bag. 'I've got a spare pair of knickers in here. I always carry some. You can have them.'

'I don't want them.'

'Go on, put them on.'

'No.'

'Listen,' the girl said. 'I've got a feather boa back at the table. You could wear the knickers and drape that about your neck. It would cover your nipples but you'd still be showing off your tits. It'd probably be even more sexy than being naked, but at least you wouldn't be so obvious. What do you say?'

'No thank you,' said Toni. 'I'd rather stay completely naked. I like being like this.'

'Oh well, please yourself,' replied the woman, shaking her head. 'I'm only doing it for your own good. You'd better get back to Masad. But I'd watch it. As I was coming in I saw a bunch of guys with a camera, planning to get some shots of you in compromising positions. And I don't think they were going to stop at that.'

Toni awoke the next morning feeling stiff and sore, her backside still aching from the whipping she had received from the women. The rest of the evening was something of a blur to her. She had returned to Bastik's side and had again had to suffer his false remonstrations for her nudity and to protest that she was naked by choice. Then a man had asked Bastik's permission to dance with her and, after feeling her up on the dance floor, had taken her out and fucked her against a tree. It was there that the group of men with the camera had found her. They had photographed her in the ballroom, the function rooms and the dining room, making her pose in every position imaginable, lying on tables or on the floor, spreading her legs and raising her crotch up to the camera whilst the other guests looked on. Afterwards they had taken her into the garden and taken shots her sucking their cocks before subjecting her to yet another gang-bang.

There followed a stream of encounters with men, and she found herself spreading her legs for them in all corners of the house and garden as they took her quickly and casually before passing her on to the next man. Toni had no idea how many times she had come that night, but by the time Bastik allowed her to leave the party she was totally exhausted.

Bastik took her to his suite, where she was allowed to shower. When she emerged, she was amazed to find Jennifer in the room wearing only her underwear. She was more surprised when Bastik asked her to strip the other woman and lick her vagina. Jennifer proved hot and responsive to Toni's tongue and came quickly, after which Toni sucked Bastik's cock to erection and guided him into Jennifer's wet hole. Then she was banished to the outer room whilst the couple fucked noisily. Toni had slumped down onto the couch in his sitting room where she lay listening to the pair next door before finally falling into a deep sleep.

Now, as she rubbed her eyes and gazed about her, she

realised it was late morning. She rose to her feet, still feeling groggy and stretched her lovely young body.

She stole a glance into Bastik's room. The bed was unmade but empty. Then she spotted a note on the mantelpiece. She picked it up and read it.

'Your clothing is on the side table. Put it on and join me in the morning room.'

She put the paper down and, with a sinking feeling, crossed to the table. On it lay a pair of knee-length black leather boots and a thick black belt. Nothing else.

Toni washed, then put on the boots, cinching the belt tight about her waist. She went to the mirror and took in her reflection with some dismay. The black leather contrasted starkly with her pale skin, somehow drawing attention to her nakedness. Her eyes dropped to her crotch, where the arrow was still as visible as when it had first been drawn on her. Her sex lips seemed thicker than usual, possibly swollen from the pounding they had taken the night before. Her nipples were stiff. She turned and examined her backside. It still bore a mesh of red stripes across it, witness to the beating she had received. All in all she was in no fit state to be seen, yet seen she would be. She sighed and went to the door.

Downstairs the staff were still cleaning up after the party, though most stopped to stare at the naked young beauty as she went past them, her eyes cast down to avoid their gazes. As she reached the door to the morning room she paused, reluctant to enter, fearful of who might be in there. She knew she had no choice, though. Taking a deep breath, she pushed the door open.

There were maybe twenty people in the room, many of whom Toni remembered from the previous night's party. A number of the men she recognised as having fucked her, and one group was poring over a set of photographs that she knew to be of her. Bastik was sitting at a table on the far side of the room and Toni crossed to him, aware of the sea of eyes cast in her direction. He was with three other people, one of whom was Jennifer.

'Ah, Antonia, there you are,' said Bastik. 'But naked again. Is there no end to your shamelessness?'

'Good morning Masad,' said Toni.

'Didn't you bring any clothes with you?' asked Jennifer.

'I just choose not to wear any,' said Toni. 'The Count doesn't mind, and it is his castle.'

'Yes, but some of us can get a man without flaunting ourselves,' replied Jennifer, smirking.

Bastik sighed. 'If I'd known she was going to behave like this I wouldn't have invited her,' he said. 'How many men had you last night, Antonia?'

'I'm not sure.'

'You're not sure, yet still you intend to go about today with your breasts and vagina bare?'

'I want to walk around like this. I love men to see my body.'

'Well, I suppose it's your choice, child. We're going for a walk in the grounds, will you join us?'

'All right.'

Toni followed them out into the garden. It felt odd to be naked in the bright sunshine. Under any other circumstances she might have enjoyed it, but she knew the boots and belt singled her out, not as a naturist, but a woman fully aware of the eroticism her nudity implied.

They had barely walked two hundred yards and were not yet out of sight of the house before a young man appeared from Toni's right and began walking beside her. He was tall and strong-looking and he regarded her body with undisguised interest.

'Hello,' he said.

'Hello,' she replied.

'You're called Antonia, aren't you?'

'That's right.'

'I watched you at the party last night. You seemed to be enjoying yourself.'

'I was.'

'You have beautiful breasts, Antonia. May I feel them?'

Toni glanced at him, then at Bastik, who was walking slightly ahead with Jennifer, apparently oblivious to her conversation.

'You can feel them if you like,' she said.

The man draped an arm about her neck and let his hand drop down over her breast. He squeezed it, rolling the nipple between his fingers.

'Your nipple is hard,' he observed.

'That's because it likes to be touched.'

'You are a remarkably sensuous woman, Antonia.'

At that moment Bastik stopped and turned to face her.

'Come on Antonia, keep up,' he said. 'Oh, I see you have found a companion.'

Toni blushed as she glanced down at the hand that was caressing her bare breast.

'We were just chatting,' she said.

'Looks like a very friendly chat,' observed Jennifer.

'I wondered if Antonia would join my friends and me?' said the man. 'We've found a very secluded spot by the river. That is if Mr Bastik will allow it.'

'These friends of yours,' said Bastik. 'Are they all men?'

'Yes Sir. There are four of us.'

'In that case I'm sure Antonia would be happy to join you, wouldn't you my dear?'

Toni forced a smile. 'I'd love to.'

'Then we'll see you later,' said Bastik. 'Enjoy yourself with them, Antonia.'

'Oh, I'm sure she will,' said the Englishwoman.

The man dropped his arm to Toni's waist, his hand closing over the soft globe of her buttock.

'Come on then.'

As they turned away he moved his other hand across to her belly, and slipped his fingers down over her pubis, seeking out her clitoris and rubbing it gently.

'My friends are looking forward to seeing you,' he said.
'I'm sure I won't disappoint them,' she replied.

During the rest of the week the ordeal went on without pause for the young beauty. Bastik made her keep her breasts and sex bare at all times. He devised ingenious costumes for her, sometimes stockings and suspenders, sometimes a basque that lifted her breasts but left them uncovered. One evening she wore crotchless panties and a cupless bra, much to her acute embarrassment. And yet her nudity brought out the perverse desires in her that she knew he intended, so that her crotch was constantly wet. When, as frequently happened, a man or men made a pass at her, she was able to give herself freely and achieve more orgasms than she could remember.

Every day she would be attended by the barber, who would shave what little growth had manifested itself about her sex, then apply the ointment again so that by the end of the week there was no sign of hair growth at all. Every two days he would renew her 'tattoo', making it dark and visible as when first applied.

She saw very little of the Count during this period, much to her disappointment. When she did encounter him he would make no comment about her state of undress, though she wanted desperately for him to remark on it. Bastik, on the other hand, was constantly goading her about it, making false demands that she cover herself, demands that Toni always ignored. For himself, he would simply demand she provide the foreplay for him and Jennifer at night, before banishing her from the bedroom.. Sometimes she would be summoned again in the morning when they woke up, often to lick the sperm from Jennifer's sex or to suck Bastik's balls whilst he fucked the Englishwoman.

The weekend arrived and Toni knew she had only one more week to go as the Count's plaything. Jennifer left that morning and she guessed that Bastik too was leaving soon, though he was unclear precisely when. Toni had just been sucking off one of the Count's guests whilst another took her from behind, and she had slipped into Bastik's room for a shower. She wouldn't normally have paid any attention to the open drawer of the bureau, but for the fact that a photograph caught her eye. It was a glossy colour shot blown up to a large size and as she came closer she gasped as she recognised what it was.

It was a shot of Toni, completely naked, her legs spread as she fingered her open crotch. It was one of the pictures taken during her fake registration when she had first arrived at the castle. It was both lewd and erotic, and she stared at it for some time. Then she noticed her name on a sheet of paper below, and she picked it up. It seemed to be some kind of legal document, naming her two or three times, as well as large sums of money.

All at once it came to her, and her blood ran cold. It was an invoice. A bill of sale in which she was the merchandise. There was a letter next to it, written in English, and she took it out and read it.

'... the aforenamed Antonia is an adept and willing slave with an almost voracious appetite for sex, despite her demure English manners. She is also excited by bondage and physical punishment and is an expert at fellatio. I will be shipping her out on the nineteenth from Adoba port, so she will be with you within the week. I know she will give you many years of enjoyment, after which she will certainly be useful as a plantation slave or maybe a whore for your servants. I look forward...'

Toni dropped the letter, her mouth agape. So the Count had betrayed her! She could scarcely believe it. She had been certain he was trustworthy, and now this letter told her otherwise.

All at once she was galvanised into activity. The nineteenth was only three days away. She had to get help. But from whom? She couldn't trust the police after the incident at the Midnight Club. Wasn't there anyone she could turn to for help?

Alex! She must get in touch with Alex. She would know what to do. Toni picked up the telephone. She knew Bastik had an outside line. Frantically she punched in the international code, followed by her friend's number.

Her first two attempts failed, resulting in the receiver emitting a low buzz. Then she tried again and was rewarded by the faint sound of a ringing tone.

It seemed to ring forever, but as last a voice sounded on the other end.

'Hello.' The voice was far away and obscured by a loud crackling, but Toni recognised it as Alex.

'Alex? Is that you?'

'Who's that?'

'It's Toni, Alex.'

'Toni? Hi. Wow, it's great to hear your voice. How are you?'

'I'm in trouble, Alex.'

'What? This line's dreadful. Where are you?'

'I'm in a castle somewhere in Estavia. Listen Alex I'm being kidnapped.'

'Kidnapped?'

'Yes. They're some sort of white slavers. They're selling me. You've got to help me.'

'Call the police.'

'I can't. I think they're in on it too.'

'Listen, how can I find you?'

'I'm being shipped out on the nineteenth. From a port called Adoba.'

'Where? I can't hear you.'

At that moment a hand crashed down onto the receiver, cutting the connection. Toni looked up to see Bastik beside her, glaring down at her.

Chapter 23

Toni lay in the back of the van as it sped along through the country roads, her mind racing. She was quite naked, her hands cuffed behind her back, her legs shackled and the chain attached to a metal ring in the floor of the vehicle. The blinds on the rear windows were drawn so that she had no idea where she was being taken. In the driver's cabin up front she could hear the two men chatting, but could understand not a word.

After Bastik had found her on the phone he had acted fast, grabbing hold of her whilst he dialled a number and shouted something down the phone. Minutes later the two men had appeared in his room. They were rough, unshaven men, quite unlike anyone she had encountered in the castle before and they grinned broadly at the sight of the naked beauty being held in an armlock by Bastik. They snapped cuffs onto her wrists and ankles and silenced her protests with a ball gag that fastened behind her head. Then one of them lifted her easily onto his shoulder and carried her out.

They took her down a back staircase to where the van was waiting, bundling her into the back and attaching her leg irons to the ring in the floor. Then the door was closed and locked and they were on their way, speeding out of the castle grounds and away.

Toni was shocked by the abduction, but she was also confused. After all, surely the castle was a secure enough fortress to keep her in. Why bother to take her away like this? She could only assume that the Count feared that his other guests would discover that she was being held against her will, though it was unlikely, since the dungeons in the castle were deep and inaccessible, and it would have been easy to hide her away.

She thought of her conversation with Alex. If only she had had more time. As it was, her friend had been left with half a message and would probably be unable to act upon it. She cursed the inefficient telephone system of the country she was in.

They travelled for more than two hours before she felt the van slow, then swing left. The road they had turned onto was rough and uneven, and she guessed that they were heading up some kind of track. They bumped and swerved along for what she estimated must be at least three miles, with Toni doing her best to hang on as her body was thrown this way and that. At last, though, they drew to a halt, and she heard the front doors open. Moments later, the rear doors were swung aside.

Toni blinked out into the sunlight. For a moment the glare obscured her vision, but gradually it began to clear. Beyond the door she could see a bare, flat landscape bathed in bright sunlight. She lay still as the man removed the cuffs from her legs

'Get out now,' he ordered.

Toni climbed to her feet and jumped out the back of the vehicle, her hands still secured behind her. She stared about her. They had stopped at a lone house positioned at the end of a dirt track that snaked away into the distance. The house was a bungalow, with a dilapidated air about it, the paint on the doors and windows blistered and peeling. In the simmering heat of the plain it seemed a bleak and unwelcoming spot.

The men took her by the arms and led her to an open veranda at the front of the house. There, on the floor, was a coil of chain of the thickness and strength of a dog's lead. There was a shackle at the end, and this was closed and locked about Toni's ankle. Only then did they remove the gag.

'Look,' she protested. 'What's going on? I...'

The larger of the two men put a finger on her lip.

'Quiet, little English beauty,' he remonstrated. 'You stay here with us for a couple of days. No talk unless we talk first.'

'But I...'

'No talk I said.'

'Listen,' she pleaded. 'Let me go. I can get money for you.'

He laughed and shook his head. 'How you get money? Whoring maybe? No customers here, just Marko and me, and we not pay. Now you be good girl and we treat you good.'

'Just help me,' she pleaded. 'Look at me, I'm naked. You could fuck me all you wanted.'

He laughed again. 'Don't worry,' he said. 'We will fuck you all right. In fact we do it right now.'

'You can't force me. That wouldn't be right.'

'We not force you, eh Marko?'

All at once Toni felt an arm encircle her waist from behind, the man's hand sliding down between her legs. She tried to struggle, but with her hands pinned behind her it was hopeless. She gave a gasp as he penetrated her with his finger whilst his other hand closed about her breast.

'No,' she protested.

'But you just say we can fuck you all we want. Now we going to fuck you.'

He delved his finger deeper into her, bringing a shudder from the youngster as he probed that most secret of places. His fingers toyed with her nipples, making them hard at once, despite her reluctance. Once again she struggled to get out of his grip, but he was simply too strong for her.

Toni knew then that it would be useless to resist this pair. They would have her with or without her consent. Out here there was nobody to hear her cries, even if she did resist. She eyed the pair of them. They were rough, masculine types and the thought of being taken by them sent a shiver of excitement through her. The bondage and enforced nudity were beginning to excite her more than she cared to admit and, much as she tried to fight down her passions, she suddenly found herself pressing down against his fingers as he turned her on with his caresses.

All at once she ceased her struggles and relaxed into his arms. The man sensed her surrender, and his grin widened.

'I think the little lady finally got the picture,' he said to his companion.

'I thought she'd see it our way. C'mon baby, we'll show you how to use that pretty little body.'

When he pulled her down onto her knees on the dusty wooden floor of the veranda, Toni made no protest. Her role was that of whore again, and she knew it. There was nothing to gain from showing reluctance to men of this type. She may as well enjoy the rough fucking she was about to get. She spread her legs and watched as the one called Marko undid his trousers. He had a long, circumcised cock that rose up stiffly from his groin, his ball sac contracted in a tight lump beneath it. He moved close until she was staring directly at his engorged penis. Then, taking hold of her hair, he pulled her head forward.

'Suck me,' he ordered.

She opened her mouth and took him inside, beginning at once to suck at his meaty penis. He tasted of salt and sweat, but she slurped at him with relish, the sensation of having a cock in her mouth arousing familiar desires inside her. At that moment she felt her cuffs being removed and, as soon as her arms were free, she wrapped her fingers about the base of his shaft, working the skin back and forth as she fellated him, whilst her other hand closed about the tight sac of his balls. She squeezed them and he gave a grunt of pleasure.

All at once Toni felt a hand slide down the crack of her behind and round to the hairless lips of her sex. She gave a little sigh as she felt it delve into her open sex. She wondered at her own promiscuity as he began to frig her. She should be fighting for her honour, she knew, but what was the point? If necessary they could simply tie her up and take her at will. Better to be in some control herself. Besides, she was too turned on now to turn back, and when she was ordered to get up onto all fours she complied at once, spreading her legs still wider and pressing her hips down against his fingers as she continued to suck hard at his companion's penis.

His fingers left her, and seconds later she felt the thick, hard end of his cock probing between her legs. She gave a little whimper of pleasure as he rubbed it along her slit, teasing her clitoris. Toni was gasping with desire now, her hips writhing, anxious to feel him inside her. And all the time she was moving her head back and forth as Marko fucked her face with gusto.

For a second longer his penis hesitated at the entrance to her sex. Then he lunged forward, and she gasped as he slid into her, pressing himself home with a series of short jabs that brought cries of muffled delight from the lustful young beauty. Once inside he paused, taking hold of her hips and pressing his body against hers. Then he began to thrust, his body smacking against hers so that she had to cling to the thighs of the man in front of her in order to maintain her balance.

Toni's pleasure knew no bounds as she took on her two captors. This was not the sex of lovers in a nuptial bed, this was driven by raw lust, two randy ruffians and a wanton young girl with an appetite for cock that seemed insatiable. The men laughed aloud as Toni was shoved back and forth between them, her delectable breasts swaying deliciously below her as she pleasured the pair. For herself, Toni was beyond caring, content simply to suck and be fucked, revelling in the double penetration and oblivious to the fact that she was practically being taken without consent.

As her ravishment continued, Toni sensed the arousal in both men increasing, their bodies stiffening as their orgasms approached. She stared up at Marko and noted the way the veins in his neck and temple stood out as his body stiffened.

All at once he let go, and her mouth was filling with spunk, his balls contracting with each spurt of thick, hot fluid. She swallowed it down, relishing every drop, her hand still flying up and down his shaft. Even as she was drinking his seed, his companion came, the delicious sensation of his seed pumping into her vagina finally sending Toni over the top, her body shaken like a marionette between them as she revelled in the joy of orgasm.

For what seemed an age the three of them remained locked together, the two men continuing to thrust their cocks hard into the writhing girl. Then, almost as one, they withdrew and she dropped to the floor, still moaning softly, her backside pumping up and down, her pubis thrusting against the bare boards.

At last she was still, and she rolled onto her back, gazing up at the pair, who were tucking their cocks back into their pants, both grinning broadly. She stared down at herself. Her knees were covered in dirt, as were her breasts and hands. Spunk was dribbling from her sex onto her thighs as she lay with her legs spread wide. Marko stretched out a hand and hauled her to her feet.

'So what we heard about you is true, little English one,' he said. 'You will make good slave I think.'

Toni said nothing, suddenly ashamed of her behaviour, but he laughed again and slapped her on the backside.

'Inside,' he said. 'First you shower, then we eat.'

Chapter 24

Toni's two days in the remote house were busy ones. She was kept chained at all times by the shackle on her ankle, though this allowed her full movement about the house. At night she was cuffed spreadeagled on a small bed, after which the men both fucked her, then left her for the night. During the day the two men, whose names were Marko and Jani made her cook and clean, keeping her naked at all times. Both men had strong libidos and would take her at any time during the day, laying her on the floor or pressing her against a tree outside and ramming their cocks into her, making her come every time. For herself, Toni could see that there was no chance of escape as long as the shackle was about her ankle, so she gave herself with enthusiasm, complying to her captors' every whim as she took her lascivious pleasure with them.

211

On the morning of the second day, a man arrived in a small van. Toni hid in the kitchen, ashamed of her nakedness but her two captors dragged her out and made her lie on a table on the veranda. It wasn't until they had cuffed her hands and feet to the corners of the table that she saw the man's tattooing needle. Despite her protests she had no choice but to watch as the man made permanent the arrow that would forever point to the object of men's desires between her legs. Toni lay on the table, her cheeks glowing as she watched him work, each tiny pinprick increasing her shame. When he had finished she gazed down at herself, aware that anyone seeing her from now on would have their eyes drawn to the mark, and to her shaven sex..

The pair paid the tattooist, after which there was a brief conversation. Toni knew what he was asking, and she knew too that her captors would concur. When he reached for the zip on his jeans her fears were confirmed. He took her whilst she was still bound to the table, fucking her with hard, rough thrusts and once again she found herself crying aloud with lust as yet another orgasm shook her lovely young frame.

The nineteenth dawned, the day she knew she was to be taken away, and sure enough Bastik arrived at about midmorning. Toni was cuffed and seated in his car, her legs shackled to the floor. He climbed in beside her and at once the car set off down the track toward the road.

'Where am I going?' she asked him.

'To Adobe.'

'I know that, but where will I be taken from there.'

'You'll find out when you get there.'

'Then I'm really to be sold as a slave?'

'That is correct.'

'Surely there's no such thing any more/'

He laughed. 'You have no idea, little one. There are men in this world who are rich and powerful enough to have anything they want. There's always been a trade in beautiful young girls. Most of them come from India, Africa and the East, where a girl can be bought cheaply from her parents. A European girl is much rarer, and fetches a much higher price. A specimen like you, so beautiful and submissive with such a high appetite for sex is worth a small fortune.'

'But it's not right. I took the Count on trust. How could he betray me like this?'

Bastik laughed again. 'The Count did not betray you,' he said. 'His offer to you was genuine. Unfortunately he lacks the eye for a business deal that I have.'

Toni's jaw dropped. 'You mean you abducted me against the Count's will?'

'That, my dear, is an understatement. The Count will have been livid the moment he realised that you had gone. He'll be out searching for you right now. Unfortunately he won't find you.'

'I don't understand.'

'Listen,' said Bastik. 'The Count is wild about you. He sent me a long letter singing your praises and urging me to come and meet you. Unfortunately for him I saw a more commercial use for you.'

'But if he feels so much for me, why does he let other men use me?'

'That's what he gets his pleasure from. Watching you being used. He knew me as one able to inflict unusually cruel treatment on a girl. Able to hurt her mentally rather than physically. He knew my methods would bring out the best in you, that's why he invited me.'

'He must be a remarkably cruel man.'

'On the contrary. He understood that, such was your perverse nature, you would revel in the harsh treatment. Despite your embarrassment you were more stimulated and more alive during the last ten days or so than you've ever been. Admit it.'

Toni reddened. 'I can't help the way I am,' she mumbled.

'The Count didn't want you to help it. He saw you with your nipples stiff and your cunt wet, and saw the number of

213

orgasms you were having. He did it for you as much as for his own pleasure.'

'Well why didn't he tell me?'

'He preferred things the way they were. I think he may have been planning to tell you his feelings before you left. Unfortunately he never got the chance.'

'You're a despicable man, Bastik.'

'And that, young lady, is the last time you will ever speak to me in such a manner. From now on I shall require complete obedience. Aboard ship there will be nobody to answer your screams if I choose to tie you naked to the mast and have you whipped. Just remember that.'

Toni lapsed into silence, still digesting the information Bastik had given her about the Count. There was an odd relief in the discovery that he had not lied to her. When Bastik had abducted her she had been shocked and saddened by his betrayal. Now, at least, she knew he was honourable, though it was scant consolation given her current plight. She wondered where it was she was being taken. There seemed to be no hope of rescue. She thought of the phone call to Alex. If only she had had more time. The motion of the vehicle was making her drowsy, and before long she settled back into the comfort of the limousine's seat and drifted off to sleep.

She awoke with a jolt as the car suddenly came to a halt. Bastik was still beside her, rummaging in a bag. He pulled out a T-shirt and a key.

'Give me your wrists,' he said.

Toni turned her back to him and held out her arms. There was a click, and they were free.

'Put this on.'

She pulled the T-shirt over her head. It was tight-fitting, so that her breasts pressed against the material, the nipples plainly outlined. She pulled it down as far as she was able, but it barely came below her crotch. Still, it was the first time for nearly two weeks that she had been allowed to cover her breasts and sex, and she was grateful for that. He undid her

214

leg irons, then pulled a small gun from the bag.

'This will be trained at your back at all times whilst we are on the dockside,' he said. 'I strongly suggest that you try nothing stupid, or you will end up another police statistic in this lawless place, a whore shot whilst trying to rob me. Understand?'

'Yes,' she sighed.

The car door opened and she climbed out, trying to pull down the T-shirt as best she could. When she stood straight it rose even higher, so that her crotch was almost visible as was the underside of her bottom. She was standing on a dockside in quite a large harbour. About half a mile away was a sweeping harbour wall with a narrow entrance guarded by a lighthouse. There were a number of freighters unloading, including a large, rusting hulk about a hundred yards away. It was toward this that she was being taken.

At the foot of the gangplank stood a small group of sailors. They whistled and cheered at the sight of the barely-clad beauty as she was led up onto the deck of the ship. Bastik took her through a heavy door and down a short flight of metal steps.

'This is to be your cabin for the voyage,' he said

Toni looked about her. It was a dull room painted in grey. The room was divided in half by vertical iron bars, set about four inches apart, with a door in the middle. Beyond was a small bunk and a porthole set high up and heavily barred. The only other piece of furniture was a wood-burning stove that stood outside the cell with a chimney that ran out through the ceiling. A man was sitting on a wooden chair by the door and he sprang to his feet as Bastik entered

'Once we are at sea you will be allowed a little more freedom,' said Bastik. 'For now, you will remain in here. Lock her inside, and see she doesn't emerge until we are clear of the harbour.'

'Sir!'

The man took hold of Toni's arm and led her to the cell.

He pushed her inside and swung the door closed. Then he turned a key in the lock. Bastik went out, leaving her alone with her jailer. He was a thin, weasel-faced man of about thirty and he leered at her barely covered body as she retreated to the back of the cell.

She sat on the bunk. It was made up with a blanket, sheet and pillow. There was nothing else in the cell. Then she noticed something black lying on the floor. It was a piece of charred wood, obviously from the stove. She was about to cast it aside when an idea came to her. She picked it up and ran it along the floorboards, making a black line across them. Then she dropped it on the floor once more and sat back on the bed.

'Can you get me a drink please?' she asked.

'What you want?'

'Just some iced water. I've been travelling all day and I'm parched.'

'No ice in here.'

'Well can't you go down to the kitchen and ask for some?'

He stared at her with narrowed eyes, then nodded. 'I try.'

The moment he had left Toni went into action. Pulling the cover from the pillow she spread it out on the floor. Then she picked up the charred wood and began to draw on it. She worked fast and in two minutes she had what she wanted. There, on the pillowcase, was a surprisingly good rendition of the crossed whip and chain that had been hers and Alex's secret sign whilst they had been together.

Toni climbed onto the bunk. By stretching as far as she was able, she could just reach the porthole and she pushed her banner through the gap, spreading it out to the best of her ability and wrapping the ends of the material about the bars. Then she dropped back onto the bunk just as her warder returned with her glass of water.

It was a small and desperate gesture, she knew, but if Alex was anywhere in the port, she would recognise what was otherwise an apparently innocent sign.

216

Time dragged on. Her warder grew bored with watching her and began to read a newspaper. Toni dozed intermittently, occasionally shaking her head to keep awake. Then suddenly, something dropped onto the bunk beside her. It was a piece of screwed-up paper. She glanced across at her guard, but he was immersed in his newspaper and had seen and heard nothing.

Toni reached for the ball of paper, placing it on the bed on the far side of her, out of the man's sight. Then she began slowly to unwrap it and spread it out on the bed beside her. There was a note scribbled on it.

'Toni. I hope to god you get this. I can't get near the gangplank, there's two armed guards. The dock office says you're leaving this afternoon. Your only chance is to get out once you're at sea. I've hired a small boat and I'll be waiting about ten minutes out from the harbour entrance. I guess the rest is up to you.'

Toni glanced across at the guard, but he was still intent on his newspaper. She slid the note under her bedclothes, then lay back on her bunk. Bastik had promised that she would be allowed more freedom once they had sailed. All she had to do now was make sure that that happened sooner rather than later. She looked at the guard again, and a plan began to form in her mind.

Chapter 25

It was late in the afternoon before the noises from outside told Toni that the ship was about to sail. There was a good deal of shouting, then she heard the sound of the ship's engines starting far below her. She could see little out of the high porthole, but the sight of a crane coming into view and drifting past told her that they were moving. She knew it would take no more than five minutes to reach the harbour mouth, which left her fifteen before they would be close to

Alex's boat. She waited another two minutes, then sat up.

The guard sat, intent on his newspaper, paying her no attention at all. Toni took hold of the hem of her T-shirt and pulled it over her head, leaving her quite naked. She lay back on the bunk and spread her legs. Then she slid a hand down between her legs and began to masturbate.

Her finger slipped in and out of her sex, making the wetness inside her begin to flow anew. It felt good to be playing with herself, and for a moment Toni forgot her predicament, loving the feel of her fingers as they moved in and out of her vagina whilst her thumb teased her love bud. Then she looked up and saw that the guard had lowered his paper and was watching her intently.

'What you doing?' he asked, his eyes wide.

'I was just feeling horny,' she replied. 'You go back to your paper. I'm okay on my own.'

'You want to fuck maybe?'

'How can we fuck with me stuck in here? Maybe when we're at sea. Mr Bastik said I could have more freedom when we've left harbour. Perhaps I'll fuck with you then. Right now I'm so horny I can't wait for that.'

He moved up close to the bars. 'Come nearer,' he said.

'Leave me alone,' she protested. 'I'm too turned on.'

'I will rub your cunt for you.'

'No. I'll get too excited, then I'll want to fuck, and we can't.'

'Come,' he insisted. 'Let me try.'

As he spoke the words, Toni caught sight of the lighthouse at the harbour entrance sweeping past her porthole. They were at sea.

She rose slowly from the bunk. her arms hanging by her side, and for the first time he got a glimpse of her tattoo.

'You like it?' she said, running her fingers lightly over it. 'It's to show men where I want their cocks to be. I like men to see my cunt. They tell me it's a very tight one.'

'Let me feel.'

218

She shook her head. 'Maybe when we're at sea. It's not your fingers I want. It's your cock.'

'Let me feel your breasts.'

'Why should I?'

'You will enjoy it. Come closer.'

'All right.'

Toni moved up to the bars where the man was standing. He reached out a hand and ran it over the soft flesh of her breast, making the nipple harden at once.

'You are beautiful, little English slave,' he said.

'You're not so bad yourself. Is your cock circumcised?'

'No.'

'Good. I like a man with a foreskin.' She ran a hand down over his crotch. 'You're getting pretty hard down there,' she said. 'What a pity you can't fuck me. I really want it bad.'

'You are teasing me I think.'

'Who's teasing who? You're the one keeping me locked up in here. Come on, we must be at sea by now.'

He gazed at her for a moment, and Toni feared that she had been too obvious and had blown it. Then he reached into his pocket and pulled out a key.

Her heart was hammering as he turned the key. She estimated she had seven or eight minutes. He swung the door open, then she was in his arms, his lips placed over hers, his tongue snaking into her mouth. She gasped as he reached down between her legs and penetrated her with a finger whilst his other hand mauled her breasts.

The kiss went on, their tongues licking hungrily at one another as he groped her lovely young body. Toni's natural lasciviousness was kindled almost at once, and she pressed herself against him, loving the sensation of his hard crotch rubbing against her own.

But time was passing, and she had to concentrate on her plan. She broke away.

'Fuck me now,' she said breathlessly. 'From behind. Come on.'

She took hold of the cell bars next to the still open door and bent her body forward, spreading her legs wide and pressing her behind backward. She turned to see him fumbling with his fly. Then his cock came into view, stiff and rampant.

'Mmm, that's what I want,' she said. 'Come on, give it to me.'

He moved close behind her, his fingers reaching for her open sex. She felt him press his glans against the heat of her vagina, then he slid into her in a single movement, bringing a cry of pleasure from her as he did so.

He began to fuck her at once, lunging against her, so that she was obliged to cling tightly to the bars in order to maintain her stance. Toni, in her turn, thrust back at him, her breasts shaking back and forth as he took her. His thick cock felt wonderfully filling within her, and she could scarcely concentrate on her plan of action, such was her state of arousal. She grunted with pleasure at every thrust, loving the urgency with which he drove hard into her.

His motions increased in power as the ravishment went on, so that she knew he wouldn't last long. She tightened the muscles in her sex, massaging his cock as it slid in and out of her and bringing fresh groans of pleasure from him. Toni too began to moan, clinging tightly to the bars as she sensed his climax approaching.

He came suddenly, his semen spurting from the tip of his knob and filling her deliciously. Toni had determined to remain in control, but the wanton youngster couldn't hold back the orgasm that suddenly overtook her, bringing fresh cries from her as her body shook with lust.

He went on thrusting until he was spent, then withdrew, leaving her still gasping as she clung to the bars. Slowly her mind came back to what she must do, though, and she turned to face him

'Not bad,' she gasped as she watched him tuck himself back into his trousers. 'Now see what you think of this.'

As she spoke she lunged forward and pushed him with all

her force, making him stagger backwards and sit down hard on the bunk. Toni didn't waste a second, leaping through the cell door and slamming it shut, then turning the key. The man gave a shout of outrage, but there was nothing he could do. Toni flung the key into the corner of the room, then turned to him.

'So long lover boy,' she said, then she was out of the door and racing up the stairs.

She flung the door open and ran out onto the deck. She went straight to the rail and scanned the sea, but there was nothing in sight. She gave a little cry of anguish, then turned and ran around the deck, heading for the other side of the ship.

As she came round the corner she stopped short. There, right in front of her was Bastik, talking to another crew member. The moment he saw her he gave a shout of surprise, but she had already turned and was running the other way.

As she came round the deck, with Bastik close behind her, she saw more men running toward her. Ahead was the ship's rail and she dashed toward it. The moment she reached it she saw a small open boat about two hundred yards away, with the unmistakable figure of Alex at the tiller. Without another thought she vaulted onto the top of the ship's rail and dived gracefully off, splashing into the clear blue waters and stroking as hard as she was able away from the ship.

She knew Alex had seen her, as the boat turned in her direction. It seemed a long way off now that she was in the water, but she was a strong swimmer and she struck out for it with all her strength.

By the time she reached the boat she was exhausted, barely having the strength to drag herself over the side.

'Alex,' she gasped. 'Thank god.'

'Don't thank him too quickly,' replied her friend. 'Look.'

Toni turned and looked behind her, and her heart sank. Already a small motor boat was being lowered from the ship with three figures in it, one of which she recognised as Bastik.

'Quick, head for the shore,' she gasped.

'I'm going as fast as I can. This thing wasn't exactly built for speed.'

The boat was some kind of fishing craft, and Toni saw at once what her friend meant. The engine was tiny, and they were making very slow progress indeed toward the harbour. There was the roar of an engine behind them, and she saw at once that the ship's boat was far faster. They had a start of about three hundred yards, but it wouldn't take long for the other boat to make that up.

'Oh hell, Alex,' she cried. 'What have I got you into?'

'They haven't got us yet,' replied her friend.

But Toni was unconvinced. Already the boat had almost halved the distance between them.

Suddenly there was a loud crack, followed by the whistle of something flying through the air.

'My god, they're shooting at us, Alex,' she cried. 'Look there's no point in both of us getting caught. I'll dive over-board. By the time they've picked me up you'll be away.'

'No, wait,' said her friend. 'That shot didn't come from them. Look!'

Toni swung round. There, approaching them at an ex-traordinary pace, was a sleek luxury yacht, plumes of spray rising up behind it as it sped along. Even as she watched, a puff of smoke appeared, followed by the sound of another gunshot.

'What on earth is that?' said Toni.

'I don't know, and I don't care,' said Alex. 'All I know is that it's a welcome sight, look behind us.'

Toni gazed out over her shoulder and saw that the launch had slowed its pace. As she watched, it turned in a wide arc and headed back toward the ship.

Toni shouted with joy and hugged her friend. 'Wow, Alex, you're the best.'

Alex smiled. 'Well I couldn't have them take you away, you're much too precious. Besides, you look as though you haven't been wasting your time. I love the shaved look. And the tattoo.'

Toni reddened. 'That's a long story,' she said.

'I'll look forward to hearing it. Meanwhile we seem to have company.'

Toni turned to see that the yacht had pulled alongside them and the sailors were throwing across a rope. Alex cut the engine, and grabbed hold of it. In no time the pair were being helped onto the deck.

A sailor on brilliant white uniform saluted them.

'Please to come below.'

Toni, suddenly embarrassed by her lack of clothes tried to cover herself with her hands as he took in her charms.

'What about the boat?' said Alex. 'I have to return it.'

'One of my crew will see to that. Follow me.'

He turned and went through a door with the two girls close behind. They followed him down a short passage, at the end of which was a door. He knocked on it twice, pushed it open and then stood aside.

'Please to enter.'

Alex stepped through with Toni following. She found herself in a large room with thick carpets and plush decor. There was a man standing at the far end, and Toni stopped short as he recognised him.

It was the Count.

Chapter 26

'You,' gasped Toni. 'What are you doing here?'

'You know this guy?' asked Alex incredulously.

'Yes. I've been staying at his castle for the last three months. This is the Count.'

The Count gave a little bow.

'Antonia, you must accept my deepest apologies,' he said. 'I had no idea that Bastik planned this. Had I known I wouldn't have let him near my house.'

Toni was slightly taken aback. He had never referred to her by name before, and it sounded strange to hear him do so now.

'I know it was none of your doing Master,' she said softly. 'Thank you for saving me.'

'Master?' said Alex. 'You'll have to tell me more about this relationship.'

'I couldn't have saved you without this lady's intervention,' said the Count. 'Even had I outrun that hulk there was no way of stopping her. The rifles we carry on board would have been of little use.'

'Yes, she's a real friend,' said Toni, and she gave Alex a kiss on the cheek.

'Meanwhile I have to give you this,' said the Count. He picked up a briefcase from the table and offered it to Toni. The youngster had been still covering herself, but now she removed her hands from her private parts and took it from him.

'What's this?' she asked.

'Open it.'

She clicked the fastenings undone and lifted the lid. Then her eyes widened. It was full of English banknotes.

'The money I owe you,' said the Count. 'Plus a fifty percent bonus to make up for what happened.'

Toni closed the case and handed it back to him.

'You don't have to give me anything,' she said. 'Not after

today.'

'But you must take it.'

'I'm not sure I want it.'

'I don't understand.'

'I'd rather think I was staying at the castle because I wanted to do your will, not because you were paying me.'

'Nevertheless, we had an agreement. The money is yours.'

Toni laughed. 'I started by giving myself for five Zluva a throw,' she said. 'Taking this makes me a higher class of whore, I suppose.'

'Not a whore. Just a beautiful and unique young woman with an extraordinarily sensuous nature.'

Toni looked into his eyes. 'I'll take it on one condition,' she said.

'Name it.'

'That you let me come back to the castle with you.'

For the first time since she had met him, the Count looked surprised.

'You want to come back?'

'More than anything. I want to continue as before. I'll even dress the way Bastik made me if you like. And this time I'll be doing it because I want to, not for money.'

'But are you sure?'

'Perfectly. I want to serve you, Master, in any way I can.'

'In that case, how can I refuse?'

'Thank you Master. Thank you very much.'

Alex's eyes were wide. 'This castle must be quite a place.'

'It certainly is,' said Toni.

'Naturally you must come and see it as my guest,' said the Count.

'Yes, do come,' said Toni excitedly. 'You'll love it. I could be your slave too when the Count allows it.'

'Sounds like an offer I can't refuse. Now, if you two would rather be alone...'

'No need,' said Toni. She stepped forward and kissed the Count lightly on the cheek. Then she turned away from him and prostrated herself on a low couch, spreading her legs and moving her fingers down to her vagina. She began to rub her clitoris gently.

'Master,' she said quietly. 'Why don't you send for one of your sailors?'

THE END

And now the opening of next months release "EVE IN EDEN" by *Stephen Rawlings*.

PROLOGUE TO EVE IN EDEN

"This other Eden, demi-paradise,
This fortress built by Nature for herself,
Against infection and the hand of war,
This happy breed of men, this little world,
This precious stone set in the silver sea,
Which serves it in the office of a wall
Or as a moat defensive to a house,
Against the envy of less happier lands."
(Richard II Act II)

CHAPTER 1 ARRIVAL

The lean Scot, hesitated as if unwilling to leave a woman alone in this place, then relaxed.

"Well,"he said,"if Mrs Borenson is coming to meet you, you'll be alright. Gordon keeps a strict rod, and has her well in hand."

Before Eve could recover from the insultingly patronising tone of his remark, he had made his farewells and walked off to his waiting car, as she sat and seethed.

When they'd roomed together at college, Daphne had made no secret of the customs of the island, and women's position there; how every woman, whatever her age, must have a male protector and how all, whatever their station, were subject to hot rods on bare bottoms, and other physical forms of discipline, but somehow it seemed remote and unreal. Anyway, it was different hearing it from a woman. She resented this man's oblique allusions to it, just as she resented his 'old world charm', his careful solicitude for her comfort, his attention to manners, stepping ahead of her to open doors, taking possession of her carry-on bag. She found it wholly patronising. She wondered in fact if

227

his anxiety over leaving her alone in the tiny airport arrivals lounge was not so much a matter of caring for her security as a dislike of leaving a female visitor, a loose cannon, at large without some firm male hand in control. She was glad to see him go.

His presence had been a burden to her since they had first come across each other on the mainland, when he had appointed himself her guardian for the flight to L'Ile de Paradis. As a liberated woman of twenty-eight, with a successful career and two husbands behind her, she particularly resented his patronisingly 'protective' attitude. At any minute she expected to be addressed as 'little woman', or 'my dear young lady'. In fact he proceeded to address her as 'gurll' in his pronounced Scottish brogue. She tried to tell him that it was `inappropriate' but he swept her protests to one side and pressed on in his male arrogance. In her present mental state it was too much hassle to try and reform such an antediluvian MCP; after all she was here to get over the trauma of a second failed marriage, and they were only committed to a few hours of flight together.

Looking back, she could see that she should have anticipated a meeting with a male of this variety, given the reputation Eden had been given by her room-mate at college. She was in fact here at Daphne's invitation, persuaded by the sympathetic and understanding letter she had received, in reply to her own, with its news of yet another failed relationship. Actually she was surprised that Daphne was not there to meet her, but an immigration officer soon explained the absence.

"If you would just wait here a minute," the official said, after consulting her papers, and the letter from Daphne's husband sponsoring her while she visited the island, "Mrs Borenson has some business to conclude in the traffic section. It should not take long."

She already knew the island's reputation for strict immigration controls, and that she was only permitted to land by the sponsorship of Daphne's husband, Gordon, and must stay at all times under his protection, or that of his representative, in this case Daphne. Ordinarily she would not have put up with such blatant discrimination against women, men were not subject to anything like the same restrictions, but she was here to mentally convalesce, and was prepared to over-look such out-dated attitudes for a while.

As the hum of the departing Scot's car faded, total quiet fell over the deserted arrival hall, save for the faint cries of birds in the trees on the far hillside. The quiet was pricked, though hardly broken, by a small sharp sound as of a folder slapped down on a desk, or a sticky drawer thrust home. It seemed to come from one of the anonymous offices a yard or two to her left. There it was again, that small crisp snapping sound. And again. It seemed to have a slow rhythm of its own, a ten second clock beat, that caught her attention and had her straining her ears to detect the next. Four came and with it a small animal sound. Five ticked by in step with four, a faint punctuation mark in the otherwise still hall, then six, and with it the animal sound again, though louder this time, and followed by what she took to be a female voice, though she could not make out any words. The silence drew out, and she thought whatever had caused the snail slow metronome beat was over when a seventh sharp cusp of sound came to her. This time the animal mewl was higher and louder, something in pain, and it was followed by two female voices, one making some sort of statement, the other merely acknowledging, then more silence, or did she detect a shuffling sound.

Suddenly Daphne was there, straining blindly in the doorway, oblivious for a moment of her guest, her body rigid, her head arched back, her face twisted in a grimace of pain, her hands bunched into fists by her sides as if she fought some desperate urge to bring them behind her.

"Daphne." Eve called, conscious that her friend had not seen her, even though she was seated barely five yards away.

"Hello, Darling," Daphne called, seeming to suddenly come back from some distant place."Sorry to keep you waiting, but I'm afraid I had a parking offence to clear. Ouch!" she groaned, clutching her behind, "That stings."

She screwed up her face in concentration.

229

"Damn, its always worst just after. And Gordon thought I needed livening up this morning, eight stingers as soon as my feet touched the floor it should have been six, but he claimed I moved. And I'm walking a pair today. Double threaded too. God, I'll be like steak Tartar down there before I can get back into decent underwear."

Eve looked at her in bewilderment. She knew about the corporal punishment of course, Daphne had warned her what to expect, although, as a temporary visitor, she would be immune during her stay, but it was one thing to hear about it in theory, quite another to encounter her friend, red-faced, clutching her behind as if it was being attacked by a horde of bees, and talking of liveners and strange references to underwear.

"Eh, what do you mean, 'walking a pair'," she began, "and what's all this about liveners?"

"Tell you later," Daphne promised, still rubbing her well developed rump. "Just now I'm in a limited parking zone and the state my bottom's in, I think a further 'fine' might be a tad uncomfortable."

Sensing her friend's urgency, Eve didn't delay her further and followed her out to the car. Daphne opened the passenger's door for her to slide in, then went round to the other side to let herself into the driver's position. Looking across, Eve noticed the driver's seat carried a small grid of triangular section wooden slats, on top of the usual upholstery. As Daphne lowered herself onto this uncomfortable looking 'cushion' she hiked up her skirt behind, so that it did not come between her and the ridges of the slatted frame. Eve's eyes widened even further than at the strangeness of the wooden mat, and Daphne's partial baring of herself, when she saw the nature of her present underwear. Her ample, but shapely bottom, in contrast to the stylish sophistication of her designer suit and acessories, was adorned by a drab grey pair of antique pattern 'Directoire' knickers, that came almost to her knees, where elastic gripped her ivory flesh tightly below the unbecoming loose cotton 'bloomers'. Before the humiliatingly clad rump touched the sharp slats of the grid, she could

230

see that there were two scarlet threads sewn across the full width of their widest part. She could see also that, on the right flank, a small smudge of red had stained the thin cotton fabric.

But there was more. Before she actually lowered her buttocks onto the slats, Daphne deftly hooked her thumbs under the waist of the unlovely garment and pulled the rear part down until her shapely rump was exposed. Eve drew in her breath at the sight of the angry red stripes that covered it. Her mind went back to the strict girls' boarding school she had attended and conspiratorial sessions in the changing rooms after discipline hour, when girls had stripped and proudly displayed just such spoor.

A pained grunt marked Daphne's first engagement of her bared striated flesh with the hard ridges of the slats, and she wriggled as if trying to find the least uncomfortable position.

"What on earth are you sitting on?" Eve couldn't help asking. "Is that some sort of exercise thing?"

"An exercise in humility, Darling," Daphne told her, "I have to put this on my seat every time Gordon disciplines me. Helps to drive the lesson home while I drive, he says. Certainly doesn't let one forget one's been caned."

"But he didn't know you were going to be caned again so soon," Eve protested. "Couldn't you just not use them, seeing that you've been so badly beaten?"

"Well," Daphne replied, "Gordon might excuse me or he might take the view that I'd brought it on myself by careless parking. In any case I'd always obey his orders until he gave permission to do ,otherwise."

"But can't you ring him at the office and ask?"

"No way. That would be a real no-no. One does not ring a man at his office about something so trivial as domestic discipline, and a sore bottom."

Eve gave up the struggle and tried another tack.

"And what on earth are you wearing? You used to tell me a girl could never be really smart, even in a designer dress, if she wore cheap undies. It had to go all the way to the skin, you used to say, not just surface."

Daphne sighed.

"I see I'm going to have to confess all," she said, starting the car, "I'd hoped to break it to you gently, a bit at a time, but that beastly Parking Offence Officer wouldn't let me commute it to another time, so you got to see me in the heat of the moment as it were. Best I explain, before you get too overcome with curiosity, I suppose."

"Yes please, Dee. I'm bound to find out sooner or later, so I'd rather you prepared me for what goes on around here. Then I won't make a fool of myself," she added, "by letting my jaw drop every time some drawers drop, as it were."

"I expect you're right. I'm probably not thinking too straight. Gordon always does maintain we women keep our brains in our bottoms, and just now mine's sure feeling battered."

She concentrated a minute on getting the car out of the park, and onto what passed as a main road on the delightfully under-developed island. Eve noticed a little tightening of her lips from time to time as the car's movement caused her weight to shift on her seat. When they were clear and bowling sedately along the highway, Daphne took up the tale again.

"It's like this," she said, "as you know all we women have to have a male sponsor, father, husband, brother, son, who is responsible for our discipline, and that is by very physical means. By that I mean, usually, the cane, though some favour the strap, the crop, or even a rope's end. Floggings are not entirely unknown either but, thankfully, rare."

Eve shuddered but held her tongue, as Daphane continued.

"We get punished for every sin of commission or omission but, sometimes, just to make sure we feel our position appropriately, for nothing in particular, just a general livener. This morning Gordon thought I'd been getting a little lazy recently; not enough exercise, a drink too many here, a few cream cakes stuffed down there. Getting a bit of a roll on my belly he said, though he'd seemed to enjoy rolling on it himself last night. Anyway, by dawn's early light I have to slide out of the warmth of our bed

232

and bend in the chill morning air and touch my toes, while he limbered up for the day by delivering six nice tight ones to my tender bottom."

"You said eight before," Eve corrected her.

"Don't remind me,"Daphne pleaded, rolling her eyes, "Normally I can take a sixer without too much fuss, but I was cold and sleepy, and Gordon was hitting really hard, to warm himself up, and I did wriggle a bit, I guess. Didn't get up of course. not a good idea to do that round these parts, but I waggled my arse and he added a couple to remind me to keep still another time."

"Oh wow! First thing in the morning!" Eve exclaimed, "I'm never at my best then. At the coll we got them in the evening usually, although I did once get a whacking before breakfast, when we used to get up early in the summer to do exercises. I remember it seemed to sting a lot more."

"It does," her friend confirmed, emphatically.

"And then you got it again?"

"Yes, my own stupid fault," Daphne admitted, "I didn't look at the notices properly. Actually, they've altered the layout since I was last here, and the short stay spaces are at the other end. I had my mind on other things, principally the sting in my tail, and the sore seat I was sitting on, and the thought of meeting you again soon, and just didn't spot the change. Drove blithely into the Airport Manager's personal slot. Might have got away with just a warning if it had been any one else, though remission is a word almost unknown round these parts, but the Airport Manager! Next thing to God round here and I had to bend and bare for six crackers. Gordon can hurt, but he usually contents himself with a school type cane, except for serious offences. Here all offences are serious and it's a penal rod every time."

She screwed up her face at the memory.

"Nasty vindictive bitch that Parking Officer, and a local tennis champ as well. My bare bottom against her penal rod; definitely no contest."

"Always on the bare?"

"Always," Daphne confirmed, "knickers down and bottom

233

up. At least they give you a desk to bend over in there; it helps, but even so she claimed I moved and gave me another for luck."

"Thinking of knickers," Eve said, this talk of seemingly endless cuts on bare female bottoms beginning to raise ambiguous feelings in her belly and her feminist soul, best diverted into some other topic, "what on earth are those monstrosities you're wearing? I used to look up to you as the dictator of taste, from your shoes to your smile. Besides," Eve added with a giggle, "we always used to quote the old adage about what would happen if you had an accident while out or, better still, were surprised by the neighbourhood rapist."

"I was rather hoping you wouldn't remind me of those," Daphne sighed, "I'm not too happy about them myself. apart from the humiliation of wearing such gross objects, I do still take a pride in my undies. Even so, I can assure you, I'm not looking forward to handing them back. I was sent them this morning by the Bridge Club Committee, and have to return them at the meeting tomorrow evening."

"Oh, that's not too bad them," Eve said, with relief. "Beastly for you to have to wear such horrid pants, but only until tomorrow. Is that what you meant by `walking a pair'?"

"Got it in one, girl," Daphne replied, "but there's more to it than just wearing them. It goes like this. If you do something that offends one of the women's groups, the tennis club, the swimming club or, in my case, the bridge club, the committee may decide to "send you a pair', and have you `walk' them until the next committee meeting, or whenever. These arrived this morning, with a Bridge Committee card attached `7.30 tomorrow' written on it."

"So?"

"So, tomorrow I have to report to the Bridge Club committee and lower these disgusting drawers and take another thrashing on my poor sore bottom. Not funny since there will already be fourteen welts on it. That is if Gordon doesn't decide on a few more liveners before then, or decides I've offended in some way," she added glumly, "He's not above punishing me himself for getting into this scrape, but I'm hoping he'll be kind and not insist this once. After all, he did give me my `liveners' on the basis that I didn't seem to be likely to get anything else in the near future. Bad forecast that."

"You poor thing,"Eve sympathised then, overcome with feminine curiosity, "how many?"

"That's the worst of it," her friend answered with a bitter laugh, "I expect you saw those scarlet threads. One thread, six strokes; two, a dozen. That makes twenty eight in two days, always assuming I don't collect any more along the way, and that I manage to stay down at the club. Not easy with Angela on the end of the rod, and she's bound to be. She'd never turn up a chance to whip my arse. Mind you," she added, "I'd do the same for her."

"Are you such sworn enemies then?" Eve said, surprised.

"Enemies! Oh no, we're the best of friends. I can see you've a lot to learn about our way of life during your stay."

"It would seem so," Eve replied drily, "it all seems over the top, and more like torture than discipline, to me."

"You poor thing,"Daphne replied, "you did rather walk into it at the deep end didn't you. Me with my sorry arse cut to ribbons, and more promised for tomorrow. Don't worry. It's not all like that. You just caught me on a bad day, I'm afraid. Usually I reckon on going at least a fortnight, and sometimes three weeks or even a month without getting myself welted to this degree. Well, not counting Gordon's liveners, of course; he'd never neglect me for that long, but they are by way of love strokes really and, if I'm really raw down there, he has been known to keep them down to two or three at a time. He doesn't say anything, but he's just an old softy underneath."

"A softy!" Eve almost squeaked in her indignation. "When he gives you even a couple on a bottom like you've got now?"

"Well, you must admit I'm no child; I've a fine broad bottom and there's plenty of room for a few. He'd never do anything to harm me, and I'd have to be pretty bad or foolish to earn a beating that would put me out of action for any time. Normally

235

I can take his canings and come up smiling the day after, especially,"she grinned evilly, "if he gives me another kind of seeing to after he's dealt with my sins. Actually I can usually rely on it, as my naked arse reddening under the rod seems to to get his rod equally red, and twice as stiff as that whippy cane. On the whole," she added pensively, "I think the afters are worth the entree. Sore but satisfied might cover it I think."

"You mean you actually enjoy it?"

Eve's outrage was beginning to surface despite her best efforts to avoid commenting on the customs of the country.

"Well not exactly enjoy it," Daphne cautioned, "but there are compensating factors. Being beaten by the women is the worst. They seem to be able to whip your soul as well as your butt. Ugh. Get right to you where it hurts your pride. They can humiliate you until you squirm and want to sink through the floor. And no real erotic compensation afterwards."

"I thought you liked girls? I seem to remember some pretty hot nights at coll.," Eve reminded her, blushing herself at the memory.

"Oh, I do," Daphne assured her, "But not in the same way as men. Can't seem to get the same cure for a burning bottom from a girl. Of course the men encourage these inter-women discipline sessions. They know they hurt physically as deep as their own thrashings, and that the effect on the soul goes even deeper. Also, greedy beasts that they are, they can take advantage of our need for a little erotic therapy when we get back."

Although Daphne delivered this last in tones of hurt indignation Eve more than suspected that her real feelings on the matter were very different, and more close to the cunt wetting type than any sense of injustice about the matter. All this time they had been driving steadily along a narrow, though well maintained highway, first through a level plain, with cultivated areas that seemed to Eve's casual glance to be mainly fruits of all sorts flourishing in the semi-tropical climate, then the foothills, where the road became more winding, with the views becoming more spectacular with every metre of height gained. A temporary notice warned of road works ahead, and Daphne slowed then came to a halt as a uniformed woman stepped into the road.

"Sorry to delay you, Madame," the official said, through Daphne's opened window,"but we've had a slight spillage ahead, and it'll take a few minutes to clear."

Eve could only gape. The spillage was little enough, just a wagon that had sunk into a ditch and tipped its load of ballast across the tarmac, it was the gang that was busy frantically shifting it with shovels and barrows. They were all women, and they were all stark naked, apart from straw hats to protect them from the sun. But that was all, unless one counted the steel bands on their ankles, and the gleaming chains that connected each woman to her neighbour on a classic chain gang.

"It's barbaric!"she exclaimed. "You can't treat women like this."

Daphne sighed.

"Just our luck to run into a road gang your first day. I was hoping to introduce you to our little ways in easier steps."

"But why are they here? Are they criminals?"

"In a way. Actually I suppose some of them might be serving time for offences you'd recognise as crimes back home; embezzlement, fraud, drunken driving, but many of them will be here for crimes against womanhood."

"You mean they attacked other women?"

"Only in principle. No-one is likely to have hit another woman over the head with her stiletto, though it has happened. Crimes against womanhood are those offences where the woman's behaviour has not been up to the standards required of women here and, hence have let all the other women down. Actually,"she said, looking carefully at the line of sweating women, "I know one of these."

"Which one? What's she here for?"

To be continued............

The cover photograph for this book and many others are
available as limited edition prints.
Write to:-

Viewfinders Photography
PO Box 200,
Reepham
Norfolk
NR10 4SY

for details, or see,

www.viewfinders.org.uk

TITLES IN PRINT

Silver Mink

UK £4.99 except *£5.99 --USA $8.95 except *$9.95

All titles, both in print and out of print, are available as electronic downloads at:

http://www.electronicbookshops.com

e-mail submissions to:
Editor@electronicbookshops.com

TITLES IN PRINT

Silver Moon

*UK £4.99 except *£5.99 --USA $8.95 except *$9.95*